ECHO
DOMINION

OTHER BOOKS BY ANNA DURAND

ECHO DOMINION

Echo Power Trilogy, Book Two

ANNA DURAND

JACOBSVILLE BOOKS · MARIETTA, OHIO

ECHO POWER

ISBN: 978-1-934631-68-3 (paperback)
ISBN: 978-1-934631-67-6 (ebook)
ISBN: 978-1-934631-73-7 (audiobook)

Jacobsville Books
www.JacobsvilleBooks.com

Publisher's Cataloging-in-Publication Data
provided by Five Rainbows Cataloging Services

Names: Durand, Anna.
Title: Echo dominion / Anna Durand.
Description: Marietta, OH : Jacobsville Books, 2022. | Series: Echo power trilogy, bk. 2.
Identifiers:ISBN 978-1-934631-68-3 (paperback) | ISBN 978-1-934631-67-6 (ebook) | ISBN 978-1-934631-73-7 (audiobook)
Subjects: LCSH: Magic--Fiction. | Survival--Fiction. | End of the world--Fiction. | Man-woman relationships--Fiction. | Romance fiction. | Paranormal romance stories. | BISAC: FICTION / Romance / Paranormal / General. | FICTION / Romance / Fantasy. | FICTION / Romance / Suspense. | GSAFD: Love stories. | Occult fiction. | Romantic suspense fiction.
Classification: LCC PS3604.U723 E24 2022 (print) | LCC PS3604.U724 (ebook) | DDC 813/.6--dc23.

CHAPTER ONE

Grant

I PLUNGE MY CUTLASS INTO THE CHEST OF THE ECHO CREATURE, punching the sword's blade straight into the beast's torso and out through its back, skewering the monster's heart. The creature gurgles. Its jaw slackens, and blood dribbles out of its gaping mouth. When I pull the sword free, the beast crumples to the ground.

Maybe I should feel a flush of triumph, but I don't. Killing is never a good thing, even when the monster before me had tried to assault a child. I'm glad the creature is dead and no longer a threat to anyone. That doesn't mean I enjoy meting out lethal punishment.

I glance around the alley, searching for my partners.

Bobby had gotten cornered by an Echo creature at the entrance, but I don't see him now. Erin did what she always does—run off on her own and get into trouble. I can't see her either, so I have no proof she's gotten herself in trouble again, but it's a safe bet she did. That woman must have a suicidal streak.

A triumphant cry of "hooh-yeah!" echoes down the alley.

That would be Bobby. Christ, I'm working with immature daredevils. I sprint out of the alley, then pause to survey the area. Yeah, there's Bobby. He stands over a creature that lies prone on the ground. I rush to him and peer down at the beast. Blood streams out of a wound in the center of the creature's forehead.

"Nice shot," I say. "But we can't be sure it's dead. The only surefire way to take out an Echo creature is to pierce the center of its heart."

"Yeah, I know," Bobby says. "But a shot to the head will at least slow him down for a good long while."

I grasp the straps of my backpack and wiggle them to get the weight more evenly distributed. The medical supplies in my pack could save lives, but it's damn hard to fight these monsters while saddled with a full load. I glance at Bobby. "Have you seen Erin?"

"Yeah. She went down that street over there." He points toward the next intersection, about a hundred yards away. "Told her not to go because you'd be mad. But you know how Erin is."

Oh, yeah. I know.

"Come on," I tell him. "Let's catch up to her."

And then I'll strangle the woman. She is single-handedly eroding my belief that I don't want to kill anybody without serious provocation.

We jog down the street until we reach the intersection, then I stop us both so we can scan the crossroad.

That's when I see her. Three creatures have surrounded Erin, circling her while they taunt her with verbal jabs I can't quite hear and fake-out lunges that keep her on her toes.

Bobby and I raise our weapons—my cutlass and his .9mm handgun—as we pelt down the road toward Erin. The creatures hear us coming. All eyes, including Erin's, rotate toward us. Two creatures break away from their buddy to sprint in this direction, clearly aiming to murder me and Bobby. He fires three shots, two of which hit one creature. Neither shot results in a kill, but the beast hits the pavement facedown.

I try to skewer the other creature, but it dodges my strike and hunches to ram its head into my stomach. The force of the blow sends me reeling backward while I gasp for breath. The creature straightens and pulls out a wickedly serrated blade half the length of my sword but just as deadly, if not more so.

The monster roars and rushes at me.

With one swift movement, I pierce its heart.

And the beast collapses.

Erin lets out a primal shout.

I leap over the dead creature and run toward her. But I know that wasn't a scream of fear. She often hollers that way right before she delivers a serious blow to an Echo creature. I see Erin and the last creature dancing around each other. She hollers again and thrusts her cutlass, but the beast kicks her in the gut. Erin drops, clearly stunned by the blow.

The creature raises its knife and plunges it toward Erin's chest.

Grasping the cutlass in both hands, I ram it straight through the creature's back and out through its chest. I wrestle the blade free while Erin lies there on the ground, her eyes wide, breathing hard as her gaze locks on to me.

"How do you do that?" she asks. "Hitting the exact center of the heart is tough enough, but doing that from behind… Nobody else can manage it."

"Glad you're impressed. Maybe you'll start listening to me now."

She pushes up into a sitting position and puckers her lips. "Never said I was impressed."

I lean over her and offer my hands. "Come on, we need to get moving."

Erin narrows her gaze, flattening her lips, but she accepts my help in getting up. "You must have Echo power in you. No way in hell anybody could punch straight through the center of a creature's heart that way every time without magic involved."

"Shut up and get moving."

I spin around and stomp down the street toward Bobby.

Erin huffs but hurries after me, falling into step beside me. "Everybody says you're such a nice guy. Did you bribe them to spread that propaganda? You're a dick."

"Yeah, I am."

"Can't understand why Willow thinks you're amazing. Must be a teenage crush caused by hormone overload."

"For once, could you please shut up?" I squeeze the words out between my gritted teeth. "We need to get back to Sanctuary before any more creatures come out of the woodwork."

Peripherally, I see her flash me a scowl.

We stop when we reach Bobby. "Okay, kid, do your thing."

He shuts his eyes and fists his hands as if that helps him focus his Echo power. But I've spent enough time with him to realize it's a crutch, not a necessity. The apocalypse that transformed the world gave certain people a special kind of magic that lets them teleport themselves and others to anywhere they want to go. I don't have that power, so I need someone like Bobby with me on every supply run.

Energy tingles over my skin, and the ruins of Phoenix, Arizona, vanish. Sunshine and greenery take its place. The scent of meat cooking on a barbecue grill wafts toward us, and birds chirp in the trees. We've come home to Sanctuary. We don't call it that just because it's a relatively safe place. This has become our home, and all these people are our family.

A teenage girl rushes up to me and throws her arms around my neck, standing on her tiptoes. "Sooo glad you're home."

I stroke Willow's hair. "Hey, kiddo. Yeah, we're glad to be home too."

Willow lets go of me and hugs Bobby, then tries to fling her arms around Erin. But she scuffles backward to avoid the girl's attempt.

Unfazed, Willow shrugs and returns to me, grasping my hand. We walk into the main area of the camp, which lies in the center of a large clearing. Forest surrounds us, and I've always thought that might be why Echo creatures rarely make it into our Sanctuary. Anybody could get lost in these woods.

Bobby jogs over to his buddies, the youngest adult members of our ragtag family.

Erin flashes me a scowl, then hustles into her tent.

Willow and I approach the group that's gathered around the barbecue grill. We had scored a huge grill a couple of months ago in Des Moines, Iowa, of all places. Now we can cook our meals without needing to gather wood. Because yeah, we find lots of bags of charcoal on our trips into the wider world.

Dax and Allison, the leaders of our community, stand at the grill. Dax flips a hamburger and slips an arm around his wife's waist. Allison smiles up at him. Nobody voted on who would lead our group. Didn't need to vote. Dax and Allison earned the right to be head honchos because they stopped the alchemy of worlds, the magically powered reaction that started the apocalypse. They know more about the apocalypse than anyone else.

The savory scent of hamburgers makes my stomach growl. Finding meat has gotten harder, since nobody has electricity anymore. As much as I don't like to kill anything, even I realize we need meat to survive, especially with a pregnant woman in our ranks. Allison needs protein, iron, and all that good stuff. I'd prefer to eat only things that were never breathing, but fighting Echo creatures and hunting for a way to reverse or at least end the apocalypse requires tons of energy.

"Grant is back," Willow announces as we reach Dax and Allison. "Isn't it awesome?"

"Yes, it is awesome," Dax says, though he still sounds uncomfortable every time he uses Willow's teen-speak. It took him a while to adopt her slang, and being British probably didn't make the transition any easier for him.

I still can't get over the fact that Dax, a man with Echo blood in him and giant muscles to boot, cooks burgers and plays go fish with Willow.

"Welcome home, Grant," Allison says. "How did your trip go? Looks like you found a lot of supplies for our little pharmacy."

"Yeah, we did. And I got you something." I shrug out of my backpack and dig inside it until I find Allison's gift. Dropping the backpack on the ground, I hand the plastic bottle to her. "It's not an exciting or fun present, but I figured you could use these."

She takes the bottle and reads its label. Then she grins and kisses my cheek. "Thank you, Grant. Look, Dax, he got me prenatal vitamins."

Dax nods at me. "That was very thoughtful. Thank you."

"No problem."

"Care for a venison burger?"

"Nah. I'm not hungry. The three of us ate back in Phoenix. We scored some MREs at an army surplus store, so we had a nice warm meal and even dessert." Prepackaged meals never used to appeal to me, though I ate MREs in the army. Can't be finicky these days.

"Did you bring home any of those desserts?" Allison asks. "I'd love something sweet."

"Our mandate was to grab as many medical supplies as possible. But somebody could go back and grab the MREs, either us or another team."

Dax gets a thoughtful look while he studies the flames inside the grill. "Perhaps we should send two teams."

"Good idea." I pick up my backpack, hooking one strap over my shoulder. "I'll drop these supplies off at the med tent, then head back to my place to do some more studying."

"Can I help?" Willow asks. "I got straight A's back when there was, like, actual school."

"That reminds me," Allison says. "It's time for your math lessons. Eat your lunch, then go find Sister Muriel."

Yeah, a former nun has become our schoolteacher. Since Willow is the only kid among us, Muriel doesn't have an arduous job. And she's technically still a nun, though we all call her "former" because there's no church here—or anywhere, as far as we've seen. I wonder if Sefton Stainthorpe planned it that way. The architect of the apocalypse was a total nutjob, after all.

I leave Willow with her adoptive parents, Allison and Dax, and head into my tent on the outskirts of Sanctuary. When I decided to make my little home in a secluded spot away from everyone else, nobody minded. Maybe I'm a bit of a loner, but I do try to matriculate with the group sometimes too.

My mission doesn't leave much time for that.

Inside the tent, I pull out my trunk I'd insisted on dragging home a few weeks ago. I needed a safe place to store the precious antique documents I'd saved from the ruins of Fallenmouth, the English manor where Sefton and his twin brother Dax had grown up. I'd seen Fallenmouth not long after the alchemy of worlds destroyed it. The place looks like a haunted house now. Feels like it too.

Pulling the key out of my pocket, I unlock the trunk and flip the lid up. My notebook lies on top. I take that out and open it to the last page of my notes, then carefully bring out the book I've spent two weeks studying. Alchemy isn't the easiest subject to master, but quantum physics is even harder. I need to understand both, though, and figure out how the magical and the scientific intersected to create the Echo.

I remember the day the world ended. Vividly.

The sky had split open, and monsters poured out of the hole to ravage our world and murder any humans they found. Fireballs and freakish lightning pounded the earth, punching holes straight through solid concrete buildings. But that wasn't the worst part. No, I'd seen things I still can't force myself to relive, not even in my own thoughts.

The flap on my tent is flung open, and Erin marches inside. "What's your problem?"

"Excuse me?"

"I said what is your problem. Getting damn tired of you treating me like dirt."

"No, I don't treat you that way. I like dirt. It smells good after the rain."

Her brows pull together, and her lips fall open.

Ignoring her, I carry the book to my desk—aka a folding table—and set the volume on the plastic surface along with my notebook.

"What have I ever done to you?" Erin asks. "You've hated me from day one."

"I have work to do. Could you please leave?"

She huffs and stomps out of the tent.

Erin Harding might drive me batty, but she's also beautiful and sexy, with long raven hair and emerald-green eyes. But I will never admit to anyone that I'm attracted to her. I can't. It has nothing to do with her reckless behavior on our supply missions. No, my reasons are entirely personal and too painful to discuss with a woman I've known for a matter of weeks. Maybe I should do what most guys would and take my pleasure any way I can, but I've never been that kind of man. As much as I'd love to have sex with Erin, I will never do that.

What's my problem? It's simple.

My wife and son died at the hands of Echo creatures, and I cannot watch that happen to anyone I love ever again.

CHAPTER TWO

Erin

GRANT LARSON IS A JACKASS. I'VE KNOWN HIM FOR SIX WEEKS AND three days, according to the calendar on my watch, but I still can't get the man to have a normal conversation with me. It took fifteen days for him to look me in the eye, and even longer before he spoke to me. I shouldn't keep track of the timing of my acquaintance with Grant, especially since my watch battery will die one day soon, but I've become slightly obsessed with him.

With his behavior. Not the man himself.

Sure, he has a hot body and a beautiful face, gorgeous blue eyes and wavy brown hair too, but his looks don't make me like him any better. What did I ever do to him? Nothing. He hated me from the moment I walked into Sanctuary. Not long after I arrived here, I asked Allison about Grant's attitude toward me. She said, "Cut him some slack. He'll warm up to you eventually."

Yeah, I'm still waiting for that warm-up.

I shouldn't have waltzed into his tent to gripe at him. I know that. It was childish and stupid, but the man honestly drives me insane. I can fight almost as well as he can, and I'm ex-military like he is. We should get along fine. He's nice to everyone else in Sanctuary, and they all love him.

Oh, for heaven's sake. I need to stop thinking about the jerk.

Since I'm always kind of wired after a trip into the hell zones formerly known as cities, I decide to blow off steam by practicing my archery skills. We have firearms in the camp, but we reserve those for emergencies. Or for Bobby. He doesn't like swords or knives, but he does well with a .9mm pistol.

I grab my bow and my quiver of arrows, then head for the outskirts of Sanctuary where we've set up a practice range with equipment we took from sporting goods stores. Nobody owned the stuff anymore. We found the owner and several employees dead and buried under a mountain of debris. Part of the roof had caved in, probably because a bolt of Echo lightning punched through it.

The world ended. What took its place… Well, the only person who wants to think about that is Grant Larson.

"Erin! Wait up!"

I spin around and see Willow sprinting toward me. She's carrying her bow and a quiver of arrows.

When she reaches me, she's breathing hard. But she still manages to grin. "Can I practice with you?"

"Sure. Come on, sweetie, let's see who can hit the first bull's eye."

"Only you do that. The rest of us are still trying to get inside the circles on the target."

"You do a lot better than that." I start walking, with Willow keeping step. "You're even better than Allison and Dax."

"Thanks, Erin. You're awesome. Did you really fight in combat?"

"Uh-huh. I was a Marine."

"Wow, that is so amazingly awesome."

Everyone around here knows Willow's favorite word is "awesome." She also likes to tell Dax, the huge and shockingly muscular man with Echo blood, that he looks like he's about to "hurl." It's an inside joke between the two of them, and Dax always fake growls at her when she teases him that way.

Willow and I reach the practice range, which already has two targets set up. They're pinned to stacked straw bales, providing a safe backdrop. I give Willow a few pointers, but honestly, she knows the rules and doesn't need my help. I hit one bull's eye, and Willow shrieks while jumping up and down to celebrate my victory. Her shots all fall within the circles on the target, and several get close to the center. She doesn't hit a bull's eye, but that doesn't matter. We had fun and got in some necessary practice.

Life isn't all warfare and devastation these days. The sun is shining, the sky is blue, and birdsong fills the air. At times like this, I can almost forget that the world was destroyed. If birds can survive, maybe there is a chance that one day we will figure out how to repair the damage.

The ground shudders.

I stumble sideways and bump into Willow.

"What was that?" she asks.

"No idea."

I stand still and tilt my head to the side to listen and watch. The air feels different somehow, and the sky turns a darker shade of blue while silence descends on the world as if someone has flicked a switch. The air feels different, smells different, though I can't explain how or why. A shiver tingles down my spine, and every hair on my body stiffens.

A ratcheting noise originates from somewhere overhead, growling louder every second.

I seize Willow's arm. "Run! Go!"

We bolt toward the main camp area.

Screams erupt as the sky above us roils and darkens. People scurry around like mice trying to find a hole to hide in while they crash into each other because they aren't watching where they're going. The barbecue grill has fallen over, spilling hot coals onto the grass and spewing sparks.

I slam into a big body and yelp.

The man whirls toward me and Willow. Grant's eyes widen for a heartbeat, then he grabs us both by the arm and drags us toward the center of the camp. He flips over a crate full of melons and stands on it.

"Everyone, calm down," he hollers, and somehow, he manages to sound calm. "I know this is scary, but someone might get injured if we panic. Come on over here, please."

Willow wraps her arms around my waist. I hold her to me, though I don't normally like to hug or be hugged. Yeah, I'm not ashamed to admit I'm terrified right now. As the others gather around us, we all bend our heads back to stare at the heavens. A circular section of the sky has begun to rotate, the maelstrom shifting to a darker shade of blue.

A deafening crack of thunder explodes. The maelstrom snaps shut.

Within seconds, the hole in the sky starts to enlarge and spin again.

The entire camp has fallen silent. No one even yelped when that unearthly thunder shattered the air. We've all seen something like this before, though the entrance to the Echo looks nothing like this maelstrom in the sky.

Dax and Allison push through the crowd to reach Grant, who still perches on the wooden crate. He stares up at the sky just like Willow and I do. Dax and Allison stare at the maelstrom too. So does everyone.

I hug Willow tighter. My pulse pounds so hard and fast that I feel a little weak and nauseous. No, we can't lose our camp. Sanctuary means more than a place to sleep and eat. It's our home, our family, our everything. Is it all about to be devoured by the Echo?

Another explosion of thunder shakes us and the ground too. I instinctively shield Willow with my body, as if that will help.

The maelstrom telescopes shut and vanishes. Utter silence blankets the world.

A breeze kicks up, then the birds resume their chirping. I loosen my death grip on Willow, but she still clings to me. The sky looks normal now, and the air feels like air with no supernatural weirdness.

I look at Grant. "What was that?"

"Not sure." He hops off the crate. "But I'm going to find out."

He pushes past Allison and Dax, whispering something to them, and they follow him toward his tent.

I release Willow. "Go hang out with Sister Muriel for a while. I need to do something."

"But—"

"Please, Willow. Go with Muriel."

She twists her mouth into an expression of teenage annoyance, then stomps off toward the nun.

I march into Grant's tent.

He, Dax, and Allison all swerve their attention to me.

"You guys know something," I say. "Don't you?"

Dax glowers at me. "This is a private conversation."

"Unless you're talking about how to manage childbirth in a tent, it's not private. You're discussing the maelstrom in the sky, right?"

"Yes," Allison admits. "We don't want to scare the others. That's why we came in here to talk."

"I get that. But I've been fighting alongside you guys for long enough that you should know I can handle whatever's going on. I was a Marine—in combat situations. Only one other person in this camp has military training and battle experience."

We all know the other person is Grant.

Dax and Grant exchange looks that I can't decipher. Then Dax and Allison exchange a similar look.

Finally, Dax nods at me. "All right. You can stay."

I wonder briefly if the three of them share a psychic bond or something, but I dismiss the idea. They've been through actual hell together, so I imagine that forged a deep connection.

"What just happened out there?" I ask.

The trio trade more meaningful looks that I can't puzzle out.

"We should tell her," Allison says. "Bringing another person into the loop could be helpful, and she can handle knowing the truth."

Dax rubs his jaw. "Perhaps you're right."

Grant shrugs when his friends look at him. "Whatever you think is best. She might be reckless, but she knows how to fight and getting into a fracas with Echo creatures doesn't faze her."

"I'm standing right here," I say, not even trying to squelch the annoyance in my voice. "You could speak *to* me instead of talking *about* me."

"Sorry," Allison says. "We've gotten used to keeping this stuff between the three of us. But it's time to initiate you."

"You guys have a cult?"

Allison smiles, though only a little. "No. But we've kept secrets for a damn good reason."

They exchange yet another group look.

"We're not sure what just happened," Grant tells me. "But it seemed like the Echo was trying to restart the alchemy of worlds."

"The what? I know I'm relatively new here, but I haven't heard anyone else talk about the alchemy of worlds. I'm assuming that's one of the secrets you three keep."

"Yeah." Grant shoves his hands into his pants pockets. "Everyone knows that Sefton Stainthorpe created the Echo and the apocalypse, and that he and Dax were brothers. They know Dax killed Sefton to save Allison, but that's all anyone outside the three of us knew—until right now."

"Okay. I'm ready to listen."

"Let's all sit down." Grant waves toward two folding canvas chairs that are set up in the corner of the tent. "You and Allison take the chairs. Dax and I will sit on the ground."

Whatever they plan to tell me, it must be awful if we need to sit down before I hear about it. I do what Grant said, though. Allison and I settle onto the chairs while the men take the dirt floor.

"Have you heard of alchemy?" Grant asks me.

"Yes. Don't know anything about it except that it's supposed to be a way to make gold out of other metals."

"Alchemy is way more than that." He has his knees bent in front of him, but now he rests his arms on them as he gazes at me. "Alchemy is the transmutation of one thing into something else. It's a medieval science that has mystical aspects too. With the Echo, it became more than that. Sefton Stainthorpe combined quantum physics with alchemy to create another world and then use that world to trigger the apocalypse."

"I don't understand."

"Yeah, it's complicated." He stares down at the ground for a moment as if he's considering how to explain. Then he meets my gaze again. "Think of it this way. Quantum physics provides the scientific framework, but alchemy fills that in with magic. You see, quantum entanglement was a key part of the apocalypse. Entanglement used to be theoretical, until Sefton used it to bind Dax and Allison to him. The science of it says that two particles can be linked across vast distances via entanglement, and whatever happens to one particle also happens to the other."

"What does that have to do with Dax and Allison?" I ask. "They're not particles."

"No. That's why Sefton added magic to the mix. He used alchemical principles to cast a spell that bound him to Dax and Allison through quantum entanglement. Sefton called it the alchemy of worlds."

Okay, I think I understand what he's saying—sort of. But it brings up a question. "Do you think what happened in the sky a few minutes ago means the alchemy of worlds is starting up again?"

Grant's eyes widen for a heartbeat, then he blinks rapidly, as if I've surprised him. "You're smarter than you seem."

Should I thank him for the compliment? No. I'm not sure it was a compliment.

"Yes," Grant says. "I'm concerned the alchemical reaction has either restarted or never completely stopped in the first place."

"What can we do about that?" I ask.

"Someone needs to visit Fallenmouth."

It's my turn to blink rapidly and stare at Grant. "Fallen-what?"

Dax clears his throat. "Fallenmouth was my ancestral home. And it's where Sefton plotted his apocalypse."

CHAPTER THREE

Grant

"WHY DO WE NEED TO GO BACK THERE?" ALLISON ASKS. SHE LOOKS TO Dax, but he shrugs and shoves a hand through his hair. "Grant, you know how dangerous it would be to go back there. Even if the house is still standing, the last time we saw it, the place had been devastated by the last gasp of the alchemy of worlds."

Dax sighs heavily, shaking his head at me. "The only way to get there is via teleportation. Only Allison, Willow, and I can manage that. Besides, Fallenmouth Manor is in ruins now."

"I know that," I say. "But the bones of it are still there, and we might be able to get inside and search for Sefton's notes."

"His notes?"

"Didn't you ever think your brother might've written his plans down in a notebook or on a computer?" I pick up one of the alchemy books. "He made a few notes in these manuscripts. But he must've had records of his calculations and plans. Sefton was a scientist before he went completely insane. Scientists document everything."

"What do you hope to gain from reading the ramblings of my mad-as-a-hatter brother?"

"Don't know. But somebody needs to check it out." I flip through the pages of the alchemy book, which makes the strange drawings inside it seem to move. It's an illusion. I know that, but watching the pictures shift and blend into each other rattles a shiver up my spine. "I need to go back to Fallenmouth. Not asking any of you to go with me."

"Then how, precisely, do you mean to get there? You can't teleport."

"No, but someone with a strong link to the Echo power can do it. You three aren't the only ones who have a touch of the Echo." I set the book down, but I swear I can feel those images licking at my skin. The sensation is a remnant of what happened in the sky a few minutes ago, nothing more. "Not asking Allison or Willow to help me get there."

"You want me to do it."

"No. We all agreed you need to stay with Allison to protect her and the baby."

Their child is barely a fetus right now, but we have no idea if Echo creatures might be able to find Allison. If they can, she needs Dax, our strongest warrior, to stop them. Since they both served as part of the Tria Prima, the reaction that started the alchemy of worlds, they might be connected to the creatures in ways we haven't recognized yet. And their unborn child might become the golden fleece of the apocalypse.

It's all conjecture. But we need to take every precaution.

"No one else in this camp can teleport," Dax tells me. "Your plan cannot succeed."

"I'm not so sure nobody else *can* do it. We only know that nobody else *has* done it."

Dax's brows wrinkle.

"Oh, I get it," Allison says. "Grant thinks that somebody else in our community might have the latent ability to teleport."

"Exactly," I say. "Some of the people in this camp got here when we found them in one of the cities and you or Dax teleported them to Sanctuary. But others just wandered into camp with no idea how they found it. We've assumed that means they have the Echo power inside them, but not strongly enough to do any magic. I think we were wrong. Maybe those people just need a nudge in the right direction."

Erin eyes me up and down, lifting her brows. "What about you? The way I heard it, you wandered aimlessly until you found the beach that's just over the hill from Sanctuary."

"I was escaping from the apocalypse. And that was before we founded Sanctuary."

"What does that matter? You found the place. According to your half-assed theory, that means you might have the Echo power too."

"I don't have it." Okay, I kind of snarled those words. I've always tried to stay calm under any circumstances, a skill I learned the hard way in the army and as a deputy sheriff. But Erin knows every way to tick me off. I take a deep breath and exhale slowly until the anger sifts out of me. "Look, I get what you're saying. But I don't have the Echo power. I've tried to teleport, tried many times, but it never works."

"You tried?" Allison says. "When?"

I avert my gaze and scratch my cheek. "It was, uh, occasionally over the past few months."

"But you never told us. Maybe we could've helped you figure it out."

"Doubt that would've worked. From what you and Dax told me about the instances when each of you teleported, it required a strong emotional connection." I hesitate because it's really not my business to point this out. But I need to convince them that I don't have the power in me. Why I need to convince them… Well, that doesn't matter. Mostly because I'm not sure of the answer. "Willow managed to teleport for the same reason. She desperately wanted to get to you when the creatures attacked Fallenmouth. Dax was desperate too, after Sefton sent him and Willow to the other side of the world. They both love you, and that emotion empowered their magics."

Allison and Dax both nod as if they agree with me.

But Erin huffs and throws her arms up. "Oh, come on. Why do you automatically believe him? He's not an expert on anything about teleportation or Echo magics. Everything he just said might be true—or it might be total bullshit."

I shrug. "You're right. But since the apocalypse hit, nothing is for certain. All we have is guesswork. That's why I need to get to Fallenmouth."

Dax rubs his chin, his gaze narrowed as if he's thinking. "Perhaps I could send you there without traveling myself."

"What makes you think that?" Allison asks.

"It's worth a try. Don't you think?"

"Sure. But how would Grant get back to Sanctuary?"

"We could arrange a specific time when I will bring them home, using our watches as a guide."

Allison bites her lip. "Well, that might work. But Grant shouldn't go to Fallenmouth alone."

Erin straightens and looks directly at me. "I'll go with him."

"Maybe I should ask someone else," I say. "You don't know how to follow orders, which is odd since you served in the military."

"Yeah, I did. And when I got out, I'd had enough of taking orders from jackasses like you."

Allison clears her throat to get our attention. "She would be the best choice. You and Erin have worked together a lot lately, and she has military training. If you need to fight your way out of Fallenmouth, you'll have a better chance with someone like Erin beside you."

I hate that she's right. The suicidal chick is the only one who has the training to fight Echo creatures. Others in our community know how to defend themselves, and a few have become good fighters, but none can claim to have genuine battle skills. None except Erin Harding.

Well, and me. So yeah, that makes us the perfect team to go to Fallenmouth. *Damn.*

"All right," I say. "Erin can come with me. But I'm in charge, which means she needs to follow my orders."

Erin rolls her eyes. "Yes, sir. 'She' will do what you say as long as your orders make sense."

She just had to tack a qualification onto her statement.

"How did you survive in the Marines?" I ask. "You should've gotten booted out for insubordination."

"I followed orders then. Had to. But I'm not in the Marines anymore, and you are not in charge of me."

"For this mission, I am."

Erin glances at Allison, who shrugs. "Fine. I'll do what he says—as long as it makes sense."

She couldn't stop herself from adding that qualification again. Whatever. I have more important things to worry about than what one obnoxious woman might do. I need to gather equipment and supplies. That means weapons and water. We can't assume we'll have access to clean, safe water at Fallenmouth, and we don't want to get dehydrated while fighting those beasts.

Yeah, I assume we'll need to fight. Fallenmouth lies within an exclusion zone, after all. We call it that, and we defined which areas qualify for that title. We had to call them something. "Post-apocalyptic wasteland" is too hard to say five times fast. "Exclusion zone" sounds official and less like hell on earth. The places we identified as exclusion zones are the areas that suffered the worst damage during the alchemy of worlds.

Nobody wants to live in those areas. Nobody except the creatures.

"Let's go," Dax announces as he marches out of the tent. He pauses to glance back at us. "It's time to test my teleportation skills."

By "test" he means "try to send you two morons to Fallenmouth and hope you survive the trip." Well, I signed on for this. If Dax messes it up, I'll probably die without ever knowing what happened.

I grab my backpack and head to the supply tent to get water and ammo, though I prefer my cutlass to firearms. Erin joins me a minute later to stock up her pack too. Dax loiters outside while we get what we need. Then we all tromp out to the edge of the camp, to an open area where no one has set up a tent. Though we stand a good hundred yards from the nearest tent, I can't help worrying we might accidentally hurt somebody if our test goes sideways. At least Allison stayed in the tent she shares with Dax. It's farther away from ground zero.

Dax waves at the air in front of him. "Stand over there."

Erin and I take our positions, facing Dax.

He fists his hands and clenches his jaw, then shuts his eyes.

Nothing happens.

Dax growls and glares at us.

"Try again," I say. "Let all the tension go and relax into the magics."

Erin shoots me a skeptical glance. Okay, it's more like a nasty glance.

I might be full of crap, but all I was really trying to do was to help Dax get in the zone.

This time, he shuts his eyes but keeps his body relaxed. He takes a few slow, deep breaths. And he seems to disappear. But I know he hasn't moved.

Instead, Erin and I moved, which I can tell because we now stand in a different spot than before.

"Over here," Dax shouts.

I swerve my gaze toward the direction of his voice. He stands about fifty feet away. I holler, "It worked."

"No shit," Erin mutters. "Thanks for the completely unnecessary statement."

We jog back to Dax.

"That wasn't so hard, was it?" I say. Then I slap his arm. "Good job."

"Don't congratulate me yet. I transported you a short distance, but Fallenmouth is thousands of miles away across an ocean."

"You can do it, Dax."

Erin snorts. "Now you're the head cheerleader."

I ignore her statement and grab her arm to drag her a short distance away from Dax. "If this works, bring us back in three hours."

"One hour."

"That's not long enough."

"I will not wait longer than two hours." Dax clenches his fists. "If I can't bring you back…"

"We know the risks." I glance at Erin. "Are you sure about this? Last chance to back out."

"I'm sure."

Don't think either of us can be positive about this mission, but we need to try. "We're ready, Dax. Do it."

He shuts his eyes again.

The world vanishes. A powerful force hauls us into a darkness deeper than the furthest reaches of outer space and sucks us down, down, down. Can't breathe. Can't see. My only tether to the world is the sensations that bombard me, things I can't describe but that disturb me at the deepest level of my soul.

Light blinds me.

I squint and struggle to sort out what I see. Not only am a little disoriented from the trip here, but I also have trouble figuring out what the ruins before me are supposed to be. I'd seen Fallenmouth before its demise. Back then, the boxy house had squatted inside a large clearing, surrounded by manicured shrubs and flowering bushes. The house itself had consisted of gray stone with windows that had wrought-iron holding the panes together, and the garden had featured wrought-iron benches. Fallenmouth also boasted a cemetery, which I assume is still here.

But everything looks different now.

Though the sun shines down on us from a blue sky, the house hunkers inside a barren clearing scarred by the scorch marks I've come to recognize as the aftermath of the supernatural lightning bolts and meteorites that had battered so much of the earth until the alchemy of worlds ended. The incident today, back in Sanctuary, might suggest otherwise. That's what we need to find out. The gravel driveway is unrecognizable, though I can see the remnants of the track that used to lead through the woods to Fallenmouth Manor. Chunks of scorched concrete serve as reminders of the fountain that had once stood inside the circular driveway.

As for the house itself… The third floor is gone. Only jagged pieces of walls hint that the building used to have another level. The second floor has suffered major damage, but it retains about half of its ceiling. The ground floor appears to be intact, though who knows what kind of wounds it suffered on the inside. The ground-floor windows have cracked in some spots and shattered in others. Only a handful of the panes have stayed intact.

This place looks even worse than the last time I'd seen it, shortly after the alchemy of worlds finally consumed Fallenmouth.

Erin stares at the house with her mouth partway open. "This used to be a mansion? It looks like something out of a horror movie."

"Yeah. That's what the alchemy of worlds did. You lived through that, so how can you be surprised by what Fallenmouth looks like now?"

"I just am." She scans her gaze over the house again. "Every time I see another devastated city, I feel this way. It should never stop being a horrific sight."

Well, she's right about that. The day we get blasé about it is the day we lose our humanity.

"Come on," I say. "Let's go inside and see what we can find."

Erin follows me to the massive wooden doors that form the entrance to the manor. They hang askew, almost off their hinges, the wood singed by the apocalypse. I pause at the doorway as a strange chill rushes over me. I feel like I'm about to walk on someone's grave. I suppose I am. Sefton Stainthorpe died in this house along with his Echo minions. Though I've never believed in ghosts, I can no longer swear they don't exist. If a madman could create a parallel world and start an apocalypse, then anything is possible.

"Are you going inside or what?" Erin asks. She just came up alongside me, and now she peers into the darkness within the house. "This is one spooky place."

"Glad you told me that. I thought we were walking into a Christmas party."

"Why are you always mean and sarcastic to me? I've seen the way you treat everybody else. They call you Mr. Zen because you're calm and easygoing."

Maybe I am usually that way. I can't explain why Erin makes me behave like a jerk. Allison suggested recently that I dislike Erin because I'm attracted to her but I'm afraid of getting involved with anyone since I lost my wife and son. She might have a point. But that doesn't change anything. I will never let another woman into my heart. The apocalypse took my family from me. That's why I must dedicate my life to reversing the alchemy of worlds. Nothing else matters.

Erin doesn't need to know any of that.

She huffs and jabs her finger into my arm. "Get moving. We'll never find anything if we just stand here staring at the doorway."

"Maybe I'd be nicer to you if you tried being nicer to me."

"Just go inside already."

I stomp across the threshold and stumble over chunks of debris. Pieces of a wall, I think. Since I'd only visited this house once before it was destroyed, I don't remember what rooms are where. There was a library, and a sitting room too. Within half an hour after Dax teleported me and Willow to Fallenmouth with him, we had been thrown into a battle with Sefton's minions, the Echo creatures who guarded the estate. I didn't have much time to explore the place.

Yeah, I had a solid plan for this excursion. Find mysterious things I've never seen before while navigating the ruins of a house that has many rooms I've never seen before.

This might be a lot harder than I expected.

CHAPTER FOUR

Erin

WE WANDER THROUGH THE HOUSE, CLIMBING OVER WRECKED FURNI-
ture and doors that got knocked off their hinges. Grant really has no
clue where he's going or what he's looking for, except that it must be something vital. Yeah, sure, I believe him. He's given me so much reason to trust
his instincts. If he has a nice-guy side, he hides it well.

I brought my bow and arrows, and he brought his cutlass. We used to
have guns, but it's gotten much harder to find usable ammo when we search
the cities and small towns. I have a machete in my arrow quiver too, but I'd
feel a heck of a lot better about creeping through an eerie mansion if I had
a fully automatic handgun or at least grenades.

The apocalypse doesn't care what I want. And neither does Grant Larson.

While we search Fallenmouth Manor, we stumble onto the decaying
bodies of Echo creatures. Though I'd known we might see those corpses, I
couldn't prepare for how I would feel when it happened. I get slightly nauseous the first time, but after the seventh body, I just feel cold inside. I've
killed creatures like these. But seeing their lifeless forms crumpled under
debris… I can't help experiencing a twinge of empathy. Then I think of
Hayley, and I lose all empathy for the creatures.

Because monsters just like the ones whose bodies I'm stepping over murdered my baby sister.

In the library, we find books. Duh. I could've told Grant we'd find those,
but they aren't the ones he wants. I've asked him repeatedly what sort of
books he hopes to recover from this place, but he just grunts and tells me to
keep searching. Great. I'm hunting for unidentified junk.

Grant's backpack looks heavy, and he's sweating like a pig roasting on a
spit. His face has turned kind of gray too.

I grab his arm to stop him just as he's about to clamber over a pile of rubble near the staircase. "We need to rest and drink some water."

"Can't stop. We only have two hours."

"Then at least let me get a couple of water bottles out of your backpack."

He exhales a heavy sigh. "Fine."

I unzip his pack and bring out two water bottles, then zip it shut again. He snatches a bottle from my hand and marches up the stairs while unscrewing the cap. Swigging his water, he climbs the stairs to the second floor.

So much for taking a break.

After opening my bottle and downing half its contents, I race up the stairs after him. I find Grant standing in the hallway, staring through a doorway that has no door. Or rather, its door no longer hangs from the hinges. It lies on the floor, half propped on the bed. The wrought iron on the windows remains intact, though the glass has shattered, leaving jagged fragments stuck to the iron.

Grant stares into the room with a blank expression, and his gray pallor has deepened. His lips have turned paler too.

I lay a hand on his arm and try for a gentle tone. "Hey, are you all right? Look like you've seen a ghost."

He shakes his head slowly. "Not a ghost. A memory."

"Of what?"

"The day we stopped the alchemy of worlds." He takes a few steps into the room, and I follow him. "This is where I entered the house. Dax teleported me, Willow, and himself into this room—the bedroom of the Earl of Fallenmouth."

"Dax's room?"

He nods. "But Sefton had locked Allison in here while he planned his next move. He was going to force Allison to marry him and use her Echo power to bolster his own."

I can't believe Grant is telling me all of this. He barely speaks to me except to gripe at me. But this room has some kind of hold on him, something more than the events that might've transpired here. If he wants to tell me, I'll listen. But I will not push him to share the details.

"We hid in the closet," he says, "while Allison waited for Sefton to come for her. She went with him. She had to, or else he would've killed us all. Willow stayed in the closet, but Dax and I went downstairs to get weapons."

Though I've heard parts of this story before, from Dax and Allison, I feel like Grant is about to tell me something the three of them have never told anyone else. So I stand beside him and wait for him to continue.

"Sefton planned to rape Allison," he says, his voice flat. "But she got away by using her Echo power to teleport into the cellar. Dax and I were on the ground floor fighting the creatures. Lost count of how many heads I sliced off with my cutlass. Back then, I didn't know you could kill an Echo creature by piercing its heart straight through the center."

All the bodies of creatures we had stepped over during our search of this house had died at the hands of Dax and Grant. I'd noticed the severed heads, though not all the corpses had been decapitated. I understand how, in the heat of battle, a person can avoid thinking about what they've done, what they had to do to survive. Later, the reality of it creeps into your psyche. I don't regret any of my kills, not even the ones that happened before the apocalypse when I'd been a Marine. But I wish I had never needed to take even one life.

"Sefton found Allison in the cellar," he says. "And he killed her."

"What? I never heard about that."

"That's because we've kept the details of what happened here at Fallenmouth a secret. We want to trust the other members of Sanctuary completely, but we don't really know all of them." He turns his pallid face toward me. "You can't ever tell anyone. Everybody knows Allison and Dax have the Echo power, but they don't know how powerful those two are. If anyone found out Willow had resurrected Allison… Well, we still keep her powers a secret for a damn good reason."

"I won't tell anyone. You have my word." But I can't believe he shared those secrets with me. Does that mean Grant trusts me? I don't know why he would since our relationship has always been strained at best. Since he opened the door to this story, I decide to walk in. "Did something else happen in the cellar?"

"Yeah. Dax killed his brother. He snapped Sefton's neck because he'd murdered Allison."

"Did you see it happen?"

"No. I was still upstairs fighting the creatures. I got to the cellar right after Willow brought Allison back." He turns toward the doorway, still seeming almost like a zombie. "The cellar was the key to Sefton's plans, and he wanted to start the next phase—the alchemy of souls. The boxes in the cellar contained powerful magics. Allison used them to stop the alchemy of worlds, but we still don't know if that means the other part stopped too."

"Other part?"

"The alchemy of souls." He looks down at his water bottle, which he still holds in his hand. The bottle quivers faintly. His voice sounds weaker when he speaks again. "Sefton wanted to transmute the souls of every human left on earth and force them into the bodies of Echo creatures."

Oh dear God. What would that do to us? Make us monsters? Or would we become normal humans trapped inside the bodies of the Echo creatures, unable to control the horrific acts they commit?

Grant's knees buckle.

I try to grab his arm to hold him up, but he tumbles to the floor before I get the chance. His eyelids flutter closed. His body goes slack. Kneeling beside him, my heart thudding, I check for a pulse. He's alive, but his pulse feels thready. I'm no doctor, but I'd learned a thing or two from Navy medics. I think Grant might just be dehydrated and exhausted.

So I drag the door off the bed and haul Grant onto the mattress, which leaves me gasping and drenched with sweat. I'm in good shape, but Grant is a tall, muscular man. He weighs a lot. Once I've got him on the bed, I wrestle with his limp form so I can remove his jacket. Taking his shoes off is much easier. Now he wears only his T-shirt, jeans, and socks. He seems more comfortable now, but I can't tell if Grant would agree with that statement since he's unconscious.

A search of the room nets me a pillow and a blanket. I carefully lift his head and slide the pillow under it, then I lay the blanket over him.

Now what? I have no idea how long it'll be before he wakes up.

I should stay in this room in case Dax needs us to be close together when he teleports us. But when I check my watch, I see we still have nearly an hour left before Dax will even try to bring us back. Might as well explore the second floor. I won't go too far from Grant, though, in case he rouses.

My exploration doesn't give me any helpful information. Most of the rooms don't have anything other than furniture in them. Unless I want to carry a few chairs home with me, I can't get anything useful out of these rooms.

I return to the earl's bedroom and find Grant still sleeping.

What if he never wakes up? I hardly know the man, but I don't want him to die or languish in a coma forever. So I dribble water onto his lips in the hopes it will seep into his mouth and refresh him. Maybe that's a dumb thing to do, but I can't think of anything else. I've seen too many people die before and after the apocalypse, and I don't want to watch that happen to Grant, however much he annoys me.

Grant told me what really happened on the day the alchemy of worlds ended. He shared secrets with me. Why? He doesn't even like me, and he thinks I'm reckless. Maybe I am. But he's obsessed with alchemy and quantum physics, though he never studied those subjects pre-apocalypse, and he exhausted himself to the point of passing out. He has no right to criticize my actions.

I've just set the water bottle on the nightstand when he groans.

Grant's eyes flutter open, and he squints at the sunlight streaming through the windows. "What happened?"

"You passed out. Have you eaten anything today?"

He ignores my question and tries to push up into a sitting position but falls back onto the mattress. "Shit. I feel like I've got the flu."

I press a hand to his forehead. "No fever. I think you wiped yourself out. So I repeat, when did you last eat?"

He screws up his mouth and wriggles, then shoves the blanket off himself. "Don't remember."

"Come on, Grant. If you had traveled to Fallenmouth alone, like you wanted, you'd be dead by now. I dribbled water into your mouth and put you on the bed."

"Didn't need your help. Still don't." He tries once again to sit up, but once again falls back down. "How long have we been here?"

I check my watch. "An hour and forty-five minutes."

"Dammit. I need to search the rest of the house."

"I already ransacked this floor. The only thing left is the cellar."

He freezes, his eyes widening the slightest bit. "No. We can't go down there."

"Why not?"

Grant scrubs his hands over his face and sighs. "Sefton's body is still down there."

"We've stepped over how many dead creatures today? I can't believe you're squeamish about the remains of one lunatic."

"Don't you care that he was a human being? He might've gone nuts and destroyed the world, but Sefton Stainthorpe was still a man. He deserves to rest in peace."

"Of course I care that he was human." I stand up and cross my arms over my chest. "You might think I'm a heartless, reckless bitch. But I care about every damn living thing that died because of the apocalypse, even the creatures. Sefton and his minions had to die. That doesn't mean I threw a party to celebrate those deaths."

He sighs again and manages to sit up this time, though he shimmies backward to lean against the headboard. "I'm sorry, Erin. I didn't mean—Well, let's just forget about that, okay?"

"Forget about what?"

"That I kind of accused you of being a heartless bitch. I don't really believe that."

But he believes I'm reckless, otherwise he would've apologized for that too. Well, he might have a point—one that also applies to him.

"How long has it been since you ate or slept?" I ask. "You've been obsessed with those books, haven't you? So I'm betting you haven't taken care of yourself."

He makes a pained face and bows his head. "Yeah, I've been obsessed. For a good reason."

"I get that you want to save the world or whatever, but you need to take care of yourself. I repeat, when did you last eat or sleep?"

Grant glances out the broken windows. "I haven't slept well for a week or so, and not at all last night."

"And food?"

He shrugs. "Lunch yesterday, I think."

"You think yesterday? Grant, you need to eat three meals a day like everybody else. Three good meals."

"What does it matter? We'll all die if I can't reverse the apocalypse."

I stare at him, frozen by the stark words he spoke in a casual tone. "What do you mean reverse the apocalypse? Is that possible?"

"Don't know." He throws his head back, shuts his eyes, and groans. "Didn't mean to tell you that."

I study him for a moment while I try to understand. No such luck. "Have you told anyone else that you want to reverse the apocalypse?"

"No."

"But that's what you're obsessed with doing. Have you come up with a plan?"

He shakes his head slowly, his eyes still closed.

"Do you have any food in your backpack?" I ask. "You need to eat something."

"Got some energy bars I took from that army surplus store."

I retrieve his backpack from where he left it on the floor and sit on the bed next to him while I search for food inside the bag. I've just pulled out an energy bar when one fact finally penetrates my brain.

"How could you have not eaten since yesterday?" I ask. "When we got back from Phoenix, you told Dax you weren't hungry because the three of us ate MREs from the army surplus store."

"Did you see me eating?"

"No." I hand him an energy bar. "You lied to Dax, didn't you?"

He nods while he takes a bite of the food I gave him.

"Why would you do that?" I realize the answer a second after I asked the question. "You don't want anyone to know you aren't eating or sleeping. Your obsession has gotten so strong that it's taken over your entire life."

"Life? I don't have one of those anymore. Nobody does."

We need to talk about his issues more, but Fallenmouth is not the right place to do that.

I hand him two more energy bars. "Eat these. Then we need to search the cellar before Dax brings us home."

"No. There's nothing down there that either of us needs to see."

"If you're scared, you can stay in the kitchen. I'll check out what's down there."

He wolfs down half of a second energy bar and glowers at me. "I'm not scared. We'll check out the cellar together."

"Can you walk? We'll need to go down two flights of stairs."

"I'll manage."

Once he's finished his snack and guzzled more water, I try to help him get off the bed. He scowls and shakes my hand off his arm. I grab his backpack. Grant does manage to walk on his own with only a little shakiness that dissipates by the time we reach the top of the staircase. We climb down the steps to reach the foyer, then swerve right toward the kitchen and the cellar beneath.

All the while, one question haunts me. Will his obsession get us both killed?

Chapter Five

Grant

I SWEAR I'M NOT A JACKASS, AND I'M NOT STUPID EITHER. MY RECENT behavior doesn't support my claim, and I can't deny what Erin said. I am obsessed. When I first began to study the alchemical manuscripts, I made it my goal to ensure the transmutation that destroyed much of the earth would never swallow up any more of it. But that goal has mutated over the past few months. Now I need to reverse what Sefton Stainthorpe did.

Is that even possible? I don't know.

The longer I obsess over the answer to that question, the less I care about trivial things like eating and sleeping. Yeah, I'm being sarcastic, sort of. I know I need food and rest, but I just can't muster any enthusiasm for either thing. How can I sleep when the entire earth is in chaos? When people are still suffering and dying out there in the world beyond our Sanctuary?

While I follow Erin into the kitchen, I can't stop the memories that unreel in my mind. Blood. Screams. Death. Destruction. Maybe I should adopt Erin's mindset and just murder everything I see that's not a human being. But I can't do that. It's not in my nature.

The doorway to the cellar stands open—because the door itself got torn off its hinges and now lies on the floor near the shattered marble island.

Erin goes through the cellar doorway but hesitates on the top step to glance back at me. "Are you coming?"

I've stopped moving, haven't I? Didn't realize that until she spoke. My feet don't want to move. Why the cellar disturbs me so much, I can't explain. I've been down there before, once, but I didn't witness what happened when Dax, Allison, and Willow stopped the alchemy of worlds and Sefton died. I have no firsthand experience of those events and know only what I saw when I finally reached the cellar.

"

A dead creature. A dead man. That's what I saw. Sefton and his minion had suffered similar fates.

"Okay, fine," Erin says. "You wait here. I'll check out what's down there."

"No. I'm coming with you."

I follow her down the stairs. Every hair on my body stiffens and tingles as if an electrical current has enveloped me. But I keep trudging down the steps into the darkness below. Even when Erin switches on a flashlight, I swear I can feel the darkness around me. Yeah, the apocalypse can make a believer out of the most die-hard skeptic of the paranormal.

We both halt when we reach the dirt floor of the cellar.

"Do you feel that?" Erin asks. "Never believed in ghosts, but I can only describe this feeling as like a spirit passing through me."

"Yeah, I feel it too."

She rubs her arms. "Suddenly, I get why you didn't want to come down here."

Well, at least I'm not paranoid. She feels the weirdness too.

Erin sweeps her flashlight over the cellar. A mostly decomposed body, not much more than a skeleton, lies in the corner a few feet from us.

"That's one of the Echo creatures," I tell Erin. "Sefton's body would be over there."

I point toward the middle of the space.

Erin swings her light toward where I pointed, revealing another mostly decomposed body that consists of bones with bits of decayed flesh and scraps of clothing stuck to it.

"And that would be Sefton Stainthorpe," I say. "Dax broke his brother's neck."

Erin winces. "I've seen that done before. Heard the crack when the vertebrae snap."

I don't need to ask when she witnessed that. Even before the apocalypse, we'd both seen things no one can ever unsee.

"What are those boxes?" Erin asks.

My gaze lands on the metal shelves that take up one wall of the cellar. A bunch of boxes occupy those shelves, with some made of metal and others fashioned from wood. Every box sports unusual symbols carved into it. I recognize many of them from my research into the alchemy books, though I haven't figured out how they relate to the apocalypse. My gaze is drawn to a circle with a dot in the middle that represents gold, the sun, and the heart. Next to that one, I see the symbol for air, a triangle with a line drawn across it, which also represents life-giving energy and blood.

"Those were the vessels for the Echo energy that created the apocalypse," I say. "The patterns etched into their surfaces are alchemical symbols. The images used to light up in a specific sequence, but only when someone with the Echo power touched the boxes."

"Used to?"

"Yes. They're dead now, apparently. When the alchemy of worlds ground to a halt, the boxes no longer lit up. Allison said she felt the energy inside them had been drained."

"She felt it? That's awfully indefinite."

"We're dealing with magics here, stuff nobody really understands. Can't give a definitive answer."

And for reasons I can't explain, I don't want to point out the gold and air symbols to her. It feels…forbidden. Or maybe I'm losing my mind and those shapes hold no darker meaning.

Erin approaches the shelves and traces her fingertips over the symbols on one of the boxes. Then she opens the lid and explores the velvet lining inside the box. "Don't feel anything."

"Told you, the magics must be depleted."

She turns toward me. "What now?"

"We go home." I check my watch. Luckily, it has glowing numbers on it so I can read the time even in the gloom down here. "It's been one hour and fifty-eight minutes. Dax should be calling us home any second."

She walks back to me, and we both stand here waiting. And waiting. And waiting. I check my watch again. Dax should've retrieved us five minutes ago. Well, we didn't synchronize our watches, which means he might think it's not quite two hours yet. So we wait some more.

After ten minutes, I know something has gone wrong.

"We're stuck here, aren't we?" Erin asks. "I knew this plan would go sideways."

"Let's give Dax a little more time. He's never done this before. Retrieving people via teleportation, I mean."

"Maybe we should get out of the cellar. If this room used to house powerful magics, it might be blocking other paranormal signals or something."

I want to roll my eyes and tell her that's bullshit, but I can't swear it is. So instead, I head for the stairs. "Come on. Might as well test your theory."

We climb up to the kitchen and stop there to wait for a little longer.

The world shifts, and sunshine blinds me for a moment. I squint and hold up a hand to shield my eyes.

"Finally," Dax growls. "What took so bloody long?"

"Don't ask me," I say. "You're the teleporter general."

Erin drops her backpack on the ground. "We were in the cellar. Apparently, something in that place blocked you from retrieving us. Once we reached the kitchen, voilà. We got zipped home."

Dax's brows scrunch up in the way I've only seen him do when Allison says something that confuses him. I guess the big guy doesn't get Erin's description of what happened. Well, he did live in the Echo for five years, thanks to the way time moves differently there. He still hasn't fully readjusted to life on earth.

For the rest of us, the apocalypse started a week after Sefton banished his twin brother to the Echo, and Dax emerged from the other world on that day.

"Did you find anything useful?" Dax asks.

"No joy."

Now he gives me that scrunched-up eyebrows look. "What does that mean?"

"It means we didn't find anything."

"Except dead bodies," Erin says. "We found plenty of those."

Dax averts his gaze to the ground. "You found Sefton there."

"Yeah," I say. "Not much of him left. The boxes in the cellar seem to be dead just like the last time we were there."

The big guy grunts. "I suppose that's good news."

"It is. If the boxes have stayed dead, the alchemy of worlds won't restart."

Erin gives me a puzzled look. "Then what caused the thing in the sky earlier? We went to Fallenmouth to get answers, but we found squat to explain it."

I shrug. Honestly, what else can I do in response to her question? I have no answers.

"Need to study the books more," I say. "The answers must be in there somewhere."

Erin squints at me. "Thought you needed Sefton's notes to solve the mystery. That's why we went to Fallenmouth."

"I hoped we would find Sefton's notes there. We didn't, so I have to make do with what I've got."

When I start to head for my tent, Dax claps a hand on my shoulder to stop me. I glance at him. "Did you need something else?"

"Yes. Allison has requested that you greet our newest arrival. She swears you are the best at 'meeting and greeting and schmoozing.' I defer to the woman I love on these matters."

"Sure, I can do that. Where is the newcomer?"

"Over there." He gestures toward the area in the middle of the camp, where we all have our tents set up in a circle around the perimeter. "His name is Roger Thompson. Willow is currently entertaining him."

That's Dax's way of telling me I need to rescue the poor guy before Willow scares him away with her teenage enthusiasm. I can see she and Roger are sitting on the logs that serve as benches positioned in a circle around where we often have bonfires.

"Allison is taking a nap," Dax tells me. "You know how I am with newcomers. Willow enjoys reminding me that I 'bite the big one' when it comes to making people feel welcome."

"No problem. I can handle it."

I trot over there and sit down beside Willow—between her and the new guy. He slumps on the log next to ours. I hold out my hand to him. "I'm

Grant Larson. Welcome to Sanctuary, Mr. Thompson. Mind if I call you Roger?"

"No, I don't mind." He shakes my hand. "It's nice to meet you too."

Despite his words, he sounds confused and looks that way too. Maybe it's more like fear mixed with confusion. That's a common reaction when a person stumbles onto Sanctuary without having any idea how they found it.

"Where are we?" Roger asks as he glances around. "I have no idea how far I traveled."

"This is the Lost Coast, which used to be in Humboldt County in Northern California." I wave toward the woods. "The beach is just over the hill there. Did you come from that way?"

"Yes. I hitched a ride on a boat with some people, but they turned out to be not very nice. That's when I struck out on my own and somehow ended up here."

"How long did your journey take?"

Roger shrugs one shoulder. "Not sure. Don't have a watch or a calendar. But I think it was at least a month."

He does look kind of thin and bedraggled, though not as bad off as some people who find Sanctuary. In the wider world, lots of horrific things happen. That's why we guard our enclave. Everyone takes turns patrolling the beach and the woods.

"We're glad you found us," I say. "This is a community of good people who want to make a better life post-apocalypse."

"Thank you for letting me join your community. I can't tell you what a relief it is to find a place like this."

He fingers the gold band on his left hand.

I nod toward his hand. "You're married?"

"Yes." He bows his head and starts twisting the ring around and around. "No idea what happened to my wife. We'd only been married for two months when the apocalypse hit. On the day that happened, she was in Tacoma visiting her sister, who just had a baby. I've been trying to get there, so I can look for her, but… no luck."

Though I want to tell him we have a way he can get there, I shouldn't blurt that out yet. I need to confer with Dax and Allison first. This guy seems nice, but appearances can be deceiving. Instead of sharing our special mode of transportation, I give him our standard newcomer offer.

"We don't have a tent available for you," I say. "But we can find someone who will share theirs. Are you okay with that? Or you could grab a sleeping bag and camp out."

"Sharing a tent is fine. I'd rather not camp out." He looks up at the sky and hunches his shoulders. "I've seen those things that can fly. They tried to get me a couple of times."

"I'll find you a good roommate, don't worry. And we patrol the area day and night just in case any Echo fliers try to penetrate Sanctuary."

"Echo fliers? I guess that's as good a name for them as anything."

I stand up. "Let's find you a roomie. But maybe we should get you some food first. Are you hungry?"

"Starved."

For the rest of the afternoon, I help Roger get settled in and make sure he eats a good meal. Lunch was over long before Erin and I got back from Fallenmouth, but she actually volunteers to scrounge up food for the newest resident in Sanctuary. She surprises me even more when she volunteers to hang out with Roger until his new roommate comes back from his turn patrolling the beach. She smiles and laughs too, telling him jokes to help him relax.

Maybe she's not a heartless bitch, and maybe her recklessness has a reason. But I will never become friends with Erin Harding.

She throws her head back to laugh at something Roger said. He smiles in response, but I'm not really looking at him. My focus gravitates to Erin. The column of her throat. Those pink lips. Her long raven hair fanning out around her face. The long locks draw my gaze down to her chest and the mounds of her breasts hidden beneath her shirt, though not hidden enough. I can imagine what her tits look like naked, can picture it in detail far more vividly than my willpower can stand. This always happens to me when I catch her behaving like a normal person. I start to see her as a woman, not just a tough chick, and that realization makes my dick twitch and my hands curl into fists. Fighting my lust for her only makes the problem worse. But I cannot, will not, ever have sex with her. She's a loose cannon, and I'm hung up on the wife I lost.

Erin will never know how much I want her. Never.

CHAPTER SIX

Erin

I LEARNED SOMETHING NEW TODAY. GRANT ISN'T AS ZEN ABOUT life after the apocalypse as he wants everyone to think. He loses sleep and forgets to eat because he's become obsessed with finding a way to save the world. I can't deny he knows how to make strangers feel welcome when they stumble onto Sanctuary. He didn't ask Roger many questions, but I've noticed he and our leaders, Allison and Dax, always wait awhile before they gently prod someone for details.

At sunset, we all gather wood to start a bonfire. Why? Because it makes us feel less like a colony of outcasts from the apocalypse and more like a family. Everybody needs that, now more than ever, considering what the sky did today. Anxiety levels run higher in our community now. No surprise. We worry the alchemy of worlds might start up again, though Grant seems sure it won't.

I share a log bench with Roger and his new roommate, Patrick. I know Patrick, though I haven't gotten close to anyone since I came here. It's hard to feel comfortable sharing my innermost thoughts and feelings with another person, but I'd had that problem before the Echo ravaged our world. Still, I try to make more of an effort for our newest member, but only in part because I hope Grant will see it and stop treating me like his enemy.

Why do I care what he thinks?

Though we all ate dinner earlier, everyone agrees it would be fun to toast marshmallows while stargazing. I saw Grant eating food at dinnertime, so at least the moron isn't starving himself, at least for the moment. Maybe I should've told Allison or Dax or someone that Grant has a tendency not to eat or sleep lately, but I feel weird about doing that. If I keep an eye on him, it won't happen again. Great. Now I've appointed myself guardian of a man who dislikes me as much as I dislike him.

Somebody has to do it.

Patrick and Roger wander off to chat with other people, leaving me alone on my log bench.

A hand thrusts a stick in front of my face, though I can't see the person that hand belongs to since they're standing behind me. "Try a marshmallow."

The sound of Grant's voice makes me twist around to look at him. "What are you doing?"

"Bringing you a toasted marshmallow. Call it a peace offering."

"Uh, thanks."

I accept the stick—just a twig, really—and face the fire again. I've been sitting at the furthest edge of the bonfire, a short distance from everyone else. Yeah, okay, I still suck at socializing. Not because I have no idea how to talk to people. I just don't feel comfortable here yet. It's been slightly more than a month since I found Sanctuary, if I've counted right with no calendar to guide me, but I haven't settled in here.

Grant sits down beside me on the log. "Have you eaten toasted marshmallows before?"

"Of course I have."

"I only asked because you're staring at the marshmallow like it might come to life and eat you."

"You're the one who has food issues."

The corner of his mouth kicks up. "Yeah. Thanks for taking care of me while I was unconscious."

"No problem. If I let you die, Allison would clobber me."

"Glad you saved her from needing to do that. Might not have been good for the baby." He watches me nibble on the warm, gooey marshmallow. "You gave me water while I was asleep."

"Yeah."

"Thank you for that too."

"Um, you're welcome." I take another bite of the marshmallow. "Mm, this is really good."

"Everything tastes better post-apocalypse."

"MREs still taste like shit."

He smiles. "Yeah, they do."

Grant looks surprisingly good when he smiles. Well, he's always attractive. But I've never seen him looking happy before. That smile lights up his face, and the bonfire casts a glimmer on his eyes and his hair, making him seem less like the jerk who snaps at me and more like a normal person. Everyone here loves him. Maybe I just haven't seen what they do until right now.

My life would be a lot easier if we could be friends.

"Enjoy your marshmallow," Grant says. Then he heaves himself off the log and saunters over to Allison and Willow.

What the… Did he just stop by to give me a marshmallow? That's weird. I assumed he'd want to talk about our trip to Fallenmouth, but instead he walked away. I will never understand that man.

For some reason, talking to Grant made me want to socialize with my fellow Sanctuary inhabitants. I start up conversations with several people until everybody gets tired and wants to go to bed. I hang around by the fire for a little longer, by myself, and watch the glowing coals. The first night shift is still guarding the camp, so they'll keep an eye on the fire too until it dwindles and eventually dies.

After a few minutes, I give up on staring at the coals and head for my tent on the outskirts of the camp. I pass by Grant's tent on my way there. A light burns inside. Grant is still awake. I wonder if he'll have trouble sleeping again tonight, and then I wonder why I should care. Well, I seem to have become his regular partner on trips into the wider world, so maybe I should care if the guy sleeps. His insomnia might jeopardize both our lives—and the life of anyone else who goes with us on our supply missions.

Damn. That means I need to talk to Grant.

Tents don't have doors, just a flap for an opening. But by the time I arrived in Sanctuary, they had already developed an etiquette for how to let someone know you want to enter their tent. We have doorbells. Yep, every tent features a small clump of jingle bells tied onto the canvas to the left of the flap. I have no idea where they found those bells, since I wasn't here then, but it was a clever idea.

I jingle the bells.

"Come in," Grant says.

Pushing the flap aside, I walk into the tent.

Grant lies sprawled on his cot, shirtless, his muscular torso gilded by the light from an oil lantern.

Holy shit, he's hot.

No, no, no. I am not attracted to him. Noticing his body is…a reflex or whatever.

"Did you want something?" he asks. "Or did you just miss me?"

He can't be flirting with me. That would be too weird. So what if I'm kind of staring at his bare chest? It means nothing. I might've taken off my denim shirt, leaving me with only a tank top to cover my upper body. But he can't be speaking in a sexier voice because he's attracted to me.

"I'm checking to make sure you're okay," I tell him. "You did pass out earlier today. And you said you haven't been sleeping, so I thought maybe I could help you relax."

He sits up, swinging his feet off the cot. "Help me how?"

Good question. How had I intended to relax him? By singing a lullaby? "I could read you a story. That always worked for me when I was a kid. My mom would read to me."

"Don't think we have any bedtime storybooks in this camp."

"I could probably remember one." *Stop yammering about bedtime stories, woman.* "Well, I guess this was a bad idea. I'll leave you alone."

Just as I turn to leave, Grant says, "Have a drink with me."

"What?" I turn back to him. That's when I notice a bottle of amber liquid sitting on the ground near his feet. "Is that bourbon?"

"Yeah." He pats the cot. "Sit down and have some."

"Where did you get booze?"

"On a mission a while back, before you showed up. I kept it in case of emergency."

"What's the emergency tonight?"

He picks up the bottle and unscrews the cap. "Can't sleep. Finally decided to try the Jack Daniels method for getting a good night's rest."

I amble over there and sit down beside him. "Getting drunk won't help. You'll wake up with a hangover."

"True. But I wasn't planning to get drunk."

He takes a swig from the bottle and sighs with satisfaction. Then he offers me the bottle.

What the hell. I grab it and take a swig. The bourbon burns down my throat, but then a delicious warmth spreads through me. Yeah, Grant's method is a good way to relax. So I toss back another mouthful. Mm, yeah, warm and cozy.

He takes the bottle and drinks more bourbon. "You're good with people, especially Willow. I didn't expect that."

"Because I'm a crazy person you got saddled with on supply missions."

"No. Because you take unnecessary risks."

I snatch the bottle from him and swig more bourbon. "I take risks because nobody else wants to. Maybe offing a few Echo creatures won't save the world, but it's a start."

"You could get yourself killed that way."

"Why do you care?"

He reclaims the bottle and gulps down a mouthful. "I have to care. Your recklessness could get someone else killed."

"I've saved lives."

"Yeah, I know." He sets the bottle on the floor and turns toward me. "Maybe I don't want you to die in the process."

"Like you care what happens to me."

He leans closer, his body inches away and his gaze boring into mine. "I do care."

Maybe it's the booze affecting me, but I suddenly feel warm in a very different way that has nothing to do with alcohol. I can't stop my gaze from traveling down to his chest and all those muscles. How does he stay in shape post-apocalypse? I haven't seen any workout equipment here. But damn, whatever he does to maintain those muscles, it works.

When I lift my gaze to his again, his pupils have dilated. He licks his lips while staring into my eyes. "Maybe we'd get along better on missions if we blew off some steam together."

Blow off steam? Yeah, the rough tone of his voice made it clear he's suggesting sex. But no, Grant wouldn't do that. He despises me.

My nipples have hardened, and slickness gathers between my thighs. Maybe we should have sex. It won't make me fall instantly in love with him, and we'll probably hate each other again in the morning. I glance at his chest again. To feel all those muscles flexing against me while he thrusts inside me...

"I want to kiss you," he murmurs. "Right now."

The bourbon has made me feel so deliciously warm and relaxed. I bet his lips are soft. When he slants even closer, his mouth brushes mine, and I realize I'd been right about those lips. His breaths whisper over my skin, and his blue eyes transfix me.

I haul him into me, crushing my mouth to his.

Grant wraps his arms around me just as he pushes his tongue between my lips. We both groan. I wriggle to get my arms around his neck while I glide my tongue around his and he devours me like I'm that bottle of bourbon and he wants to get drunk on the taste of me. God, this man knows how to kiss. He lays me down on the cot, his body covering mine, and I feel his erection mashed to my belly.

The bells jingle.

We keep kissing and start groping each other.

And the bells jingle again. "Grant, are you awake?"

He freezes. We both open our eyes while we still have our tongues in each other's mouths. Then Grant leaps off the cot and hurries to the entrance, pulling the flap back just enough to speak to whoever is out there.

"Oh hey, Allison," he says with a nervous little laugh. "What's up? Thought you'd be asleep already."

"I was. Then I got nauseous, but I realized I'd run out of that herbal tea you found for me. Do you have any?"

"Sure. Just a sec." Grant lets the flap fall shut as he races to a box in the corner. After rifling through its contents, he brings out a small cardboard box of tea. Then he rushes back to the flap to hand it to Allison. "Here you go."

"Thanks. Do have a friend in there with you?"

"No. Just me."

"Uh-huh," she says, like she doesn't buy his story for one second. "Well, I'll see you in the morning."

"Good night, Ally."

He closes the flap almost all the way, but leaves enough of a gap that he can peek out. After a moment, he returns to the cot, towering over me. "Better go to your tent and get some sleep."

Grant skims his gaze over me from head to toe, and his tongue darts out to wet his lips. Then he moves aside, waving for me to leave.

I want to tell him I don't appreciate being groped and kissed and then ordered to leave, but there's no point. I can tell he's in stoic mode again, which he seems to reserve only for me. I jump off the cot, straighten my shirt, and walk out.

What just happened? No idea, but it will never happen again.

CHAPTER SEVEN

Grant

I MANAGED TO SLEEP LAST NIGHT, THANKS TO THE BOURBON, BUT I endured long and erotic dreams about Erin. I might enjoy that if I didn't know the woman is reckless and destined to get somebody killed—herself or an innocent person, maybe both. No idea why I kissed her. It must've been the alcohol. Okay, maybe I enjoyed kissing her, and maybe I wanted to fuck her right there on my cot.

Thank goodness Allison showed up.

So sure, I slept last night. But only after waiting half an hour for my erection to go away. Of course, I woke up with another one, but that's a normal thing that happens every morning. It has nothing to do with Erin. I'm attracted to her, and I hate myself for feeling that way. That's why I've decided to blame the booze and forget about it.

Problem solved.

Yeah, I'm highly skilled at self-deception.

When I head out to the main area where we always gather for meals, I don't see Erin. Willow tells me she went down to the beach. The teenager also offers me food and won't leave me alone until I eat something. Since I don't think Erin would've told anyone about my forgetfulness when it comes to meals, I decide Willow just wants to be helpful. I appease her by eating a breakfast burrito. Yeah, somebody found tortillas during a recent supply mission. Beans, rice, and salsa taste better than ever post-apocalypse. Even rice cakes taste better, though I don't have any of those for breakfast.

After eating, I tell Willow I'm going to find Erin so we can discuss our next mission. The girl wants to go with me, but I convince her that she should stay with Allison. A pregnant woman needs company. Yes, I actually spoke those words to Willow. Maybe my IQ dropped overnight thanks to the bourbon.

Finally, I leave the camp and head through the woods on my own. We've all worn down a path by walking over the mountain so many times to get to the beach. Salt water isn't ideal for bathing, but we also found a natural spring. And yeah, we've worn down a trail to that too. Right now, I'm headed for the beach to find out what Erin is up to down there. Fishing? I doubt that.

I shouldn't care what she's doing. I'm not her keeper.

Just as I crest the mountain, I notice a lone figure on the beach. That must be Erin. I'm too far away to recognize her, but I don't see anyone else.

While I hike down the hill and onto the beach, I get closer to the person on the beach and see I was right. That is Erin. She had been standing on the sand gazing toward the ocean, but now she crouches to untie her shoes. While I amble toward her, she removes her shoes and socks, then takes off her shirt and pants.

I freeze. She can't be about to… No, Erin wouldn't take off her bra and panties.

But then she does.

Erin drops her underwear on the pile of clothes she made on the sand. Though she hasn't noticed me, I get a clear view of her body from the side.

I can't move anything except my eyes, which insist on following her as she wades into the surf and finally jumps into the deeper water just offshore. I clench my fists, struggling to stave off the lust that threatens to seize control of me. I've never experienced such intense desire before. It's wrong and weird.

Last night, it hadn't felt wrong or weird. Kissing Erin had made me feel something I haven't allowed myself to experience in months, not since I lost the love of my life to the apocalypse. No, I can't want Erin. Adele was the only woman I ever loved and the only one I ever wanted. To lust for someone else must be adultery.

Erin dives under the water, then springs up out of the waves with her eyes closed and a rapturous smile curving her lips. She stands amid the swells, visible from the waist up, and brushes her wet hair back with both hands.

Fuck, I'm getting hard.

I long to go over there and pull her into my arms to kiss her right before I drag her onto the beach and lose myself inside her body. I grind my teeth, breathing so hard my ears start to ring.

What else can I do? I spin around and stomp back toward the mountain path.

"Grant?" Erin hollers. "Is that you?"

I don't stop and do not look back. She calls out again, but I walk faster and disappear into the trees before she can run over here to stop me. I maintain my breakneck pace until I crest the hill and start down the mountain's rear flank. Then I slow just enough to keep from getting overheated. But yeah, seeing Erin naked has ensured I will feel overheated for quite a while. Thankfully, by the time I get back to Sanctuary my lust has faded.

Still, I march past everyone I come across in the camp, even Willow and Allison, without speaking or acknowledging I notice them. I glare down at the ground instead. Back inside my tent, I drop onto the cot and rest my elbows on my knees so I can cover my face with my raised palms.

The doorbell jingles.

"Go away," I snarl. "Wanna be alone right now."

"It's Allison. Are you okay, Grant?"

"Fine, yeah. Just need to…take a nap."

"Um, you just woke up two hours ago."

Shit. Of course I did. And I'm not at all tired. But I need to be alone right now, and I don't want to insult Allison by lying. I have no choice, though. If I tell her the truth, she'll want to play matchmaker or something. I love Ally like a sister, but I do not want to get involved with any woman ever again.

That means I have to lie. "I want to study the alchemical manuscripts for a while. Need peace and quiet for that."

"Oh. Sure thing, Grant. I'll let everybody know you're in monk mode."

I hear her footsteps recede.

Monk mode? I guess she means because monks holed up alone in their monasteries to create books. But they didn't make these manuscripts. I'm celibate, so that kind of makes me seem like a monk.

A memory of Erin's nude body blasts through my mind.

"Shit," I grumble. Then I grab the bottle of bourbon. But no, that won't make me feel better. I set the bottle down. "Shit, shit, shit."

I need to calm down and forget about that woman. The best way I know how to do that is with meditation. I get down on the floor, seated cross-legged, and rest my hands on my knees. Then I close my eyes, take a deep breath, and exhale it slowly. Starting from the top—literally, since I begin with the crown of my head—I let all other thoughts go and focus on feeling my skin without moving a muscle. I picture my scalp, ears, nose, and eyelids while sinking into the experience of feeling each of them.

The rest of the world fades from my perception.

I envision the rest of my body in the same manner as I let my psyche travel across my cheeks and lips, down my throat and over my shoulders. I sense every inch of my skin, and my breaths have become slow and regular, whispering through me on a level much deeper than sound or touch. A soft, warm sensation begins in my chest as I let my awareness glide ever downward. That warmth spreads throughout my body as I feel a soothing weight settle onto me. And my lips curve into a slight smile, relaxing the muscles there.

At last, I've reached a state of total relaxation, floating on a sea of warm, tingly contentment.

Bells jingle, but I barely notice the sound. It drifts out of my consciousness a split second later.

The bells jingle again. "Grant? Are you in there?"

My quiet bubble pops, and all the noise of the world rushes back into my awareness. *Aw, shit.* Why can't that woman leave me alone? "Go away, Erin. I'm busy."

"I think we need to talk. About what happened on the beach."

"Nothing happened."

She lifts the flap on my tent to peer in at me. When she notices me sitting on the floor with my hands on my knees, her brows knit together. "What are you doing?"

"I was meditating." With a groan, I push myself up off the ground. "Until you shattered my Zen moment."

"You actually meditate."

"No, I sit here pretending to meditate as a joke to make myself laugh when I'm all alone in my tent."

She steps inside, and the flap falls back down. "I'm serious, Grant. We need to talk about—"

"Wrong. We don't need to talk about anything." I glance down at the bottle of bourbon. Yeah, I'd really love to guzzle the entire contents right now. Erin drives me to drink. "You were being reckless again, end of story."

"Reckless? I took a bath in the ocean."

"Nobody bathes in saltwater."

"I do." She stalks up to me and plants her hands on her hips. "How can someone who meditates be so uptight?"

"Go away, Erin."

"No. I want to know why you were secretly watching me bathe in the nude."

I huff. "Nothing secret about it. I went down to the beach and stumbled onto you acting like a brainless bimbo. I turned around and left as soon as I saw you."

"Bullshit. You stood there gawking at me."

Maybe I had. Even a man who practices meditation has a weak moment now and then. I saw a naked woman and needed a minute to recover from the shock.

Erin moves a little closer. "Did you like what you saw?"

"Anything I think or feel is irrelevant and none of your business."

She opens her mouth—to chew me out some more, no doubt—but the jingling of my doorbell stops her.

"Who is it?" I call out, sounding grumpier than I would've liked.

"Allison. Everyone can hear you two arguing in there. Might want to dial it back a little."

"Sorry. We'll try to keep it down."

"I'd rather you didn't argue. Should I come in there and help you guys talk through your issues?"

"No, we can handle it ourselves. Thanks, Ally."

I hear Allison walking away.

Erin is still staring at me, but now with her chin lifted and her arms crossed. "How are we going to 'handle it' when you won't discuss the 'issues'?"

"You leave, that's how."

She puckers her lips and jabs a finger into my chest. "I will not leave until we talk about—"

An explosion detonates above our heads, the ka-pow sending palpable shock waves through the air that flutter the tent and rattle my eardrums.

Erin and I race outside and halt so fast that I stumble into her.

Above our heads, a black disk spins in the sky while streamers of blood red snake out from it, whipping around like the tails of demonic serpents. A crackling noise erupts in the wake of the explosion, and static electricity tingles over my skin, raising every hair.

"What is that?" Erin asks, her voice hushed.

"No idea. We need to find Dax and Ally."

I seize Erin's arm and drag her with me as I sprint through the camp to Dax and Allison's tent. I don't need to ring the bell. They're already standing outside with their heads tipped back, staring at the heavens.

A mechanical grinding noise originates from the sky and reverberates all the way down to ground level. The earth begins to shudder. I instinctively throw an arm around Erin just as Dax pulls Allison against him. What can we do? Nothing, except gaze in rapt horror as the entrance to the Echo opens wider and wider, grinding along at a snail's pace, accompanied by that earsplitting mechanical noise.

Everyone in Sanctuary has rushed outside to do the same thing—gape at the heavens.

Suddenly, the expanding radius of the Echo freezes.

A silence deeper than anything I've ever experienced falls over the world. No one moves. No one speaks. I'm pretty sure not a single one of us breathes either. The only sound I can hear is the pounding of my own heart.

The entrance to the Echo slams shut with a thunderous racket that shivers through the ground.

I glance at Erin and realize I've been clutching her to me. She doesn't seem to care. Her wide eyes remain glued to the sky, and her face has turned a shade or two paler.

"What the hell is going on in the Echo?" I ask, though I don't expect anyone to respond.

Dax does. "This is an omen. The Echo is struggling to reassert itself and expand to swallow the world."

"Let's not go all 'oh shit, we're about to die' just yet," I say. "The only thing we know for sure is that the Echo is having conniptions."

"Perhaps. But until yesterday, the entrance to the Echo could only be seen from the cities and some of the small towns."

"A few rural areas have seen it."

"But the entrance vanished from those places shortly after the alchemy of worlds ended."

"True." Dax hugs Allison more tightly, though his attention stays focused on the sky. "We need to figure out why this is happening. If the Echo has become volatile and unstable…"

"I have an idea for how to get answers."

Dax, Allison, and Erin swivel their heads toward me at the same time, though Erin does that while still nestled against me.

"What idea?" Allison asks. "I thought you didn't find anything at Fallenmouth."

"That's true. But I came up with this idea while I was meditating this morning." Right before Erin ripped my Zen serenity to shreds. But I won't mention that to Ally. "My plan is radical and crazy dangerous, but I think it's our only option for getting answers."

"What's your idea?" Erin asks. "You're the expert on the alchemy of worlds, which means it's your call."

I look at her, surprised by the sincerity in her voice and her expression. Maybe I like having her tucked against me with the warmth of her body chasing away the chill that had shivered through me while the Echo expanded overhead. Maybe I shouldn't like it, but I do.

"Here's my plan," I say. "We go inside the Echo."

CHAPTER EIGHT

Erin

G O INSIDE?" I STARE AT GRANT, BECAUSE HE MUST HAVE GONE IN-
sane. The Echo is a hell world populated by, as Dax phrases it,
desecrations of the human form. Every creature living in that world was
created as a twisted copy of someone in this world. "Dax barely survived
the Echo. Now you want to jump in there just for the hell of it?"

"Not for the hell of it." Grant squeezes words out between his gritted
teeth. "We need to get into the Echo so we can find answers. I still believe
Sefton kept notes on his plan to create another world and an apocalypse,
and he must've left those notes in the Echo. Otherwise, we would've found
something at Fallenmouth."

"The house had been destroyed. Sefton's notes probably got burned up."

"I don't think so. But Dax knows more about Sefton than I do."

Dax lifts his brows. "Do I? My brother changed, and I didn't realize it until
he created an apocalypse. Not sure my opinions will be helpful. The only thing
I can tell you for certain is that Sefton was very clever and completely insane."

"True," Grant says. "But a smart guy would want to keep his most
important notes in a place where no one would ever think to look for
them. Got any ideas?"

"No."

"Then it's my plan or bust."

Are we seriously talking about going into the Echo? Into hell? The creatures that live there are wickedly strong and vicious. We've gotten a taste
of their power and brutality during our supply missions, but we only see a
handful of creatures at one time. A world full of them…

I push away from Grant, even though I kind of liked feeling his body
plastered to mine. "Your idea is reckless. Wouldn't you say?"

"Yeah. But that doesn't mean we have to go about it in kamikaze fashion. We can come up with a game plan."

"Oh, I get it. My recklessness is dangerous, but yours is mature and thoughtful."

"Exactly."

I want to deck him. Or possibly rip his clothes off. *Ugh*. I wish we hadn't made out last night in his tent because that experience has knocked me off balance. Never again will I kiss Grant Larson or let him kiss me, and we will absolutely never have sex. He's too infuriating.

"No one is going into the Echo," Dax pronounces. "We will find another way to get answers."

"We don't have time for that," Grant says. "Two days in a row, the Echo had a conniption. And it was worse today."

"He's right," I say. "We can't wait. Grant and I need to go into the Echo today."

Grant raises his brows at me. "You're volunteering us both? Could've asked me first."

"We both know you want to do this. I'm volunteering. You can't volunteer for your own plan."

"This is a bad idea," Allison says. "Time moves differently in the Echo. You might get trapped in there for years while only a few days have passed in this world."

"That might not happen this time," I say. "Things have changed. The alchemy of worlds has stopped, and the Echo has clearly been altered because of that."

Grant nods. "She's right. But even if we wind up living in the Echo for years, it will be worth it to save the world."

"If you can save it," Allison says.

"We can. We will."

The intensity in his voice almost convinces me that we can save the world.

Dax exhales a long sigh. "All right. But you should take more volunteers with you."

"No," Grant says. "Just me and Erin. I won't risk anyone else's life. We both have military training and saw combat before the apocalypse."

Just the two of us? In the Echo? Yeah, I'm not ashamed to admit the idea terrifies me. But I've lived in a war zone before, and I can handle it again. I must do this.

"If you're determined to do this," Dax tells us, "you'll need to start your journey at the epicenter of the apocalypse. You need to go to Fort Worth, Texas."

Grant's lips curve into a grim smile. "Well, at least we've got somebody who can teleport us there."

"Once you're inside the Echo, no one can bring you back. You'll need to find your own way out."

"We'll manage."

How can he sound so positive of that? Neither of us has ever been to that world before.

"Even if you escape the Echo," Dax tells Grant, "we won't have any way to know when I should bring you back to Sanctuary."

"When we leave the Echo, we'll wait at the library. You can try to bring us back every day at noon. Agreed?"

"Yes." Dax makes a pained face. "I should go with you, but..."

"Ally needs you more than we do," Grant says. "I know that, and nobody expects you to take an insane risk like this. Besides, you're the best defense this community has."

"When would you like to go?"

"As soon as we can gather supplies."

Grant and I spend the next hour scrounging up whatever supplies we can reasonably carry in our backpacks. I never use a backpack, but Grant found one for me after he declared that I must have it. We can't carry everything we might need with us. Once we breach the Echo, we will need to find more supplies on our own.

I've experienced real war, and I know fear is a necessary and reasonable reaction to a situation like this. The key to survival is not letting the fear hold you back. Not that a war in the mundane world can compare to what the apocalypse has done or what might await us inside the Echo.

We run into Willow during our search for supplies, and she already knows what we plan to do. Allison and Dax had felt that everyone should know. Though we do keep some secrets from the others, this is one instance where we all agreed we should inform the community. If Grant and I fail, the Echo might swallow our world.

"Please don't go," Willow says as she hugs me. "I love you guys."

"We love you too, baby," I say while I stroke her hair. "And we're coming back. Don't worry. We've got a solid plan."

Grant lifts his brows. Yeah, maybe I shouldn't have essentially promised we will come back. But I can't let Willow spend who knows how long worrying we might never make it home.

Now that we have our supplies, Grant and I find Dax. The three of us tromp out to the edge of the camp, away from any other people.

It's time to go.

Allison rushes up to us, breathing hard as if she ran all the way here from the other side of the camp. She thrusts a canvas bag at Grant. "You forgot the books."

He accepts the bag, gripping it in one hand. "Thanks, Ally."

"Good luck." Allison hugs Grant and kisses his cheek, then hugs me too. "Be careful."

She walks away.

Once Allison has disappeared from view, Dax faces us. "It's time."

Grant and I take a few steps backward.

Dax clenches his fists and grits his teeth, his eyes narrowed to slits.

Whoosh. The world shifts around us in the space of a single heartbeat.

I glance around and try to get my bearings. We've landed in a city, I can tell that much for sure. "Is this Fort Worth? I've never been here before."

"Yeah, it's Fort Worth." Grant surveys the building directly in front of us. "I'd been here a few times on supply missions, before you showed up at Sanctuary. This is the public library."

The building once had tall columns that supported a portico. I know that because I see the columns, though they've been shattered, and the roof of the portico has collapsed on top of them. The remains have spilled down the steps and onto the street.

"Last time I was here," Grant says, "only the front pillars had been broken. Not sure what happened since then to cause more damage."

"If this is the epicenter of the apocalypse, then what happened earlier might have been much worse here and destroyed the rest of the portico."

"Yeah, you could be right." He removes his backpack to stuff the bag full of books inside it. At least, he tries to do that. The bag won't fit. "You got any room in your pack?"

"Maybe. Let me try." I slip out of my backpack and rummage inside it to make room for the books. "I can probably fit some of the books, but not all of them."

"For now, I'll just tie the bag onto my pack. Might find a better way to carry them as we make our way through the city."

"We're going into the Echo, not exploring Fort Worth."

"But we have to walk to the epicenter. It's thataway." He gestures vaguely behind and to the right of the library building. "Let's get moving."

I have no choice but to follow him since I know nothing about this city, before or after the apocalypse. When I'd caught him meditating in his tent earlier, the peaceful look on his face made me wonder why he never looks that way when we're together. I peeked into the tent before I rang the bells, mostly because I wasn't sure if he was in there. Okay, it might've partly been that, but mostly it was my nosiness. I wanted to snoop, just a little, to peek at those alchemy books. But he had been there, and I saw his blissful expression.

Have I ever felt that way? Don't think so. Maybe I need to meditate.

As we hike through the ruined city, I have nothing to do but ask questions. "Weren't you a deputy sheriff before the apocalypse?"

"Yes."

"And in the army before that?"

"Why are you interrogating me about things everybody knows? I should get to interrogate you too. What did you do for a living back then?"

"I owned a little sporting goods store." I stumble over a piece of rubble but catch myself, so I don't fall. "I thought we could get to know each other while we're trudging through the remnants of doomsday. We're about to go inside the Echo. Before we do that, we need to trust each other."

"We've been traveling into exclusion zones together for more than a month. Now you suddenly need to hug it out so we can forge a wartime bond?"

"Don't get sarcastic about it. I'm serious. You don't trust me, and that's a problem."

He stops walking and turns to look at me. "You don't trust me either. Why else would you take off on your own during every single mission we go on together?"

"You always need to be the big man, the hero, the only one who knows how to kill an Echo creature by driving a sword straight into its heart." I grip the straps of my backpack and gaze straight into his eyes. "Have you ever showed anyone else how to do that?"

He screws up his mouth and shifts his weight from one foot to the other. "No."

"Why not?"

"Because it's hard to do, and if you miss the exact center… Well, let's just say you won't be home for dinner that night."

"What does that mean? Did someone get killed on one of your previous missions because they tried to skewer a creature?"

He turns his head to stare at the huge black disk in the sky that is the entrance to the Echo. "Nobody died doing that. Nobody else almost died either."

I'm about to say something when I suddenly realize what he said. "Nobody *else*? Did you almost die trying to kill a creature that way?"

Grant bows his head and sighs. "Yeah."

"Were you alone when that happened?"

He winces and still won't look at me. "I made a stupid mistake. I let a creature lure me away from my team. Once he had me alone, he went for me. I tried to pierce the center of his heart, but he parried at the last second, and I missed. He kicked me in the chest so hard I couldn't breathe, and the cutlass fell out of my hand. Luckily, Dax came looking for me and killed the creature before it could kill me."

"Did he stab its heart?"

"No. He beheaded the creature."

I tip my head to the side while I study him. "You've always told me that the only surefire way to kill an Echo creature is to pierce its heart."

"That's true. The creatures seem to have a slightly different anatomy than humans, and their hearts are the weakest points. I learned that the hard way. Beheading a creature in the heat of battle is damn hard work." He lifts his head. "Trust me. I've done it before."

"I've heard Dax mention that their spines are much harder than the human version, almost like stone."

"Some of them have spines like that. We got lucky early in the apocalypse and fought creatures that had weaker cervical vertebrae. That's how we managed to behead them." He rubs his neck and winces again. "Another lesson we learned the hard way, before you found Sanctuary."

I want to ask him if someone died because no one understood the anatomy of Echo creatures or if not all creatures have identical bone structure. But I've quizzed him enough for now. "Thank you for answering my questions, Grant."

His eyes go wide, but only for a second. "Uh, you're welcome."

"You can ask me questions too."

"We should get moving again."

No, I won't get any other information from him until he decides to tell me.

CHAPTER NINE

Grant

I LEAD THE WAY AS WE START OFF DOWN THE WRECKED STREET AGAIN, and I avoid looking at Erin, even peripherally. She wants to understand me, I guess, but she shouldn't care about that. I've given her no reason to want to know me better. But after wending our way through the rubble for three more blocks, I realize I should give her what she wants—information about me—whether I feel comfortable telling her or not. "There are a few things you should know."

"Like what?"

I feel my expression tighten, and I'm pretty sure I wear a grimly determined look. Can't be Zen when I'm about to share the details of the worst moments in my life. But I keep my gaze riveted to the road ahead while I speak. "My wife and son died in the first wave."

"I'm so sorry, Grant. What happened to them?"

"We left our son, Billy, with a babysitter while Adele and I went hiking in the mountains near our home." I halt and glare up at the Echo, but inside I feel cold and hollow. "When the apocalypse hit, we were fifty miles away from our son. We tried to get home, but the fireballs and the lightning made it almost impossible. The forest was on fire. Creatures poured out of a hole in the sky."

Erin waits for me to go on, almost as if she's giving me time to collect myself before I finish the story. The fact that I've decided to tell her doesn't mean I have feelings for Erin, not even the friendly kind. But we need to learn to trust each other, and that requires sharing personal information.

I bow my head and suck in a shaky breath. "A creature took Adele. Two of his buddies grabbed me, and I wasn't strong enough to get away from them." I squeeze my eyes shut, but nothing can ward off the memories. "I watched while those monsters…did things to my wife that I won't describe."

Erin doesn't speak. Well, at least she has a modicum of good sense.

I remember every second of what those monsters did, though I wish I didn't. Life post-apocalypse is bad, but life in the early days of the alchemy of worlds was beyond hell. "Luckily, Adele passed out pretty quick. Never felt the worst of what they'd done to her. Then they just let me go and went who knows where to do who knows what. I collapsed on the ground and sobbed."

"Oh, Grant, I… That's horrible."

"Yeah." She has no idea how horrible it was, and I will not explain it. Some things should never be spoken of again. "I managed to get back to our house, though I couldn't carry Adele's body, so I had to leave her in the woods." My throat goes thick, and I want to stop talking about that day, stop thinking about it. Instead, I pull in a deep breath, blow it out, and continue. "Our house was destroyed—by the crazy-powerful lightning, I think—but I found the remains of my son and his babysitter. After that, I fought my way out of Los Angeles County, eventually found an abandoned boat that still had fuel, and made my way north."

"That's when you ran into Dax and Willow."

I almost smile as I remember bumping into them, but the expression crumbles away as memories of Adele and Billy torment me. I marshal all my Zen training and force myself to focus on the here and now. "Yeah, that's when I met Dax and Willow. They happened to stumble onto my little campsite on the beach. The same beach where we all go to fish and swim now."

"It couldn't have been easy to relive those events, and I'm grateful you shared it with me."

She's grateful? I can't see why. When I look at her, she seems almost…sympathetic. I've never shared my whole story with anyone, not even Dax and Allison. Why did I spill my guts to Erin? "You are the only one who knows the details. Guess that means I trust you."

"Maybe we only thought we didn't trust each other because we're still recovering from our losses."

"Who did you lose?"

"My sister. Our parents died years ago." She bites her lip and gazes at me for a moment, then seems to reach a decision—to tell me her story. "We flew to New York City on vacation. Hayley had just graduated from Penn State, with honors, and I was so proud of her. The trip to New York was a graduation present. But when the apocalypse hit, we got separated. I searched and searched for her, fighting my way past Echo creatures and dodging fireballs and lightning."

"Did you find her?"

She bites her lip again, harder this time so the skin turns white. "Kept searching for two months. When I finally found Hayley's body, she had been…eaten. But her face was the least damaged, and I knew it was her. She was still wearing the little diamond earrings I'd given her for her birthday."

I experience a strong urge to hug her. But I doubt Erin would appreciate that.

"The creatures in New York had blocked every borough," she continues. "I had to find ways to break through their barricades, but I finally discovered a weak spot and escaped the city. Caught rides with people whose cars still had gas, even rode a horse for a while until somebody else needed that mare more than I did. Walked and walked and walked."

"You hiked all the way to California?"

"No. I met a woman who had an airplane. Her husband had been on a business trip to San Francisco, so she offered to let me fly there with her because she'd heard a rumor the apocalypse hadn't touched that part of the state. But we ran out of gas. Made an emergency landing in a clearing maybe ten miles from the beach where you met Dax and Willow. Kept walking until I met someone from Sanctuary."

"I wish you'd never had to go through all of that. I wish none of us had."

"Me too. Things were getting really bad in New York by the time I got out of there. I mean, the deepest level of actual hell kind of bad." Her gaze goes distant for a moment, as if she's concentrating on a memory or devising a plan. "I think New York might be the capital city of the apocalypse."

"Why would you think that?"

"The way they fortified the whole thing." A sigh gusts out of her, and she lets her shoulders sag. "Even if that's true, it doesn't help us. Does it?"

"Not sure. Right now, we need to focus on our mission." I cup her elbow with my hand while we start walking again. "We need to get inside the Echo."

We travel at a brisk pace, and soon the Paddock Viaduct comes into view. The bridge spans the West Fork of the Trinity River. I've come to this city several times with Dax and other members of our community, but never with Erin. She joined our group about a month ago, after we'd given up on scrounging for supplies here. It's too dangerous.

If the Echo creatures have a capital city, it should be Fort Worth, not New York. This was ground zero for the apocalypse, after all.

"Why haven't we seen any creatures?" Erin asks. "I thought all the cities were overrun with them."

"They are." I stop dead, mere feet from the on-ramp to the viaduct. "You're right. We should've seen some creatures."

"Does it matter that we didn't? Maybe they've killed each other off."

"I doubt that. All the creatures I've met stuck together." I turn in a circle to survey the area, but I still can't see or hear anything other than the whispering of a breeze and my own heartbeat thumping in my ears. "I don't like this."

"Neither do I."

"We don't have time to explore the city for answers." I grasp her elbow again, urging her to walk with me. "Let's get into the Echo fast."

As we step onto the bridge, we walk faster and faster until it becomes jogging, then sprinting. The entrance to the Echo hovers directly above our heads. The black disk at its center rotates like a whirlpool, and spinning serpents of black and golden yellow unfurl from its edges. A faint mechanical sound emanates from the opening.

I stop us when we reach the center of the viaduct.

"What now?" Erin asks. "How do we get inside the Echo?"

"Not sure. It's up in the sky, so we need a way to climb or jump in there."

"Climb or jump?" Erin's voice is filled with genuine disbelief, and her jaw has gone slack. "Are you insane? I don't see any way that either of us can jump into the sky high enough to climb inside the Echo."

I scratch my jaw as I gaze up at the spinning black disk above our heads.

Erin plants her hands on her hips. "You didn't have a plan at all, did you? No, you just dragged me here and… What? Hoped for a miracle?"

Maybe I had brought us here with a plan that amounts to squat. That doesn't change the fact that we must get into the Echo. *Think, moron, this was your idea. Find a way.*

Growling originates from directly behind us.

We both turn sideways to see the other end of the viaduct. Echo creatures have swarmed the on-ramp. Every sort of monster imaginable stalks across the bridge toward us. When I glance in the other direction, I notice shadowy figures approaching the off-ramp.

Aw, shit. I got us trapped on a bridge. What a fantastic job I'm doing.

I channel all my Zen energy to remain calm and seemingly unaffected by our situation. Then I wave to the creatures coming toward us. "Hey, nice to see you guys. We were getting lonely out here by ourselves. Any of you know how to jump into the Echo, by any chance?"

Erin gapes at me again like she thinks I've gone insane. Maybe I have. My cutlass is inside the scabbard attached to my backpack, and I know Erin has a sword too. We've got handguns, but those are reserved for only the most desperate situations. We don't have an unlimited supply of ammo.

The creatures jog toward us, growling and snarling and gnashing their teeth. Some sport scaly skin, others have horns and bumpy flesh, and even more display other types of weirdness. The beasts approaching from behind will reach us soon too.

"Got any brilliant ideas?" Erin asks. "You're the genius who got us into this mess."

"Shut up and let me think." Yeah, Erin always knows how to shatter my Zen energy.

"Maybe we should ask one of those nice monsters to give us a ride on his back."

"Sarcasm doesn't help."

Erin saunters toward the creatures and waves her arms in the air. "Hey, y'all! Wanna play?"

What the hell is she doing? And why is she speaking with a southern accent?

The largest and scariest-looking beast stops within ten yards of Erin, towering several feet above our heads. His long hair flies wild around his face and shoulders while yellow liquid oozes from the two horns on his forehead. "Yeah, girlie, I'd love to play with you."

"You can have me any way you want." She whips out her cutlass. "After you give me what I want."

The sultry tone of her voice has a bizarre effect on me. My dick twitches. Oh great, that's just what I need—to get an erection in front of a horde of monsters. Can't believe my dick thinks now is the right time to wake up and beg for sex. Maybe it's her fake southern accent that gets me aroused, or maybe it's something weirder and darker that I don't have time to think about right now.

Since I have no other options, I decide to play along with her game. I come up beside Erin and sling an arm around her waist. "Hey, baby, are you starting the fun without me?"

The crazy chick gives me a sexy smile. "Don't worry. I'm sure this guy would be glad to share me with you." She winks at the creature with the weeping horns. "I bet you'd like to screw us both, huh?"

"Yeah," the beast growls. "Let's do that now."

She wags a finger at him. "Uh-uh-uh. Not until you take us into the Echo. I've always wanted to fuck in a hell world."

Erin is more than a crazy chick. She's stark-raving mad.

And I'm beginning to have doubts about her so-called plan. "Erin, maybe we should—"

The weeping-horns beast flies at us, scooping us both up in his massive arms, then bends his knees and vaults into the sky.

I crane my neck to peer up at the entrance to the Echo. It zooms closer and closer while the beast holding us growls and snarls. The mechanical noise we'd heard from ground level grows louder, but it doesn't deafen us. I can still hear the monsters below making all sorts of bizarre noises.

We crash through the portal—and the creature lands flat on his feet. He does not release us.

"Great plan, Crazy Chick," I mutter under my breath.

Erin flashes me a scowl, then aims a sultry smile at the beast. "Let us go and I'll give you the best striptease you've ever seen."

The creature growls softly. "Then I fuck you."

"Uh-huh."

Amazingly, the beast releases us.

We back away quickly. Erin still has her cutlass in her hand, so I whip mine out too.

The creature chuckles. "Stupid humans. I'm stronger than you puny things."

I rush at the beast and ram my sword straight into his heart. But the tip breaks off. *Oh, shit.* "Run, Erin! Now!"

Erin seizes my hand, and we bolt.

Chapter Ten

Erin

WHY DID WE RUN? BECAUSE EVEN I'M NOT RECKLESS ENOUGH TO fight an Echo creature that outweighs us, is six feet taller than us, and apparently has armor plating. Jeez, who knew that might happen? Piercing a creature's heart kills it, but only if we can penetrate its skin. Now we're trapped in the Echo with who knows how many beasts that have armored bodies. Our best offensive tactic has been stolen from us.

"Got any ideas?" I ask while breathing hard because we're racing around a corner and down an alley. This place is clearly a city, but I've never seen another one like it. No time for sightseeing, though. That beast is still on our tails.

"Yeah, I've got an idea," Grant says. "Keep running."

Like I needed him to tell me that.

We race out of the alley and onto another street, this one featuring a wide roadway that could accommodate four lanes, though I don't see any lines demarcating them. I'm in the Echo, so I shouldn't expect the rules here to mirror those on earth. But the creatures in this world are twisted copies of human beings, which makes me wonder if they share more than a passing resemblance.

No time to ponder that idea.

When I glance back, that damn beast is still rushing after us with his massive feet pounding so hard that I feel tremors beneath me. I haven't seen any vehicles in this world, but I glimpse a shape up ahead that might be an SUV or a similar-size car.

Grant veers left as if he intends to turn down another street.

I grab his arm, halting us both. Though I'm gasping for breath, I manage to tell him, "Go straight. Think there's a car."

"Are you hoping a creature left his keys in it?"

"Yeah. But if not, I can hot-wire it."

His brows shoot up, but he doesn't get the chance to speak. That creature barrels toward us, and needing to stop to talk to Grant has given the monster a chance to narrow our lead.

We run.

The shape I'd noticed in the twilight gloom resolves into a familiar object—an SUV-type vehicle, though it looks quite different from the versions back home on earth. Its boxy shape has many sharp angles, almost like the exterior of a stealth fighter jet. When I yank on the handle of the passenger door, it doesn't give. Damn, the car is locked.

"Allow me," Grant says as pulls out a Beretta .9mm handgun he had kept holstered under his jacket. "Stand back."

We both move away a few yards.

Grant fires at the car window. The glass shatters.

I guess Echo creatures haven't reinvented tempered glass.

Grant reaches inside the vehicle to unlock the doors, then pulls it open and waves for me to jump in.

"I need to hot-wire this thing," I say, "so I'll drive."

"No way. You start it, then I drive."

The creature roars as he barrels toward us, only one block away now.

"Fine," I hiss.

Grant smirks as we hurry around to the driver's side. He yanks the door open, and I shrug out of my backpack, handing it to him once I've retrieved my mini toolkit from an outer pocket. I hope to hell this car isn't the kind that requires unscrewing the steering column to hot-wire it. I lean inside and find the ignition tumbler on the right side of the steering column. Still can't tell for sure. So I bring out a mini screwdriver and shove it into the tumbler, then twist it.

The engine rumbles to life.

Hallelujah. We caught a break.

"Want my due!" the creature bellows, while his footsteps pound even louder, their vibrations rattling my bones.

That beast will reach us in a matter of seconds.

I leave the screwdriver in the ignition tumbler and sprint to the passenger door while Grant leaps in on the driver's side. I've barely slammed my door shut when the vehicle launches forward like a rocket with the engine snarling.

Our big, gnarly friend throws an arm out to sideswipe our car, but he misses. His infuriated roar makes my ears hurt.

"Got any idea where we're going?" I ask. "Because I have no fucking clue."

"Neither do I. We'll wing it."

I twist around in my seat to check on our angry buddy. His figure is swiftly receding from view. Guess he can't run sixty miles an hour. Good to know.

"Thanks for getting us into hot water with your recklessness again," Grant says, his gruff tone not unlike that of the beast we just swatted off our tails. "That was really helpful."

"Hey, I just saved your sorry ass. Try being grateful."

"I said thank you."

"Sarcastically. That doesn't count."

Grant veers around a corner so fast that I get thrown against my door. "At least we're in the Echo now. But you ticked off a huge monster. What if he comes looking for us?"

"Keep driving until we get well away from where we left him."

"Glad you had a solid plan when you got us thrown into a hell world."

"Shut up and drive."

My partner in this insanity continues driving very fast and swerving around corner after corner. I search for a seatbelt, but the car doesn't seem to have those. It could stand to get some new shocks, but otherwise, it isn't half bad—for a post-apocalyptic vehicle.

"The Echo has only been around for a few months," I say. "How did the creatures make all these buildings and cars and who knows what else in such a short time?"

My partner grunts. "How do you think? Magic. For all we know, Sefton didn't just create twisted copies of humans, but also warped versions of everything else, including cars and buildings."

"Good point. I didn't think of that."

He glances at me sideways and smirks. "Did you just give me a compliment?"

"I said you made a good point. Don't read too much into that."

Grant relaxes into his seat while he slows the car a bit. "I might not agree with your methods, but you did get us here. Your crazy idea got us in."

"You can say it. I won't gloat or make fun of you."

"I can say what?"

"Do the words 'thank you' ring a bell? And this time, you could try being sincere when you say it."

He doesn't respond, but instead focuses on the road ahead.

Though I have no idea if the time on my watch corresponds in any way to the time here in the Echo, I have no other way to gauge how long we've been driving. Ten minutes go by, then fifteen, and then twenty. Finally, he pulls over at a gas station. The charred sign hangs at a sharp angle, seeming to dangle from a single nail, and the pumps look like they survived a gun battle. A giant hole gapes in the center of the roof, probably thanks to one of the Echo's ultra-powerful lightning strikes or a hit from a fireball.

Grant parks near one of the pumps.

"What are you doing?" I ask. "Kinda doubt the Echo takes Mastercard. If these pumps even work."

"Need to try. Not much left in the tank."

"But gas pumps need electricity to work."

He swings his door open and hops out, then points toward the left side of the building. "There's an emergency generator. I'll check if it's got any juice left."

"Oh. Okay." I hadn't thought of that, but I'm still not convinced it'll work.

"Stay in the car," he says. "I'll be just a minute."

I watch Grant jog over to the generator that sits on the ground near the gas station's wall. He kneels to fiddle with the thing. Soon, the generator grumbles to life. He grins at me over his shoulder and gives me the thumbs-up sign. Then Grant jogs back over here. I roll down my window, which I have to do the old-fashioned way by cranking a handle, and peer at Grant while he unscrews the fuel tank cap and slides the pump nozzle inside. When he squeezes the handle, he once again grins and gives the thumbs-up sign.

He is kind of cute when he smiles.

Okay, all right, he's completely adorable when he does that. I've seen him grin at other people, though not often. He never smiles that way at me. Until now. And I suddenly realize I'm grinning at him too.

I pull my head back into the car and face forward. Not because he caught me smiling. No, what disturbs me is the fluttery sensation in my tummy when Grant grinned.

Once he's filled up the tank, he screws the cap back on and trots into the half-destroyed gas station building. I'm just about to rush in there to make sure a creature hasn't eaten him when Grant trots back out carrying four plastic gas cans. He fills them up and stashes them in the rear cargo area of our vehicle.

Then he jumps into the driver's seat and pulls the door shut. And he smiles at me again. "Well, you might've dropped us into the deep end with no life preservers, but at least we have gas now. Enough to last awhile."

"Why are you suddenly Mr. Optimism? Five minutes ago, you were preaching doom and gloom."

"I never preach."

"But you don't deny the doom and gloom part."

He shrugs one shoulder while he twists the screwdriver to start up the engine. "Think what you want. I believe everyone should have the freedom to believe and behave as they like."

"Oh really." I turn partway toward him while he steers the car back onto the road. "Then why do you harass me about my recklessness? You are a hypocrite."

"No, I worry—Never mind. You're too pigheaded to listen, anyway."

Did he just almost admit he worries about me? Can't be sure. He didn't finish the sentence.

"Got any clue where we're going?" I ask. "You're the one who wanted to get inside the Echo, but we seem to be aimlessly exploring this city or whatever it is."

"I'm looking for a hideout."

"We came here to hide from the Echo creatures? Jeez, we could've done that in our own world."

He huffs, then snarls, "Not hiding. We need a relatively safe place to hunker down while we figure out our next move."

"And you complained that I didn't have a plan."

"Stop bitching and help me look for a hideout."

I open my mouth to issue a scathing retort, but decide against that. We're partners now, whether we like it or not, and we'll both need to make concessions if we have any chance of figuring out why the Echo is having conniptions. I stare out the window and watch for a good hideout. Grant does the same, though he also has to keep an eye on the road. We travel into an area of the city that has fewer buildings and no houses, which I take for an industrial zone. I see warehouses but also buildings that look like abandoned stores. This whole world seems abandoned, at least the parts I've seen so far.

"How about there?" I ask. I'm pointing to one of the smaller buildings that has a parking lot, though the asphalt has been reduced to rubble. "It's away from other buildings, but not conspicuously separate."

"Yeah, that looks pretty good. Let's check it out."

Grant pulls into the wrecked parking lot. Its pitted surface makes my teeth clack together, and I wind up tensing my jaw to keep from breaking my molars. He parks right beside the building's main doors. Grant pulls the screwdriver out of the ignition tumbler and hands it to me.

I stuff it into my backpack.

He climbs out, leaving his pack in the car.

Following his lead, I leave my pack too and trail after him as he pushes through the double doors and wanders into the building. Without electricity, we have no lights to guide us. But Grant pulls a flashlight out of his jacket pocket and flicks it on. The glow spreads out to illuminate a radius of maybe fifteen feet around us, with most of that area ahead of us.

We stand inside a hardware store.

Grant halts near a bin full of penny nails and turns in a circle to take in our surroundings. "Not exactly the Hilton, but we can make it work. Don't you think?"

Am I hallucinating, or did he ask for my opinion? I need a moment to process that fact before I can respond. "Sure, I guess so. Maybe they've got sleeping bags in here. You know, as part of a display."

"Let's go a little deeper and find out exactly what supplies we can find here."

We walk side by side into the bowels of the building, discovering more than just hardware supplies. Though I'd first taken this for that kind of store, I soon realize it's more like a home improvement center than a hardware store. We find a furniture department too, with a full bedroom set on display, bedding and all. Damn, I could live here. Sleeping on an actual mattress? I vaguely remember when I did that every night.

I can't resist. I flop onto the bed on my back and sigh with deep contentment. "Oh yeah, let's make a home right here."

Grant sits on the bed's edge. "We're making this our hideaway, then?"

"Sure. Might as well take comfort where we can find it." I rise to a sitting position, propped up by my straight arms, with my legs outstretched. "Doesn't it seem weird that the Echo was apparently devastated just like the earth, but it seems like it was a normal world before that?"

"Yeah, it's weird."

"What does it all mean?"

"No idea. But we're going to find out."

CHAPTER ELEVEN

Grant

WISH ERIN HADN'T JUMPED ONTO THE BED AND SIGHED WITH ALL the satisfaction of a woman who just had amazing sex. Now that she's sitting up, I still wish she would climb off the damn bed. Something about seeing her lying on a cushy mattress while smiling with sheer pleasure makes me horny. Yeah, that's exactly what I need right now—to get a hard-on. I cannot and will not have sex with her.

Okay, I *can* do it. I'm fully capable of performing the act. But slaking my lust would be a mistake.

I jump off the bed. "Let's bring our stuff in here and find a way to get more light."

We grab our junk from the car and stash our backpacks in the bedroom display, then hide the gas cans in the front among the aisles of hardware. We find food too, though it's all the prepackaged and not entirely healthy variety. Apocalypse outlaws can't be picky. I'll even eat pork rinds if it comes down to that. But I doubt it will be necessary since I plan for us to take surreptitious trips out into the wider world of the Echo—to find more supplies, but mostly to search for answers. We came here to uncover the reason for the strange things emanating from this land that have bled into the normal world, and I will never forget our goal.

After gathering some stuff we found inside this building, we return to our new "bedroom" to talk about our next moves. But first, Erin has a different topic in mind.

"Doesn't it seem a little too easy?" she asks. "I mean the way we found a car that could be hot-wired, found a gas station that had a generator, and found a store that has almost everything we need to survive."

"What's too easy about hot-wiring the car? You did that."

"You're not a car guy, are you?"

"No. I can change a flat and fill up the wiper fluid, but that's about it."

She moves the puffy pillows to make them into a pile, then she wriggles backward to lean against them. "In our world, not many cars can be hot-wired anymore. Every break we got seemed way too coincidental for my taste. One break, sure. But three? And we found exactly what we needed every time."

"Maybe you have a point, but I prefer to be optimistic."

Erin snorts out a laugh. "Since when? You're Mr. Doom, not Captain Optimism."

"You haven't seen me at my best. I'm usually upbeat and relaxed."

"I've heard a rumor to that effect, but I assumed it was baloney. All you do is growl and snarl and snap at me. Oh, and let's not forget the dirty looks."

She's right, but not the way she thinks, and I will not explain to her that I only act that way when she's around. The annoying woman will think that means something. I refuse to consider what it might suggest. Yeah, denial is my best friend.

"I apologize for treating you that way," I tell her. "We're stuck in the Echo together, so we should find a way to get along without beating each other senseless."

"Sounds like a reasonable idea."

"The sun is setting out there, so I think we should hunker down for the night. Okay?"

"Yeah." She bites the inside of her lip and scrunches her brows. "I wonder how long day and night last in this world. Would it be the same as on earth since the Echo is a twisted version of our world?"

"Not a clue."

"But you've been studying physics and alchemy. You're the expert on the Echo."

I laugh, but it's a bitter sound. "Expert? Nobody can claim that title except for Sefton Stainthorpe, and he's dead."

"Complain about my word choice all you want. The fact is that you know more about Sefton's original plan than anyone else."

Maybe I do, but I haven't been able to make sense of that information yet. Sefton must have left his notes here in the Echo. I just need to figure out where. Does he have a place like Fallenmouth here in this world? I'm too damn tired to think about that right now.

I climb onto the bed and crawl across to the other side, lying down next to where she sits. "I'm going to sleep now."

"Just like that?"

"Yeah."

"Mind if I leave the light on?"

"Do what you want."

Though I don't open my eyes, I can hear her moving around on her side of the bed and feel her movements jostling the mattress as she settles in for sleep. We had found a battery-operated lantern and some batteries earlier. If she wants to keep a light on, that won't bother me at all. I can sleep anywhere. Well, not lately. I've had trouble getting any shuteye, and knowing our home world might be razed at any second if the Echo consumes it doesn't help me relax.

Naturally, I toss and turn, though I avoid bumping into Erin.

After a while, she blows out an annoyed sigh. "How am I supposed to sleep while you're bouncing around?"

"I'm bouncing? You wriggle and jump more than anybody I've ever met."

"Me? I haven't moved in the past twenty-three minutes, but for you, tossing and turning is an aerobic workout that apparently lasts all night."

"Shut up and let me sleep."

"Happy to—if you ever do fall asleep."

I grumble and roll over onto my side, facing away from her. But I still can't sleep. I sneak a look at my watch several times and learn the dismaying fact that I've been trying to rest for an hour and a half, not including the first twenty-three minutes that Erin counted. I gently turn onto my back, so I won't disturb her.

"Still awake too," she says. "This has to stop."

I mumble things that don't turn out to be words.

Erin wriggles closer and reaches for the zipper on my pants.

"What are you doing?" I demand.

"Helping you relax." She bats my hand away when I try to block her from pulling my zipper down. "Close your eyes, be quiet, and you'll feel better very soon."

She can't intend to—No, Erin hates me.

Well, we did almost have sex last night.

No, I must be misinterpreting her motives. She wants to remove my pants to make me more comfortable. Yeah, because her hand brushing my dick makes me feel totally relaxed.

She finishes unzipping me, then slips a hand inside my pants to pull my dick out.

"Erin, what—"

"Shush. Lie back and enjoy the gift I'm about to give you."

Considering the way my heart is pounding, I won't get any sleep for sure. Guess I might as well let her do what she wants. Yeah, it's a common-sense decision. I haven't surrendered because I know she wants to give me head and I haven't experienced any kind of orgasm in a long time.

She closes her fist around the base of my cock. "Can't deny you have a gorgeous dick. And you got hard so fast." She drags her tongue up my length and back down again. "Mm, you taste good too. Can't wait to suck you off and swallow everything you give me."

Fuck, she's actually going to do this.

Erin massages my balls with one hand while she swallows my cock. Her cheeks cave in while she gently sucks, and her other hand pumps me in sync with her mouth movements. I groan and sag into the mattress. While she keeps working me, I can't stop myself from watching everything she does, and I start breathing harder. She closes her eyes and moans as she pumps faster and sucks harder.

A strangled sound emerges from me.

She removes her mouth from my dick and wriggles around to crouch over my thighs facing me. Then she sets her hands on my hips and swallows me again, licking and sucking while she makes little grunting noises and my back arches. I clench the covers under me, and though my body wants me to shut my eyes, I need to keep watching her. Erin's gaze remains nailed to mine, which is the hottest thing I've ever seen.

"Fuck, Erin, ah…" Pressure mounts inside me, and I feel it barreling down my spine. Any second now…

She reaches up to pinch my nipple.

Rapid-fire spasms grip my cock, and I shout wordlessly while I come inside her warm, soft mouth. She keeps working me until I'm done, then sits up and licks her lips. "Mm, yeah, that was good."

"What was good?"

"You, Grant. I could devour you all night long." She returns to her side of the bed, rolls over, and sighs. "Good night. I'm sure you'll sleep better now."

I do feel more…relaxed now. So I close my eyes and try to let what she just did for me slacken my muscles and ease me out of consciousness, down into sleep.

"Time to rise and shine, Grant."

"What?" I mumble.

"Get up. We have world-saving to do, remember?"

"But I just fell asleep."

She laughs. "Just? You've been asleep for eight hours."

My lids fly open. I spring into a sitting position and glance around, whipping my head left and right several times. Though we're in the back of the store, I can see the first rays of sunrise throwing their pink and gold light all the way into our little sanctuary. "I haven't gotten more than one consecutive hour of sleep in weeks. I toss and turn, wake up repeatedly, and—"

"You're welcome." She's being sarcastic, of course. Erin doesn't know how not to harass me.

I rub my eyes. "Excuse me?"

Erin gives me a wry smile from her perch at the foot of the bed, where she kneels. "I said 'you're welcome,' to save you from needing to lavish me with your gratitude. I did give you amazing head last night, after all."

Oh yeah, she did that. But I still can't understand why.

"Men always fall asleep after sex," she says. "At least, that's been my experience. You are a stereotypical guy."

"Gee, thanks." A yawn overtakes me, and I stretch my arms out. "I do feel better. Rested, I mean."

But also feel kind of weird about what happened last night.

I suddenly notice what she's wearing—gray shorts that hug her hips and barely cover her ass, a blue tank top with matching blue socks, and a pair of hiking boots. "You changed clothes? What you're wearing barely qualifies as clothing, but still—"

"Ugh. I made sure you're well rested, and all you can do is complain about my outfit." She slides off the bed to stand near the foot, which lets me see nearly all of her sexy body. "My clothes were dirty, so I found new ones."

The way her hair hangs in loose waves around her face and kisses her shoulders doesn't help me avoid the morning erection issue. I feel myself getting firm already, but I don't think I can pass it off as completely because I just woke up. She looks too damn hot in that outfit.

I jump off the bed. "Think I'll find some new clothes too. But you really need to change into something more appropriate for battling monsters. I'm sure we'll meet plenty of those when we go out to search for Sefton's private hideaway."

"Wear whatever you want, but I am not changing my clothes. It's already hot outside. Since our car doesn't seem to have air conditioning, I need to dress for the weather, so I don't get heat stroke."

"Your legs are fully exposed. Any creature that attacks you will go for your vulnerable areas." I point at her thighs. "Like your legs."

"They won't get the chance."

"You aren't invincible."

She rolls her eyes.

"Grow up, Erin. Acting like a spoiled child doesn't suit you."

I stalk over to the clothing section of the store and hunt around for appropriate stuff to wear. She's right about the weather here, or at least in this part of the Echo. I have no idea how big this world is, and Dax couldn't tell me either. I guess he stuck to one section of the Echo, though he never mentioned anything that resembles this region.

Erin didn't follow me, which makes me suspicious of what she's up to now.

I pull on fresh clothes and new boots, then march back to our bedroom. She isn't there. That woman loves to tick me off, so she's probably hiding somewhere watching me look for her. "Erin! Where the hell are you?"

"Over here. I found awesome stuff."

I jog in the direction her voice seemed to originate from and see her standing behind a glass-topped counter in front of a display of firearms, knives, and other weapons. She's holding a machine gun and test sighting it.

When I reach the counter, she gives me a smug smile. "While you were feeling self-righteous, I found us loads of weapons."

"Yeah, I can see that." I nod to her machine gun. "Does that have a full magazine?"

"Not yet. I need to load the rounds. But I think it's fully automatic."

She dry fires the machine gun, and her lips curl into a satisfied smile.

"Got another one of those?" I ask.

She hooks a thumb over her shoulder. "Take your pick. This store has every kind of weapon you could want."

Well, maybe the Echo isn't quite so awful after all.

CHAPTER TWELVE

Erin

GRANT HAS STOPPED COMPLAINING ABOUT MY CLOTHES EVER SINCE he discovered we hit the jackpot—in terms of weaponry. I've got new knives, a fully automatic machine gun, a fully automatic handgun, grenades, and a bulletproof vest. If any armored creatures attack us now, we'll give them a hell of a fight.

And we might even win.

Despite bitching about my clothes, Grant chose similar items for himself. He wears olive-green cargo pants, big black boots, and a black tank top with an olive-green, short-sleeve shirt over it. He left the shirt half unbuttoned, so I get a nice view of his pectoral muscles. It's not fair that he saw me naked, but I still have no idea what he looks like in the nude, except for his dick. That part of him is impressive.

I still can't believe I gave him a blow job. My only excuse is that his constant tossing and turning, combined with the irritated little breathing noises he kept making, drove me bonkers. I needed some serious rest, but I couldn't get even forty winks until I found a way to make him fall asleep. So naturally, I went down on him. Well, at least it worked. We both slept after that, though I dreamed about Grant doing naughty things to me with our naked bodies entangled. Maybe I, um, kind of loved taking him into my mouth, and maybe I want him to screw me for hours and hours. I doubt he wants that. Yes, he clearly enjoyed the gift I gave him, but he seems to have reverted to his usual uptight demeanor.

He did smile in the sexiest way when he saw my machine gun. I guess Mr. Zen has a hard-on for powerful firearms. He chose a similar complement of weapons as I had, minus the machine gun, so we are both now heavily armed.

We replenish our backpack supplies and load big water-cooler-size bottles into the back of our vehicle. Don't want to get dehydrated while battling Echo creatures. I insist that we also put some cardboard boxes full of nonperishable food items into the car too. I search for any kind of electronics that might help us navigate this world, but it seems like the Echo doesn't have computer technology.

Grant seems not the least surprised by that fact. He gave me peevish looks while I searched for electronic items, but I refrained from pointing out he was behaving in the "childish" way he accused me of doing earlier. Guess that makes me the adult in the room. No, I don't tell him that. Despite what he thinks, I am not immature.

I don't find any paper maps. How do these creatures find their way around this world?

Once we've returned to the car, I ask, "So, wise and grumpy master, where are we going?"

"To find Sefton's hidden lair."

"You had a vision of where it is?"

He flashes me a nasty look. "No. We're going to search for it."

"With no clue where it might be. How do you know it's even in this city?"

"Because the entrance to the Echo leads here." He starts up the engine and rolls the SUV out onto the street. "Sefton traveled back and forth between the Echo and the earth. He would've done that via Fort Worth."

I won't point out that for all we know the entrance moves around and drops people off in a different place every time. He's clearly in no mood to discuss the issue.

But I can't keep my mouth shut about something else. "How are we going to find our way back to our base camp, meaning the store we slept in last night?"

Grant slams on the brakes, which shoves me forward. I throw my hands out to keep from smacking into the dashboard or the windshield.

"Shit," he hisses. "I didn't think about that."

I twist around to reach behind my seat and dig a spiral-bound notebook out of my backpack. I'd snagged it this morning, thinking it might come in handy. Smiling, I hold up my notebook. "I'll make notes to keep track of where we turned. And I'll even draw a crude map."

"That might work. Good thing you thought to grab a notebook."

"Gee, somebody rolled his eyes and frowned at me for doing that."

He wrings the steering wheel with both hands. "I was wrong. You have good instincts, Erin."

"So do you, but your insomnia gets in the way of it sometimes."

"You're right about that." He throws me a sly sideways glance. "But you helped me with that problem."

"For one night." I cross my legs, which draws his attention to my bare legs, though I didn't intend to lure him to look there. "Unless you think I'm going to give you blow jobs every night so you can get some shuteye."

With his gaze still riveted to my legs, he licks his lips. "Maybe it could be reciprocal next time."

Did he just offer to go down on me tonight? I can't believe Grant would say something like that. "Don't you hate me?"

"No, Erin. I don't understand you, and I worry about your gonzo tactics."

"Fair enough. I don't fully understand you either, but I'm sure we'll get better acquainted now. I mean, there's nobody else to talk to—unless you like chatting with slavering monsters who want to screw you."

Grant gives me a sexy smile. "The beast we met wanted to screw *you*, but I can't blame him for that."

I feel tingly all over because of that simple statement. "Actually, he wanted a threesome with you and me."

"Sorry, I only make love to women, and only one at a time." He taps my notebook. "Start taking notes."

I dig a pen out of my pack, set the notebook on my thigh, flip it open, and poise my pen over the paper. "Ready when you are."

"The faded and almost unreadable sign on that store seems to call it the One-Stop Shop. Guess Echo creatures aren't very creative."

I scrawl the name on my paper. "What did you expect? They're vicious monsters."

"But they were created to be like their alter egos in the normal world, albeit with warped bodies and minds. You would think they'd be as intelligent as the humans they resemble."

"Well, I always thought ninety percent of the human race was stupid."

"You're an optimist, then." He starts the car rolling down the street again. "I figured it was more like ninety-nine percent."

We're both cynics, apparently. That means we share not only military experience but also the same opinion about our fellow humans. I don't think we both believe that, not deep down, but our war experiences have left us kind of jaded. Since the apocalypse began, I've witnessed humans of all ages and nationalities coming together to fight for our world. I can't view my fellow humans through the same lens as before the world was destroyed. The aftermath brought us together.

"I don't really think all people are stupid," I say. "Not anymore. Do you?"

"Nah. It's just what everybody likes to say, right? Even before the worlds collided, I preferred to see the good in people."

"That's your Zen attitude. Wish I could achieve that kind of serenity."

His gaze flicks toward me. "I needed years to cultivate it. Give yourself time."

I write down the street name and draw a line on my map when he turns a corner. "Why have you been treating me like a criminal you want to arrest? I never did anything to you."

Grant stares out the windshield while apparently trying to strangle the steering wheel. "I don't feel that way."

"But why—"

"Just keep making notes and watch out for some kind of clue to where Sefton might have hidden his notes."

"No problem. I'll get out my crystal ball."

He doesn't speak anymore as we turn down street after street, but I have to speak up when I realize my makeshift map shows something disturbing. "We're going in circles."

"What? No, that's not possible."

I thrust my map in his face. "Here's the proof."

Grant jerks his head back and squints at the paper, then he brings the car to a halt. He snatches the map from me, frowning at it. "Dammit."

"Aimlessly wandering through a strange city is not helping."

"What do you suggest we do?"

He's asking for my opinion, at last, but I have no idea what to say.

"You don't know either," he says. "We're the dream team that was going to save the world, but now our plan has ground to a halt before we even got started."

"Saying 'we suck' is not useful."

He tosses the map back to me and stares out the windshield while drumming his fingers on the steering wheel. "Let's get out and walk around. Maybe we'll bump into some Echo creatures we can interrogate."

I try not to laugh, but it turns into snorting instead. "Interrogate them? Are you nuts? They don't want to chat, they want to murder us."

"Must be some who aren't homicidal."

"Sure, you hold your breath for that. I'll catch you when you pass out from lack of oxygen."

He flashes me a scowl, then throws his door open and jumps out. "Come on. We're walking."

Grant slams the door, rocking the vehicle.

He left the screwdriver in the ignition, so I remove it and shove the thing into my backpack. Naturally, he left his pack in the car. I grab that one too and climb out. "If your hissy fit is over, you might want this."

I hold up his backpack.

Lips flattened, he plucks the pack out of my hand and stalks off down the street while struggling to get the straps over his shoulders. I pull my backpack on and jog to catch up, but he refuses my help when I try to tug his left strap into position. It takes him another thirty seconds or so to get his pack situated.

That stubborn idiot. Well, no, he's not stupid. But sometimes he does a fine impression of a moron, especially when the pigheaded beast within rears its head.

He keeps glancing at my legs and wincing.

"My clothes really bother you, huh?" I shake my head. "Get over it, Grant. We need to work together, not snipe at each other."

"I'm not bothered."

"Bullshit." I grab his arm to stop him. "Tell me what your problem is—right now."

He grinds his teeth, which I know because I can see his jaw working and the muscles pulsing. "It's none of your concern."

"Everything about you is my business now. Your behavior affects both of our safety."

He squeezes his eyes shut and hisses something I can't make out, but it's probably a curse word. Then he turns toward me. "You're right. What affects me puts both of us at risk, so I need to tell you."

The guy says that like he's just been convicted of murder and condemned to death row. Whatever he needs to tell me must be a doozy.

"It's just that—" He bows his head and shoves both hands into his hair. "I couldn't save my own family. How can I possibly save the world?"

All the annoyance floods out of me as I realize he must've been carrying that guilt around for months, ever since the apocalypse hit. No wonder he's been hell-bent on studying those alchemy books and finding a way to reverse the destruction.

I clasp his face in my hands, touching my forehead to his. "You need to stop blaming yourself for what happened to your wife and son. No one saw the apocalypse coming, and no one had the power to stop it or save themselves, much less the people they loved. It's not your fault."

"But I was a cop and former military. I have the skills—"

"Nobody had the skills to battle Echo creatures, not in the beginning. Since then, we've learned the hard way."

"But I let everyone believe I could find a way to save the world, maybe even put things back the way they were."

I tug to make him lift his face to me, then gaze straight into his eyes. "Only you laid that burden on your shoulders. The rest of us don't expect you to save us. We hope somebody might find a way sometime, but no one told you it's your fault if you can't do it."

He just looks at me, his expression unreadable.

What else can I do to convince him? Nothing. But I need to make him feel better, for reasons I can't understand or explain, so I do the only thing I can. I kiss him. The moment our lips meet, I swear I feel electricity crackling through me, and I press my mouth more firmly to his and just hold that position so I can relish the feel of his warmth and the softness of his lips.

Then he slides his tongue into my mouth.

I moan and coil my tongue around his.

He wraps his arms around me, pulling me tightly against his muscular body. I push my fingers into his hair, then latch my arms around his neck while we ravish each other with our tongues, our lips, and our bodies. The flavor of his mouth excites me though I can't describe what he tastes like, and it hardly matters. To feel every contour of his body molded to mine, it makes me crazy with the need to get us both naked and finally do what I know we've both wanted since the day we met—to have sex.

"There you are. I want what you promised me."

We both freeze. I peel my lids apart to find Grant staring right back at me, though we haven't moved any other parts of our bodies yet. The voice that spoke those words is all too familiar. The creature who had given us a lift into the Echo has found us again.

And he wants to ravage us.

CHAPTER THIRTEEN

Grant

I STARE INTO ERIN'S EYES FROM INCHES AWAY, OUR MOUTHS STILL fused and our arms still around each other. That armor-plated creature has found us again, and neither of us has any idea how to stop him from capturing us. We've traveled too far from our car to safely get back to it. I got us into this mess. My "hissy fit," as Erin called it, pushed me to act like a moron yet again. That means it's my responsibility to get us out of trouble.

Grasping Erin's shoulders, I peel her away from my body.

She glances at the creature. "Got any bright ideas? My brain is stuck in neutral right now."

"Uh..." I notice the machine gun strapped to her backpack. I've got weapons too, but I have no idea if we can get them out and ready to fire before that beast tramples us. Of course, that creature is armor-plated, and we don't have any armor-piercing rounds. "Our good buddy over there must have a weakness. Don't you think?"

"Sure. But how do we find it without getting killed?"

"You're the expert on being insanely reckless. Can't you think of anything?"

Erin lifts her brows. "Now you want me to be reckless?"

"Yeah. Do it quick."

"No more talking," the beast growls, his deep baritone voice echoing off the buildings. "Time to fuck you."

Yeah, that's exactly what I want to do right now. I doubt either of us will survive sex with that thing.

Erin turns sideways to me, facing the creature, and plasters on a sexily teasing smile. "Where have you been, honey? I was hoping you'd catch up. It's a fun game, isn't it? Hide and go seek."

The creature takes two hulking steps, and the ground shudders. "Hide and go seek? I never knew of this game."

"It's lots of fun. Want me to tell you how it works?"

The beast's brows wrinkle, as much as they can with those horns in the way. "How what works?"

"Well, you close your eyes and count to ten. Then you try to find me." Erin trails her fingertips over her breastbone, exposed by her tank top. The beast's gaze tracks every movement of her fingers. "Wanna play, don't you? So start counting."

Our huge buddy squats and closes his eyes. "One—"

He thumps his fist on the ground as he counts.

Erin snatches her machine gun off her backpack while I rummage around in mine to grab the extra magazines for her gun and the rounds for my shotgun. I toss her the magazines, and she catches them.

"Three," the creature says. "Four, five—"

He keeps striking the ground with every count, the noise giving us perfect cover. We spin around and race back the way we'd come. We have our weapons ready if we should need them, but I'm hoping Erin's clever little ruse has granted us enough time to escape before that big dumb beast realizes what we've done.

"Six, seven—"

We stumble as the creature thumps the ground even harder, but we manage to reach the car and climb inside. I reach for the ignition and freeze. "Where's the screwdriver?"

"Oh, shit, I forgot. It's in my backpack."

"Nine," the creature hollers, and we can hear it even inside the car with the windows rolled up.

Erin struggles to get her pack off her shoulders and dig the screwdriver out. She hands it to me.

I crank the thing in the ignition, and the engine sputters but doesn't catch. I try again, with the same result.

"Ten!" the creature bellows as he rises to his full height. "Here I come!"

Erin rolls down her window and roots around inside her backpack. She brings out two grenades.

I crank the screwdriver again. More sputtering. *Fuck.*

She pulls the pin out, thrusts her arm out the window, and hurls the grenade at the creature. It lands halfway between us and our buddy. The explosion rattles my eardrums, but it only makes the creature pause for a few seconds.

The engine catches at last, and I gun it, wrenching the wheel to turn us around and speed off in the opposite direction from the horny beast. Erin rises off her seat to hang halfway out the window and throw the other grenade. In the rearview mirror, I see the grenades strike the beast's calf and erupt. Our buddy roars, but not in agony. He sounds pissed to the extreme.

Erin grabs her machine gun and starts raining rounds on the creature.

I veer around a corner, hoping to hell I can find a place that monster can't get through, but having no clue what such a place might look like.

The rapid-fire rounds from the gun cease. Erin leans into the car to grab another magazine and starts shooting again.

In the rearview mirror, I see the creature still barreling toward us. I lean over to slap Erin's leg.

When she pauses in firing rounds at our buddy, she glances at me with a questioning look.

"That thing must have a vulnerable spot," I tell her. "We need to find it."

"No shit. Thanks for stating the obvious." She raises her gun again, but stops when I slap her thigh again. "What, Grant? I don't have the magical power to know where that thing is vulnerable."

"Try his groin." I'd seen a bulge under his enormous pants. Maybe he's got a dick that's as easy to injure as the ones we human guys have.

Erin drops the gun and digs a couple more grenades out of her pack. Then she pulls the pins and hurls both of them toward the creature's groin.

I watch in the mirror while the grenade strikes the monster's groin and explodes.

The beast screams. He stumbles over an abandoned vehicle, staggers sideways, and clutches his groin.

Our car sideswipes a lamppost.

Erin kicks my arm. "Watch where you're going, genius."

I return my attention to the road ahead. Just as I swerve around another corner, a massive explosion makes the earth beneath us ripple like the waves of an earthquake.

"What did you just throw at him?" I ask. "Did you hide some C-4 in your bra?"

Erin drops back onto her seat, breathing hard. "That wasn't me. The creature collapsed and created a mini earthquake."

I twist my head around to glance backward.

The beast lies prone on the ground, rocking slightly, both hands cupped over his dick.

"Guess we got him," I say, facing forward again. "Score one for the humans."

"That was a smart idea. But I don't think we should assume our ugly friend is out of commission for good."

"I know. But we managed to knock him down once, which means we can do it again." I look at her at the same moment she looks at me. "We make a good team."

"Yeah, we do."

Something ripples through me, a sensation like excitement and relief coupled with desire. My gaze flicks to her legs and the expanse of tanned skin revealed by her minuscule shorts. My dick jerks. How can I be horny when we barely survived an assault from a massive Echo creature just seconds ago? I guess it's the adrenaline rush.

I focus on the road, doing my damnedest to ignore what my body wants, and execute several more turns that seem to take us further away from the creature. I'm trying to make sure I don't drive us in circles again by turning left, right, left, right.

The engine sputters and dies. The car rolls to a stop.

"We're out of gas," I say. "Need to fill up the tank with our handy gas cans."

I get out of the car and retrieve some of the cans. Just as I've finished gassing up, Erin climbs out and stretches her entire body while moaning as if it feels so good.

My attention swerves to her legs. Those long, slim thighs that have strong muscles under the surface. I can tell that much from the way she stretches. My dick jerks again. But then Erin plants her hands on her lower back and stretches again, bending backward. The action lifts her tits, and I can see her nipples stiffening. She's not wearing a bra.

I screw the gas cap back on, suddenly breathing harder.

Erin stretches backward again, this time with her arms extended.

Lust grips me so hard that I can't breathe. I shouldn't want to screw her right now, but I can't resist the impulse. I stalk over to Erin, sling an arm around her waist, and haul her into my body. Despite her taut muscles, she has all the soft curves I love in a woman, and I can't stop myself. I mash my mouth to hers.

She doesn't react for a few seconds. But then she plunges her tongue into my mouth, and we consume each other with a passion so intense that it verges on insanity. With my eyes closed, I fumble with the zipper on her shorts until I finally grasp it and yank the thing down so I can shove my hand inside her panties. She doesn't have any underwear on. My hand slides through the silky curls on her mound. I hesitate there, but only for a moment, then I push my fingers between her folds to revel in the realization of how wet and ready she is.

For me.

This is insane. And a bad idea. But I've careened off the cliff already, and there's no going back now, especially when Erin moans and latches one leg around my hip. I scrape my fingers up and down her slick folds while I peel one eye open just enough to help me find the back door and yank it open. Then I toss her onto the backseat and jump in, straddling her body while poised on my knees. I keep rubbing her cleft even as I bend my head to take her clit in my mouth and suckle it.

She cries out, arching her back.

Though I should make her come first, my desperate need to fuck her overrides my brain. I shove her shorts down to her ankles, unzip my pants, and thrust into her hard. She cries out again, but then grips my biceps and bends her knees. I pound into her so fiercely that the car starts to shake and creak. Braced on my straight arms, I stare into her eyes while she stares right back at me, her mouth open and frantic noises tumbling from her lips. I grunt and gasp while I fuck her like a demon, pumping faster and faster while the wet sucking sound of our bodies colliding fills the interior of the car and her cream coats my cock.

I retain just enough willpower to give her what she needs. I reach down to rub her clit.

She comes so hard and fast that her body curls inward and her scream gets choked off. The spasms of her inner muscles push me over the edge too, and I let out a string of hoarse shouts while my own spasms rack my cock and the sweet bliss of orgasm barrels through me with the power of lightning strikes. After a few more thrusts, I'm done.

I collapse on top of her. We're both struggling to catch our breath.

"Holy shit, Grant," she says while still breathing hard. "That was, um, unexpected."

I suddenly realize I still have my dick inside her. Pulling out, I rise to my knees and gaze down at Erin. "Did I hurt you?"

She laughs softly. "No, I'm fine. That was incredible."

"Can't believe I did that." I glance down at my waning erection. Her cream glistens on it. "Shit. What if I got you pregnant?"

"From one time? I don't think that's likely since I had my period last week." She sits up and shimmies backward so she can get to her knees and pull her shorts up again. "Relax. I won't be demanding you provide child support for our baby. There won't be one."

"Why aren't you mad? I didn't even ask if you wanted to have sex. I just...assaulted you."

Erin waddles across the seat toward me and takes hold of my face. "You didn't do anything wrong. What about me makes you think I'm afraid to say no to a man? I wanted you, and I didn't care how you took me. It was amazing."

She's not upset, but I'm disgusted with myself. Not because of the way I fucked her. No, it's something much worse.

"What's wrong?" Erin asks. "You look like you might throw up."

Maybe I will, since bile is rising in my throat, scorching a path toward my mouth. I can already taste the acrid flavor of it. But I can't move or speak to answer her question. What's wrong? Everything.

She inches closer until our noses brush against each other. "Please tell me why you're upset."

I grasp her wrists and pull them back to peel her hands away from my face. "I betrayed Adele."

"No, Grant, you—"

"When we got married, I didn't promise to honor and cherish Adele until death do us part. I vowed to love her forever." I scuffle backward and fall off the seat, tumbling to the ground. My fly is still open. I yank it closed and struggle to get to my feet. "I'm sorry, Erin. I shouldn't have done this, any of it. Kissing you. Letting you give me head. Fucking you. I've become the kind of bastard I never wanted to be."

She starts to speak, but I slam the door to silence her.

Then I stalk around to the driver's side, get in, and crank the screwdriver in the ignition until the engine snarls to life. Erin climbs over the center console and onto the passenger seat. I gun the engine, rocketing our car down the street.

I wanted Erin since the day we met, but I fought it. I don't deserve to feel good, not even for a minute. Because I betrayed Adele the first time I looked at Erin.

CHAPTER FOURTEEN

Erin

WE DIDN'T DO ANYTHING WRONG, BUT I KNOW I CAN'T CONVINCE Grant of that. He needs to punish himself. I've never been into self-flagellation, not even the mental kind, and I refuse to lie and tell him what we just did meant nothing. When a man tormented by his past finally opens the floodgates of his emotions, he's destined to sink under the water for a while. He'll surface again. By the time he does, maybe I'll have thought of a way to talk him out of the idea that he betrayed his late wife.

I'm not dumb enough to try that right now.

So instead, I gaze out the windows. "The way Dax described the Echo, I expected more fire and brimstone and less…normal stuff."

"What's normal about a destroyed city?"

"I just meant that this place looks an awful lot like Earth. Dax described this world as literal hell."

"He lived here for five years before the alchemy of worlds began. When that happened, he was thrown into the normal world again. Maybe everything here changed post-apocalypse, just like things changed on Earth."

"Maybe." I chew on the inside of my cheek while I contemplate our surroundings. Something still doesn't feel right about this place and our amazingly good luck in finding supplies and a car. "This is supposed to be a copy of the earth, right? Sefton Stainthorpe created the Echo to be a twisted mirror image of the real world, and that's why the Echo creatures look like demonic versions of the people on earth. Right?"

"If you keep repeating everything we've already talked about, I'll go insane."

"Newsflash—you've already done that."

"Yeah." He scowls out the windshield, his fingers wrapped around the wheel so tightly that the knuckles have turned white. "Must be a clue somewhere in this city."

We drive past a dilapidated building that has faded words painted on a scorched sign.

"Stop!" I shout.

Grant slams on the brakes. "What is your problem now?"

"Back up. I saw something on that sign, but we went by too fast for me to read all of it."

He shifts the car into reverse and backs up.

"Stop here," I say. Then I stare up at the sign. The damage has made it harder to read the words, and the muted daylight in this world doesn't help either. But finally, I'm sure of what I see. "It's a shop called Maps of the World."

"Maps?" Grant sounds baffled, and I'm right there with him. "Are you sure you're reading it right?"

"Yep. Look for yourself."

He leans across the center console and peers through my window. His brows furrow. His mouth falls open a touch. Then he swivels his gaze to me. "It does say Maps of the World. It can't mean…"

"Maps of the Echo? Yeah, I think it does mean that."

Grant shuts off the engine and stares blankly at nothing. "This is insane."

"Uh-huh. Still think all our good luck has been nothing but a series of random coincidences?"

"I'll reserve my judgment for after we check out that shop." He climbs out and lays one hand on the top of the driver's door as he bends forward to look at me. "Hurry up, Erin."

He must have seriously sublimated what we did a few minutes ago. I still feel tingly in places that aren't at all helpful to my powers of concentration, but he acts like we didn't just have sex in the backseat so hard that the car shook—and possibly the earth too.

Wow, I loved that. But he thinks it was a horrible sin.

I climb out of the car and follow Grant into the shop. The windows have been shattered, but jagged pieces clinging to the frame make it impossible to enter the building that way. The door is locked.

But Grant doesn't care about that. He kicks it open.

That's hot. Really hot.

"Wake up, Erin."

Grant's snarly command jerks me back to reality. I'd been enjoying a memory of our encounter in the backseat. "I am awake, jackass."

I follow him into the shop, and he turns on a flashlight to sweep its beam over the interior. Metal racks fill the space, but most are empty. I pull a folded map out of its slot, but the paper has been badly scorched. I can read the title, though—Capital City. The Echo has a capital? That implies it also has some type of government. It must be a dictatorship, considering what I've heard about Sefton Stainthorpe. He was not a nice guy or a sane person.

That begs a question. "Who's in charge of the Echo now that Sefton is dead?"

"Nobody, I guess." Grant picks up a hand-size globe. "This world must be a separate planet. We've assumed it's purely a magical construct that doesn't exist on a physical plane the way planets do, but this globe suggests otherwise."

"Maybe it's a parallel universe. Or maybe it's both magical and physical."

He jerks his head up to look at me. "That's a smart observation, Erin."

Why does he seem shocked? I'm not an idiot. I went to college, for heaven's sake.

"You're the first person who suggested that," he says. "Not even Sanctuary's resident expert on the Echo thought of it."

"Dax didn't realize that? Has he ever mentioned the Capital City?"

"No. Unless he found this city and this shop, he wouldn't have any reason to know about it. The Echo is a magical construct, but it must also have a physical presence in some kind of universe."

"This is a fascinating discussion. But aren't we looking for a map of the city we're in right now?"

"Yeah." He rolls the globe in his palm, then sets it down. "Better keep searching."

I wander among the racks but don't see anything useful, just maps that are so damaged they're unreadable. But then I notice something on the sales counter and trot over there to get a closer look. I hold up the booklet. "Found something."

Grant hurries over to me. "What is it?"

"A map booklet." I flip through the pages to let him see. "It's an undamaged map of the Capital City. I think that's where we are. It would make sense that Sefton headquartered his new world in the city where the entrance to the Echo resides."

He picks up the map booklet to thumb through it. "I think you're right about all these convenient discoveries. We just happen to drive by a shop that has a single pristine map for us to find? That's one too many coincidences for my taste."

"You finally came over to my way of thinking. About time."

"Why do you always have to be snarky? I liked it a lot better when you were gasping and moaning."

He said that while casually browsing the map booklet, and his expression stayed neutral, his tone of voice too. I can't figure this guy out. He snarls at me, then screws me, then tells me he betrayed his dead wife, and finally he reminds me of what we did in the car a little while ago. I have no frigging idea how to respond to that.

"I especially liked it when you screamed my name," he says in that same neutral tone as he hands me the map booklet. "You should keep this. I'll drive, and you can navigate."

Yeah, I'm getting whiplash from his mood swings.

But I do what he wanted. Once we get back to the car, I use the map booklet to figure out where we are. It's the Capital City, like I thought. The names of the streets we pass match up with what the map shows. Apparently, this city has no real name, just the generic one. Most of the streets get their names from scientists I've heard of, both modern and historical figures. Other streets are named after alchemical terms like quicksilver and quintessentia. I wouldn't have known what those terms are, but Grant explained they're related to alchemy. Other street names related to alchemy include Alembic, Solifaction, and Touchstone.

He wants to explain to me what those terms are about, but I tell him not to bother unless those things become important to our quest to reverse the apocalypse.

Grant stops the car at an intersection. He compresses his lips while he studies the street signs. We're on Ignis Boulevard, and the cross street is called Decknamen Way. I remember enough of my college science class to know ignis means fire. But that other word? Not a clue.

"Do you have any idea what the word decknamen means?" Grant asks.

"Of course I don't. I'm not obsessed with alchemy."

He eyes me sideways. "A decknamen is basically a pseudonym for an alchemical substance, something that hides its true identify."

"Fascinating. How does that help us?"

He scratches his cheek and winces. "This will sound kind of nuts."

"Like everything else you've said and done was completely sane?"

"Fair point." He sags into his seat, letting out a long sigh. "I have no rational reason for believing this, but I have a hunch we should take Decknamen Way to wherever it ends."

"Okay. Let's do that."

He glances at me. "You don't want to complain about my half-assed plan?"

"Nope. Just get moving."

Grant steers the car around the corner onto the street with a weird and kind of spooky name. "Decknamen" sounds like German or Latin or something, but I won't waste time asking Grant about that. The term's origins hardly matter.

After a few blocks, I stop staring at the buildings along the streets because something else has captured my attention. Directly ahead, at what seems like the end of this street, I see a hulking skyscraper that I swear wasn't there a few minutes ago. "Do you see that? I think that building appeared, like poof."

"You just didn't notice it before."

"Did you?"

He screws up his mouth as he stares straight ahead at the building in question. "No, I didn't see it either—until right now."

"I'm pretty sure that building wasn't there before."

"Okay, I trust your instincts. But a mysterious building that materializes out of nowhere just confirms my suspicion that we're on the right track."

"Or on our way to a horrifically painful death."

"Pessimism isn't helpful."

"I'm not being pessimistic. I'm keeping both eyes peeled and all my senses on high alert for whatever might magically appear next."

Grant braces his elbow on the door frame, tapping his fingers on the steering wheel. "Let's both be hypervigilant."

"Agreed."

The closer we get to the spooky building, the more the hairs on my arms lift and my skin tingles with an eerie kind of anticipation. What awaits us there? Soon, we will learn the answer to that question.

At the end of the street, Grant stops the car and shuts off the engine, but he just sits there staring up at the massive gray structure. Its curving lines and smooth planes remind me of fairy tales, but I doubt a valiant king resides in this castle. The building has suffered no visible damage, but I'd expect that if Sefton created this as his private sanctum. When Grant finally opens his door, I do the same. We grab our backpacks, but first, we gather as much ammo as we can stuff into our bags. I have the machine gun strapped to my pack while Grant slings a shotgun over his shoulder.

We're armed. But are we ready for what might come next? Are we prepared to meet whoever lives in this structure?

Grant holds my hand as we push through the glass doors into a vacant lobby that has no furniture, not even a reception desk. A large clock on the wall ticks off the seconds and minutes without making the slightest sound. I glance at our hands, expecting Grant to let go of mine. But he doesn't. He leads me toward an elevator instead.

The doors glide open for us.

I look at Grant just as he looks at me. He raises his brows. I shrug. We waltz into the elevator, and the doors shut. The car begins to rise while a clock-like device counts off the floors, one for every tick of the minute hand—though the device doesn't make a ticking sound. Like everything we've seen so far, the elevator makes no noise. We know it's rising only because we felt the movement when it first started to lift.

The dial counting floors glides through the numbers. Seven. Eight. Nine. Ten. I suddenly realize I've shuffled closer to Grant, and my body is touching his. I wonder if I should move away, but then he snakes an arm around my waist to tug me closer. Floor eleven. Twelve. I reach for my gun but realize I shouldn't do that yet. Maybe we're about to meet someone nice.

In a hell world? Yeah, right.

My throat has grown tight, and my pulse is racing.

At the thirteenth floor, the elevator stops. The doors glide open.

Grant clasps my hand again to lead me out into a long, blank hallway. "I'd swear this building has more than thirteen floors, based on how tall it looked from the outside. But then, Sefton was obsessed with the number thirteen. Maybe he built more floors just for show."

"Could be."

The elevator doors slide shut behind us, making me jump.

We stand here looking around, searching for anything that might explain what this building is and why we've apparently been lured here. A door at the far end of the hall eases open just as I glance that way.

"Look," I say. "Guess we're supposed to go there."

"Seems like."

We approach the door and slip inside the room, which has floor-to-ceiling windows on three sides and a stunning view of the post-apocalyptic city. No one waits for us in the large room that I take for an office. But footsteps clap in the hallway, coming our way. We both turn toward the door.

A blond man walks into the room.

Grant's eyes flare wide. "Sefton Stainthorpe?"

CHAPTER FIFTEEN

Grant

I TRY DAMN HARD TO CHANNEL MY ZEN SIDE AND KEEP MY EXPRES-sion neutral, but I have trouble doing that under these circumstances. The man whose decaying corpse I saw just a few days ago at Fallenmouth now stands ten feet away from us. This can't be. Dax told me he snapped his brother's neck, and I know he wouldn't lie. The body in the cellar must have been Sefton.

The man eying us with curiosity is an Echo of Sefton Stainthorpe. That's the only explanation that makes even a minuscule amount of sense.

"Hello," I say once I've reasserted my calm demeanor. "May I ask who we have the pleasure of meeting?"

The blond man has begun to stare at Erin in a way that makes me uneasy. "Allison Dahl?"

She shakes her head.

"Who are you?" he asks, glancing back and forth between me and Erin. "The signs were meant for Allison, to bring her to Sefton."

This guy looks like Sefton, who was British, but he speaks with an American accent.

I think it's time for a strategic sharing of information—but only a little of that. "I'm Grant, and this is Erin. Who might you be?"

"Call me Will."

"You remind me of someone I met once. Are you related to Sefton Stainthorpe?"

"In a way."

"You must know Dax too."

"No, I haven't encountered him." Will tugs at the collar of his dress shirt, which has the top button unhooked, and he grimaces. "How did you find the Capital City? No one comes here."

"We did."

Will hasn't met Sefton's brother, though he clearly knows who Dax is.

Our new friend stares at Erin again. "Are you sure you're not Allison? You followed the signs, didn't you?"

Erin clinches my hand more tightly.

"If you mean the literal signs," I say, "as in the ones attached to buildings that drew us here, yeah. We followed the signs. Did you leave those breadcrumbs for us?"

"For Allison, not for you." He sounds befuddled rather than annoyed. His fingers twiddle while he glances around like he's hunting for an escape route. "Sefton will be quite angry when he learns I've let uninvited guests into his city."

"No, he won't. Sefton Stainthorpe is dead."

Will jerks his attention to me, his eyes wide. "That's impossible. The master cannot be killed. He surrounds himself with powerful magics that repel all attempts to assault his person."

This guy talks like a prig with a big stick wedged up his ass, but he mostly seems terrified. Of what? Sefton? Like I just told him, that man is dead.

"Where are all the Echo creatures?" I ask.

"No creatures live in the Capital City—except for the one you two brought here."

"Are you going to kill him?"

Will shakes his head. "I don't have the power."

Erin releases my hand, leveling her gaze on our new friend. "Do you mean Echo power?"

"Yes," Will says. "Only Sefton has that."

Does this guy really not know that other people share the Echo power? That would have to mean he hasn't left the Echo since the alchemy of worlds began on earth. But who is this man? I want answers, and I want them now.

"What are you?" I demand. "You look just like Sefton, but you sound American. You know about Allison but had no idea Sefton was dead. You hide in this building, but as far as I can tell, you're the only living thing in this city other than me, Erin, and that creature."

Will shuffles over to the windows, gazing out at the cityscape illuminated by the glow of a full moon. "I am Sefton's Echo. He called me Will because that's his name too—Sefton William Stainthorpe."

I stop myself a split second before I blurt out something that might get us into trouble and temper my question. "But I thought the Echo versions of humans all had scales or horns or something."

"You fail to understand the scope of what an Echo is."

"Enlighten me. Please."

He touches his fingertips to the glass and begins to draw invisible patterns with them. "Sefton invented the concept of an Echo, which is essentially a copy of a human being. But he took it several steps further. Each

Echo is both an exact copy and a mirror image. What was once hidden inside the person becomes visible on the outside."

"Yeah, we know about that."

"But an Echo is more than a copy. It is the result of turning a human soul inside out. If Sefton had succeeded in creating the alchemy of souls, every person on earth would have been forced to merge with their Echo."

We already knew about the alchemy of souls, but I decide it's not smart to point that out. Will seems timid, but I won't make the mistake of trusting what appears to be true. He's hiding something, for sure.

"There are good creatures in this world," he says. "They each have the appearance of a monster but the heart and soul of a human. Sefton did not anticipate that, and the realization enraged him." Will turns toward us, his expression pinched. "You see, he assumed that if his magics created an Echo of him, that creature would be more powerful than Sefton himself—in bodily strength and brutality. But instead, he got me."

"If you're his doppelgänger, do you know everything he knew?"

"Afraid not. I know only what he told me and what I learned from experience."

I study him for a moment, trying to gauge his honesty, but I'm no mind reader. During the initial phases of the apocalypse, Allison had encountered the Echo version of a woman she'd worked with at the Fort Worth Public Library. Luckily, I haven't come across anyone I knew. Not yet, at least. "A friend of mine bumped into an Echo creature who was a copy of someone she knew. That creature shared the original woman's memories."

"Other Echo creations retain some of the knowledge of their originals. I do not." Will clamps a hand over his nape. "Sefton was disappointed that I have no knowledge of magic, alchemy, or science. He called me a useless byproduct."

As interesting as learning about Will's creation and existence might be, we have more important matters to discuss with him. He's our only lead and our only link to the madman who instigated hell on earth and in the Echo. If he is a copy of Sefton, maybe he knows something useful.

Erin has been unusually quiet until now, but she finally speaks up. "Why does this building seem empty? Devoid of everything including furniture? The way I heard it, Sefton loved the creature comforts."

"Oh, this isn't where he lived," Will says. "I assume that's what you were implying. Only Allison would ever visit his home, if she had come to him as he planned."

But she didn't because he returned to Fallenmouth instead. Based on what Will said, it sounds like Sefton had assumed Allison would find her way into the Echo alone despite the fact he left her a note urging her to wait for him at the library on the day the apocalypse began.

"I've told you all I know," Will says. "Apologies for not being able to answer all your questions. I might be Sefton's Echo, but I do not share all his memories."

Does he share Sefton's insanity? I shouldn't assume this guy is genuinely pleasant and not evil, but my gut isn't giving me any advice. As a deputy sheriff, I'd needed to hone my instincts, so I'm not gullible. I will remain wary of this man even while I trust him with a vital piece of intel.

"I have reason to believe," I tell him, "that Sefton kept notes on everything he did. Magic, alchemy, quantum physics, everything. Do you have any idea where he might've hidden those notes?"

Sure, I have no proof the documentation exists. But my gut tells me it does.

Will grasps his upper arm, almost as if it pains him. "I'm sorry, no. If Sefton kept notes, they would most likely be in his home. The one in this world."

"You really have no clue where that home is?"

"None."

Shit. We'll need to find another way to get what we need.

"We should go," Erin says. "There's nothing for us here."

"You can't leave," Will announces. "The building is warded. Once you enter, you must remain here. You're trapped, just like me."

A coldness rushes through me, and I can do nothing but stare at him. Trapped? Oh, hell no. There must be a way to escape, and we'll find it. Maybe Will is too timid to even try, but Erin and I have skills and training he can't imagine.

"We're getting out of here," I say. "Will, you can come with us if you want. But being trapped is not an option for us."

I seize Erin's hand and turn toward the doorway, which remains open. We march down the hall, and I hear footsteps behind us. A quick glance back shows me Will is following us. Maybe he only wants out of this building. Fine, we'll help him escape. After that, I'm not sure if we should let him tag along on our quest to find Sefton's notes because I'm still not sure we should trust him.

The elevator is gone. A blank wall occupies the space where it had been.

"What now?" Erin asks.

No fucking idea. But I don't say that out loud. "We keep searching for a way out."

"None exists," Will says. "Believe me, I've tried."

Isn't he a ray of sunshine? I need to keep thinking positive and keep trying.

While we all stand here like a trio of clueless morons, Will chews on his bottom lip.

I raise my brows at him. "You got something to say?"

"No. Well, yes, sort of. I was just curious."

"About what?"

"Ah, how did you two and your very large friend get inside the Echo?"

"How do you think? We came in through the front door."

"He means the entrance to the Echo," Erin says. Then she mutters under her breath to me, "He knows nothing."

Maybe she's right. But he's connected to Sefton, literally, and I can't believe he holds nothing useful in his brain, not even a speck of information. Yet he seems utterly ignorant. It's a puzzle, for sure. Why can't anything be simple? I'm damn tired of sorting out mysteries.

"The entrance?" Will says. "But only Sefton can travel through it. The gateway remains locked at all times."

I shake my head. "Maybe it used to be locked down, but it isn't now. Sefton's death might've changed the whole dynamic of the Echo."

Will's eyes widen. "If that's true, then…he might come back."

"Sefton's dead and gone, trust me."

"Not Sefton." Will grasps his upper arm again, this time hunching his shoulders too. "I was referring to the golem."

Erin stares at Will. "The what?"

"Golem," I say. "Dax and Allison told me about that. Sefton had a gigantic creature, part flesh and part machine but completely suffused with magics. It trapped Dax and Ally in Fort Worth and held them hostage until Sefton arrived."

"How gigantic is it?"

"About half the height of this building."

She blinks once slowly. "Oh. Is that all?"

"The golem sleeps," Will says. "But Sefton mentioned he could reactivate his pet anytime he liked."

Oh yeah, things just keep getting better. "Where is the golem now?"

Will shrugs.

I still don't get why he seems relatively sane, but he did mention not all Echo creatures are evil. So maybe whatever glitch made that happen might also have affected Will. Honestly, we have worse problems right now.

Our new friend suddenly freezes, and his eyes widen though his gaze goes distant. "The creature you brought here is on the move again. He will be here any moment." Will swerves his gaze to me. "He is not happy."

Gee, I'm glad he told me that. I might've thought the monster wanted a hug instead of a massacre.

Erin and I still have our backpacks and our weapons. Maybe we can fight our way out of this building. If the creature realizes where we are, I suspect he can shake this building down if he wants. Maybe he won't destroy it, but all he'd need to do is smash the lower floors to destabilize the whole thing. When that beast stomps his feet, the city shakes.

"Stay here," I tell Will. "Erin and I need to have a private moment."

Without waiting for his response, I grab Erin's arm and drag her down the hallway until we've gotten far enough away from Will that he won't hear what we say. Unless he has superpowers. These days, I can't rule out anything.

"Can't stay in this building," I whisper. Guess it's my optimism peeking out, assuming Will can't hear us this way. "We need to blow our way out."

"Not sure even a grenade could do that."

"Worth a shot. If our big, gnarly buddy really is awake again, we need to scram."

"Okay." She pulls out her machine gun and whirls toward the wall, then fires off a volley of rounds that makes my ears ring. She shakes her head. "Damn."

The wall sports pockmarks now, but it's intact.

We are screwed.

CHAPTER SIXTEEN

Erin

GRANT GLANCES BACK AT WILL WHOSE EYES ARE BULGING, AND HE'S hugging himself too. Yeah, Sefton Stainthorpe's Echo has no balls, not in the metaphorical sense. But I guess being created by a madman probably scarred him, and I imagine Sefton bullied the guy too. I mean, he wasn't expecting to create a duplicate of himself, only of everyone else on earth. From what I've heard about Dax's brother, the guy did not like competition. That's why he turned Dax into a part-Echo beast of a man and threw him into the nightmare world he'd manufactured.

"Better try a grenade," I say to Grant.

"Might just wind up deaf but still trapped here."

I smirk. "You're starting to sound like me."

"No, I'm sounding like Dax. You got it from him too."

I roll my eyes. "Please. I have my own style that doesn't come from anyone else."

"Yeah, that's for sure."

Whump.

The thunderous noise seems to emanate from outside the building, though it makes the floor beneath us shudder.

"It's the creature you brought here," Will calls out to us. "I can sense him."

Okay, I didn't expect that. But it makes sense, I guess, considering that Sefton created both Will and the beast.

Grant digs half a dozen grenades out of my backpack and offers me three of them. "Let's try it your way."

About damn time. My way might be louder and more dangerous, but it usually gets the job done.

We jog back to Will.

"Plug your ears," Grant instructs him. "Then shut your eyes and brace for impact."

Will shoves his fingers into his ears and huddles against the wall with his lids tightly sealed.

Good enough, I suppose. Grant could have been more specific and told the guy to assume the tornado warning position with his ass in the air and his head on the floor. But this way will probably do.

"Throw your grenades toward the left wall," Grant tells me. "Then plug your ears. I'll throw mine toward the right. Pitch them as far as you can."

"I played softball in high school. You don't need to coach me on how to throw."

"Good. Then we'll do it on the count of three. That means three, two, one, throw."

I give him an oh-please look, but then palm my grenades and face the end of the hall.

Grant bends his knees slightly, holding two grenades in his left hand and the remaining one in his right, ready to lob his first pitch. "Three, two, one, go!"

The two of us hurl our first grenades at the same time, then quickly throw the rest. They land close to the walls. We both plug our ears and turn our backs to that end of the hallway, huddling near the wall as we squeeze our eyes shut. The explosions reverberate through the air, the concussions rattling my bones as the floor shudders hard enough to make Grant stumble sideways into me. Once the dust has settled, literally, I peel my lids apart and shuffle around to see what damage we've done. Grant does the same.

Chunks of drywall or whatever these walls are made of have crumbled away to reveal metal underneath.

Aw, shit. What is this building made of? Steel walls and magic, apparently.

"The only way we're getting out," I say, "is if one of us develops Echo power."

Will shuffles away from the wall to face us. He wears a confused expression, like he thinks I said something weird. But he knows about the Echo and the power it confers on some people. Or does he? Maybe Sefton never told him that.

The building shakes as the Echo beast's feet stomp outside. *Whump. Whump.*

"At least one of you does have the Echo power," Will says. "I sensed it the moment you entered the building, but I was afraid to let on that I knew."

Yeah, he is one big bundle of nerves and fear.

"It's Grant," I say. "Has to be."

Will shakes his head. "It's you, Erin."

"Me? That's crazy. If I had that kind of power, I wouldn't have needed to stumble through the woods for days before I found sanc—a good place to stay."

I almost blurted out that I stumbled onto Sanctuary. Though Will can't know what that really means, I won't risk him figuring it out. He seems okay, but trusting strangers is always a risk these days. The people in Sanctuary welcomed me into their community, but they didn't loop me in on the bigger picture until recently. That means I need to treat Will in a similar fashion. He is the doppelgänger of a madman, after all.

Grant's eyebrows hiked up a touch when I almost revealed the name of our new hometown. He recovered from his surprise quickly, though.

"Perhaps you fought your Echo power," Will says. "You seem averse to the idea."

Averse? Yeah, I guess I am. Having freaky apocalypse powers doesn't appeal to me. But we need a way out of this building. That creature's footfalls pound louder and closer every minute, and the building shivers more with every concussion. Bits of the walls keep falling off. It's also getting harder for us to stay upright.

Grant seizes my upper arms and pulls me closer. The intensity of his gaze ripples a shiver through me, though not the bad kind. His voice is imbued with that same intensity. "You can do this, Erin. You need to do it. Please try."

Or we will die a horrific death. I already got that memo.

I gaze into his eyes, and for some reason, I flash back to the times we kissed and what we did earlier today in that SUV. My breaths quicken, and a warm tingle sweeps through my entire body, settling between my thighs. My tongue sneaks out to moisten my lips, but I swear I didn't mean to do that. How can I be getting horny when we're about to die?

Grant drags me into his body and slants his head to murmur into my ear. "Listen and don't complain. Just believe what I'm about to say. Desire and pleasure can trigger the Echo power."

He can't seriously be suggesting we get it on right here, right now.

"I have an idea," he says, "but I need to know you trust me. I trust you, Erin."

Boom. The building shudders and...sways. Did that really happen? Or am I so high on hormones that I imagined it?

Will lets out a sharp whimper. "Do something quick."

Grant clasps my face in both hands and kisses me.

For a few seconds, I don't move or react. He's kissing me now? Why? But I can't resist the feel of his lips pressed to mine and his rough hands cupping my cheeks. My lids flutter closed of their own volition. While the building shudders and sways around and beneath us, Grant pushes his tongue between my lips and wildly explores my mouth like he wants to devour every inch of me, and I can't stop myself from thrusting my tongue into his mouth too while I moan and clutch at his shirt. When he drops a hand to my ass, I melt into him. Maybe I'd be embarrassed if I weren't lost in a haze of lust. I feel his dick starting to stiffen. My nipples ache and grow sensitive.

Whoosh.

I swear I hear that sound just as I sense we've shifted through space, landing in a different location. My lids drift open.

Grant slowly peels his lips away from mine, though his eyes remain hooded. "Good job, Erin."

"Huh?" Somewhere in the back of my mind, I know what I've done. But that kiss fried most of my neurons. They need time to recover. I need time. But I manage to say, "Did it work?"

I sound kind of dazed, not like me at all.

Grant steps back and pats my upper arm. "You did it. You transported us out of that building."

My senses recover quickly, but my wits need a little more time.

He chucks me under the chin. "I knew you could do it. With a little help from me."

The smug tone in his voice snaps me back to reality. I plant my hands on my hips. "You knew it? Get over yourself, Grant. Kissing you isn't a life-changing experience, much less a world-shifting one."

I've never seen Grant smug before. It's hot, but I will not tell him so.

That kiss was definitely hot. Sizzling, actually.

"Is it over yet?" Will asks, almost whining.

"Yes, it's over." I tap his fingers, which are glued to his eyes. "You can look now. We got away from the big bad Echo beast."

He lowers his hands, but his gaze darts like he's not one hundred percent convinced we've gotten away scot-free.

I settle a hand on Will's arm. "Relax. We're safe now, relatively speaking."

Grant shakes his head, his lips puckered. "You just can't be optimistic all the way, can you?"

"Me? You've been Mr. Gloomy Pants lately." I turn in a circle to take in our surroundings. "Looks like we're still in the Capital City, but we got shifted to another part of it."

"It is the Capital," Will says. "But since we and that beast are the only living things in this sector, he will find us again rather easily."

Throwing my head back, I groan at the sky. "I take that back. Grant is Captain Grouchy, and you are Mr. Gloomy Pants."

Grant slings an arm around my waist and tugs me into him. "Maybe we are those things, but you are the Great Teleporter."

"Wow, thank you," I reply with more than a hint of sarcasm. "Your compliment is making me blush."

"Don't downplay your accomplishment, Erin." He gives me a quick kiss. "I'm proud of you."

"Um, thank you." This time I mean it. No sarcasm. "We need to figure out how to find Sefton's hideout."

Yeah, I changed the subject because I'm embarrassed. Only Grant has ever made me feel like a schoolgirl having her first crush on a boy. But it's more than that. He makes me feel alive again for the first time since the apocalypse ravaged our world. I think I might also be experiencing something far more shocking—hope.

"Perhaps you can wish yourself to be there," Will says. "Teleporting is an intuitive art, or so Sefton always told me."

"Can't hurt to try," I say. "What do you think, Grant?"

"Sure, try it." His hot smirk returns. "Should I kiss you again?"

"I think I can handle it this time without your lips involved."

"Maybe I can't." He nuzzles my neck. "I might get scared."

"Sure, I believe that. Mr. Zen is terrified."

A steamy thrill shivers through me when he flicks his tongue out to tease my throat. Oh, what the hell. I grasp his face and lift his head, then crush my mouth to his. It's like no time at all has elapsed between when he pressed his mouth to mine a moment ago and when I just did the same. We resume our wild, hot kiss, but this time we grope each other just as wildly as our tongues tangle.

The world spins, but I think that's only in my mind.

Will yelps.

Grant and I can't stop kissing.

"What have you done?" Will says in a panicked tone. "No, no, I don't want to be here."

Something in his voice shatters the lustful haze around me, and I jerk my head back. Grant still has his eyes closed, so I give him a quick shake. "Wake up, Romeo. You need to see this."

His lids flutter open. "What?"

"Look around."

Grant takes a few steps back, then scans the space. "Well, I'll be damned."

We've wound up inside an underground cavern that has rough-hewn walls and no visible means of exit or entry. Bookshelves line one wall, while a table in the middle holds scientific equipment like beakers and petri dishes. All the containers are empty. On the table, one book lies open.

Grant and I walk over there, and he picks up the book to flip through it. "Quantum physics. It's on loan from the Fort Worth Public Library. Way overdue."

"I doubt Sefton Stainthorpe will pay the fines, considering that he's dead."

Will keeps whimpering off and on, and now he hugs himself.

"Hey, what's wrong?" I ask. "Look like you saw a ghost."

"I have. The ghosts of the magics he invoked in this place." Will glances around, his face growing paler by the second. "This is where I was born."

He means that literally, I think. Well, he didn't emerge from a mother's womb, but Sefton created him with the magics he invoked to trigger doomsday. That's a kind of birth. A very creepy kind.

"Sefton is long gone," I say. "And his magics are gone too."

"No, they aren't. I feel their remnants nipping at my skin."

Grant starts wandering through the cavern, picking up books to flip through them, bending over to peer under the chair and table.

I cautiously slip an arm around Will's shoulders. "Take it easy, hey? Maybe what you feel is triggered by your own anxiety."

"That could be the case," he says cautiously. "You're a smart person."

"No, not really. I do a good impression of a smart person, though."

My lukewarm attempt at humor does not make him laugh or even make his lips twitch.

"Eureka!" Grant shouts. He jumps up from where he'd been perusing books on the shelves and hoists one bound volume above his head. He grins. "I found it."

"Found what?" I ask.

"Sefton's notes."

CHAPTER SEVENTEEN

Grant

I CAN'T STOP GRINNING, WHICH IS IDIOTIC. I FOUND SEFTON'S SECRET notes, and I want to jump up and down and whoop. No one knew if the madman kept any records, but I had a hunch and risked everything to get into the Echo to find the book I now hold in my hand. God, I hope it was worth the trouble. If the handwritten notes scrawled in this journal turn out to be the incoherent ramblings of a lunatic, I just might lie down on the floor and sleep for ten years.

Maybe the apocalypse would be over by then. Of course, that would probably mean the world exploded, leaving nothing behind but cosmic dust.

Erin rushes over to me and plants a firm kiss on my mouth. "Congratulations, Grant. You rock."

"I haven't actually found anything yet. Just a book."

"Haven't you read any of it?"

"Just a few sentences to verify that it seems to be what I think it is. I'd need Dax to confirm the handwriting belongs to Sefton."

Erin pats my cheek. "Stop looking for reasons to be bummed out. Open the damn book and read it already."

I used to hate her bossiness, but now I kind of like it. Erin knows what she needs to do and doesn't waste time vacillating. So I do what she would. I flip the book open and start reading. "I, Sefton Stainthorpe, vow to commit to the pages of this journal every bit of information I need to achieve my goal. The world has become too dirty and vile to go on as it is. A change is required. Only a massive and violent upheaval will bring about the necessary alterations."

Erin sidles up to me, leaning against my side, and peers down at the journal. "This is super creepy."

"No shit." The rest of the first page consists of complex equations I don't understand. I flip to the next page. "I know what the world needs, though no one would agree with my assessment. My fellow humans have become unconscionably addicted to technology and creature comforts, too settled in their hedonistic ways, more like animals than highly evolved beings."

The rest of this page is taken up by a rendering of Da Vinci's *The Vitruvian Man*. I've seen that image before—just about everybody has at some point—but for some reason, today the careful reproduction of Da Vinci's study of human anatomy sends a shiver through me. Why would Sefton care about making beautifully rendered drawings and equations when he planned to destroy the world?

Well, maybe I'll find answers on the next page.

But that page contains more ramblings about how evil and unworthy of life human beings are, plus more equations that I can't figure out. My studies of alchemy and quantum physics didn't prepare me for wickedly advanced math. Maybe these equations are nonsense, anyway.

I look at Will and hold up the journal, turning it so he can see the math gobbledygook. "Do you understand these equations?"

He shakes his head. "Sefton never taught me math."

But he is the madman's Echo. Other doppelgängers I've met knew things their originals knew, which suggests they inherited their original's memories.

I grasp Erin's arm and turn us both around, so we face the wall with our backs to Will. Then I whisper, "Something about that guy doesn't add up. He claims to be Sefton's Echo, but then he says he knows nothing about math. He should have at least some of Sefton's memories."

"Because Echo creatures do remember."

"Yeah. We shouldn't trust Will. He might be lying about everything."

"Does he look like Sefton?"

I shrug. "Guess so. But I only saw the man once, and he was already dead. Well, make that twice, counting when you and I visited Fallenmouth. His decaying corpse was hard to identify, though."

"Let's not read anymore of the journal aloud. Okay?"

"Agreed."

She leans in until her lips meet my ear, then whispers even more softly. "We can't just ditch Will, in case he's on the level, but we can't risk keeping him with us or sending him to earth."

"I know."

"Let's rummage through the rest of the books in here, then get back outside to come up with a plan."

"Good idea."

We thumb through the other books, but most of them are just textbooks on alchemy and physics. I've already read similar information in the papers I rescued from the remains of the Stanford University library. We don't need to bring these books with us. I stuff the journal into my backpack, and we're ready to go.

Erin can't seem to teleport. She didn't want me to kiss her again because she claimed it's unnecessary. But she seems to have suddenly become shy about what we need to do to get out of this cavern. No more waiting. We need out now, so I pull her into my arms and kiss her like there's no tomorrow. Which there might not be. I'm not doing this because I need to kiss her. It's an exit strategy.

Okay, maybe I just wanted to feel her up and taste her lips again. The exit strategy thing is an added benefit.

We pop out inside the Capital City, but nowhere I recognize. Since we'd driven through a lot of this town yesterday and this morning, I can't help wondering why I don't see anything familiar here. The skyscraper we had gotten trapped in earlier is nowhere on the horizon. Did our creature buddy destroy the whole building? Grenades couldn't pull that off, so I kind of doubt his big ugly feet could do it.

"Are you done fondling my ass?" Erin asks.

I jerk my hands away from her body. "Yeah, sorry."

"Don't apologize. I liked it, but we have stuff to do. Like, you know, saving the world and other inconsequential things."

Yeah, I've even started to like her snarky attitude.

The pattering of footsteps erupts behind us, retreating swiftly.

We both turn to look—and see Will fleeing. What the hell is he doing?

"Hey!" I holler. "Wait up."

Will does not stop or even slow down. He pelts down the street like an Olympic athlete and disappears around a corner. Erin and I race after him, but our backpacks hinder our speed. We get there too late. Will has vanished.

No, that's not weird or suspicious.

Erin and I halt halfway down the alley, breathing hard from sprinting while wearing fully loaded backpacks. Sweat dribbles down my temples.

"Where did he go?" Erin asks, and I take it for a rhetorical question. "Why did he run? I thought he was terrified and wanted us to protect him."

"Either he panicked, or he's a liar." Since we don't have our car, we can't search for Will. Even our eerily handy map of the city won't tell us where Sefton's Echo might have gone. "We have no choice. Let's find a place to hunker down and study the journal. If Will hasn't turned up by this evening, we should head back to earth."

"Okay." Erin bites her lip while she scans the alley in both directions. "Still not sure about Will, but I feel bad about leaving him behind."

"We didn't abandon him. He ran. That's his choice, and we need to move on."

"Maybe I should whisk us away to someplace outside the Capital City."

I consider the idea while we amble back onto the street. "I'd rather wait a few more hours to see if Will finds us. Then you can whisk us away."

"Fair enough."

The signs that led us to Will and the creepy skyscraper had also shown us where to find supplies and a safe place to sleep. We have no such luck now. Whatever magics had helped us before seem to have evaporated. But we find a building that hasn't been trashed inside as much as the other ones we checked out, so we decide to hunker down here. The vacant store is part of a larger building that extends down the entire block. This seems like it was an auto parts store, but it's hard to tell for sure what any post-apocalyptic structure might've been originally.

We don't have sleeping bags, but we find a partially scorched fabric car cover that we fold over to create a makeshift bed on the floor. Lying on our backs, we take turns reading the journal aloud. Do we learn anything? Yeah. We realize just how irretrievably insane Sefton was. Do we learn anything of practical use? Not really. Not yet, at least. But Erin keeps poring over the journal after I've given up. I'm staring at the ceiling when she speaks.

"Look at these weird symbols," she says, pointing at the book. "What are they?"

"Alchemical symbols. I saw the same designs in one of the medieval manuscripts Sefton stole from a university library, but I didn't understand why he had drawn them in the margin. Still don't."

"What do the symbols mean?"

"One is the sun symbol, which also represents the heart. The other is the symbol for gold, and it illustrates the concept of blood or the essence of life." I study the notes on the page and suddenly realize something. "Look at that. Sefton wrote that the heart and the lifeblood must be joined with the Tria Prima after the alchemical reaction has begun or else control can't be established."

"And that means what?"

"No idea."

She dog-ears that page and flips to the next. After an hour of scouring the journal, we take a break to eat some energy bars. We need real food soon, but that can wait a little while longer. I'm already feeling not up to my usual energy level, despite the name of those bars we ate. Red meat, that's what I need. We both do. But I also need to understand the journal because I feel like the fate of the world depends on it.

"You're so tense," Erin says. "Mr. Zen seems to have forgotten how to relax."

"We're in shit so deep we can't see the sky above us. Excuse me for feeling less than Zen right now."

"Try meditating. I'll do it too."

I glance at her sideways. "Have you ever meditated before?"

"Nope. You can teach me."

Erin the hardcore badass wants to learn about meditation while we're trapped in another world full of evil creatures. Go figure.

"All right," I tell her. "Let's get you up to speed on meditation. It's pretty simple."

"How do we start?"

"Ideally, we would find a comfortable place to settle in. That's not likely around here, so we'll have to make do." I sit up and get into a cross-legged position facing her. "You can sit however you like or stay lying down. I prefer a half-lotus position."

"Might as well try that too." She sits up and mimics my cross-legged pose. "I'm ready."

"We'll start with a basic mindfulness routine. It's all about staying in the moment."

"So, it's nice and vague. Which moment? This one? The next moment?"

"Right now. Are you ready?"

"Mm-hm."

"Good." I straighten my spine and take a deep breath. "Sit up straight, but keep your overall posture relaxed."

"That makes no sense."

"Shut up and do what I say."

Erin sputters like she's desperately trying not to laugh at me. "That doesn't sound very Zen, oh wise master."

I groan. "Just listen to my instructions and follow them. Okay?"

"Sir, yes, sir."

This time, I ignore her sarcasm. Telling her to shut up does no good. Instead, I channel my inner calmness and speak in a soothing voice. "Close your eyes and take slow, deep breaths to relax your entire body. Begin with your head and gradually move down to your toes. Keep breathing deeply while you do this and feel all the negative energy sifting out of you."

I peek through my mostly closed lids to watch her and make sure she does what I said. To my surprise, she obeys my instructions. Her lips curl into the barest of closed-mouth smiles.

"Next phase," I say. "Continue breathing deeply and slowly while you take note of every sensation in your body. Warm, cool, painful, whatever. Just let yourself experience all of it while remaining still and relaxed."

Her lips curl up a little more. Perfect. She's getting into the gentle relaxation of mindfulness. I'm feeling more peaceful too.

"If your mind drifts away from you, just ease it back into yourself," I say. "Your thoughts might wander occasionally, but keep bringing your focus back to your deep breathing and the sensations your body gives you."

My mind wanders, for sure—to her breasts and their enticing roundness. Her skintight tank top lets me see every contour of those tits as well as the flatness of her belly and the muscles in her arms. But I drag my focus back to the routine and close my eyes all the way, inhaling deep breaths and releasing them little by little. "How do you feel?"

"Good. Relaxed." Her voice has an almost dreamy quality. "Feel like I'm floating on a cloud while the sun warms my face."

"I feel that way too." I've never experienced this kind of sensation while I meditate. The warmth spreads down my throat and into my chest, sliding down toward my belly. "Keep breathing, slow and easy."

At this point, I would normally open my eyes. I've achieved relaxation and should move on to another exercise, but I can't make my lids part. That warmth spreads even lower, encompassing my groin, and I suck in a breath when my dick jerks and starts to swell. I've never gotten aroused while meditating, but then, I've never done it with a partner before.

The warmth suffuses my entire body now.

I hear soft whispering inside my mind, but it's not my voice. Whose, then? I sink into the mindful meditation and let go of all questions, but that voice keeps whispering to me in a sultry tone, though I can't understand the words yet.

Touch me, Grant.

Erin's voice shimmers through me like a wave of heat radiating off pavement in the summer. I inhale a deep breath, exhaling gradually while an arousing sensation ripples through me, almost like fingers caressing my skin. Erin's fingers. A blurry vision of her nude body intrudes on my meditation, and I can't resist allowing myself to dive into the fantasy. Everything remains slightly out of focus, but the feel of her skin brushing against mine grows more powerful every second.

My dick is rock-hard.

And I need to fuck her right now.

Chapter Eighteen

Erin

GRANT," I WHISPER, SOUNDING NOTHING LIKE MYSELF. I'VE BECOME A sex addict who needs another fix right now. My Zen master didn't warn me mindfulness meditation would lead to scorching sex and a strangely hot mental connection. My nipples have gone hard, and I can't shut my stupid mouth. "Oh God, please, Grant. Touch me everywhere."

"Fuck," he growls. His voice has become a rough and growly whisper that I swear I can hear in my own head. "Look at me, Erin."

His Zen tone has turned rough and rife with hunger.

I slowly part my lids, but I still feel dreamy and warm in all the best ways. "I want you."

Like I've never wanted anyone in my life, but I manage not to blurt that out. What I've said so far is embarrassing enough. The ardent desire I feel seems rooted in magics, though I can't explain why I believe that. I know it with a strange conviction.

His gaze gravitates to my lips. "I want you too. But this isn't the time."

"Please. Don't make me wait. I'm so turned on, and it feels incredible. But I need you inside me right now or I think I might go crazy."

Based on his expression and the iron hard-on straining his pants, I know he's experiencing the same phenomenon. What is happening to us? I swear I can feel him inside me already, like a sexy ghost inhabiting my body while giving me an erotic massage.

"Oh, yes," I moan. "Take me deep inside you and penetrate me to the core."

What the hell? Why am I begging for sex? And why do I kind of not mind that I'm begging?

Grant strokes his dick through his jeans.

I can't stop myself. I palm my tits and flick my thumbs over my nipples, gasping when a bolt of pleasure fires down my nerves and straight into my clit.

Grant surges forward and pins me to the blanket with his entire body, rotating his hips to grind his erection into my belly. His breaths come as short, harsh gasps, just like mine. I wrap my legs around his hips and drag my tongue up his throat, afflicted with a sudden craving to taste every inch of him. Groaning, he pushes up on his straight arms so he can reach down to unzip his jeans and push a hand inside his boxers, pulling his dick out as if plans to fuck me any second.

I latch on to his earlobe and suckle it.

He growls something unintelligible.

A ratcheting noise erupts outside, the mechanical sound echoing off the buildings.

Whump. Whump.

Grant and I both freeze, our gazes locked. Our horny friend from the Echo made a similar sound when he tromped through the city, but this noise is so much louder and imbued with a mechanical undertone.

"What is that?" I ask as if Grant could possibly know the answer.

Instead of responding, he leaps up and hauls me to my feet with him. He holds my hand as we approach the broken windows of the former store and peer out into the darkening twilight.

"Don't see anything," I say. "But that noise seems to be coming closer."

Grant compresses his lips as he stares out the window with his head cocked to one side and his gaze narrowed. "Something about that sound is familiar. Not like I've heard it, but like somebody told me about it once."

"Who told you?"

The ground trembles as massive footfalls crash down on the asphalt, and the cracking of the roadway reverberates through the city. I feel the vibrations in my body. The city itself begins to shiver visibly, from the subsurface all the way up to the tops of the buildings.

I grab Grant's arm. "We need to get out of here. Fast."

He tears his focus away from what's happening outside and looks at me. "You should teleport us away right now."

"Okay, I'll try." I seize his shirt and pull him into me, then squeeze my eyes shut as I concentrate all my willpower on one task—*get us away from here*. Nothing happens. I peek out between my half-closed lids to make sure. Nope, we haven't moved one inch. "Didn't work."

Grant cradles my face in his hands and kisses me.

I pull my head back to see him. "Still nothing. Sorry."

"Where did you try to go?"

"Anyplace else."

He squints like he's thinking hard. "Try aiming for a specific place."

"Like where?"

"The gateway to the Echo. From there, maybe you can whisk us back to earth."

The whumping footfalls of whatever lurks out there grow louder every minute, and the shaking beneath our feet may soon become a genuine earthquake. I have no choice. I must do what Grant suggested—and do it now.

"Should I kiss you again?" he asks.

"Why not? Can't hurt."

He plasters his mouth to mine and plunges his tongue deep while I concentrate harder than ever, so hard that my head starts to hurt. I don't sense any change. When I open my eyes, I realize we haven't moved at all. Grant still has his tongue in my mouth, so I slap my hands on his chest and push him away.

"Did it work?" he asks.

I spread my arms to indicate our surroundings. "Does it look like it worked?"

"Dumb question, you're right. I got a little, uh, mentally scrambled."

He can't mean because he kissed me. Well, his lips and his body turn me into a human omelet too, so I probably shouldn't judge him for that.

Whump. Whump. Whump.

The bits of jagged glass that still cling to the store window's frame begin to rattle with every step our mysterious visitor takes. I grab Grant's hand and haul him out the door, onto the sidewalk. There, we stop. As one, we tip our heads back to glimpse whatever is coming for us. The crown of a monstrous head pops up above the buildings on the cross street two blocks over, and the little of it I can see does not ease my anxiety in the least.

"What on earth is that?" I ask, my tone hushed and filled with a terrible awe I can't disguise.

Grant shuts his eyes and grimaces. Then he blows out a breath. "That is Sefton's golem."

"His what? You and Will mentioned that before, but I don't understand what the word means."

"A golem is a creature created by magic and bound to obey its master's commands. I never saw the golem, but Allison and Dax told me about it. They described it in detail." He throws an arm around me as more footfalls slam down and their concussions make the ground shudder so much that I might've fallen over if Grant hadn't held on to me. "Sefton said he put the golem to sleep after he captured Dax and Allison. Either this is a different golem, or somebody woke it up."

"Will could've done it. Don't you think?"

"Maybe. He claims not to know about Sefton's plans or his alchemical experiments, but he might've been lying."

The crown of the monstrosity's head rises above the buildings again, giving me enough of a glimpse that I know that thing can't be more than two blocks away now. I close my eyes and slide my arms around Grant, hugging him tightly. Then I try one last time to whisk us away.

Pain slams into my head like a lightning bolt.

I scream, and my legs buckle. Grant catches me. The intensity of the pain makes me feel like my skull has exploded and my brain has melted, but I force myself to suck in the tiniest of breaths to quell the ringing in my ears and prevent myself from passing out. What on earth is this? I got shot during my time as a Marine, but that was nothing compared to the mind-shattering agony I'm experiencing now.

Grant holds me to him and kisses the top of my head. "Easy, Erin. Remember the mindfulness routine. Try to focus on one thing—my voice. Can you do that?"

The golem stomps ever nearer, and the ground pulsates with every footstep.

But I manage to nod weakly.

"Good," Grant says. "Just listen to me. Tune out everything else. I won't let anyone hurt you ever again, so you don't need to worry about that. Just relax and take slow breaths, shallow ones at first, then try taking deeper ones as the pain subsides." He combs his fingers through my hair in a soothing gesture. "Shh, it's okay. Picture a sandy beach, blue skies, palm trees, and a hammock. You walk over to the hammock and lie down on it, letting the hammock rock gently side to side. I'm there with you, massaging your feet."

A tingling sensation begins in my arms and blossoms out through the rest of my body, reaching my head last. The soft, sensual tingling relaxes my muscles. The pain subsides while I focus on the lovely sensation of his fingers in my hair and the image of a tropical beach.

I lift my head. "I'm okay now. Thank you."

He kisses me. "Glad to hear it."

We turn toward the cross street again. With no options left, we stand here to await the arrival of the golem. Oddly, I experience only a twinge of anxiety. Grant got me so Zenned out that I can't worry at all, but I know the feeling will pass. I also know I can get it back anytime I need to, thanks to the man who taught me how to relax.

All of the golem's head emerges as he passes the shorter buildings near the intersection.

I glance up at Grant. "That thing looks like it's part machine and part living thing."

"Looks that way because it is that way."

The asphalt on the cross street buckles and rises like waves on an ocean, the ripples racing across the intersection to follow the track of the cross street. Their motion causes much smaller ripples in the asphalt where we stand. Though they might be smaller, those waves create enough energy to make the brick building across from us crumble.

The golem steps into the intersection and swivels to face us.

Holy shit, that thing really is man and machine combined. The metal plates fused to its skin flex with every muscle in its body. Solid metal shoes cover its feet. The dark gray and black shades of its flesh seem to shimmer as if its entire body is infused with metal. The monstrosity's eyes shimmer an electric crimson, like demonic headlights.

The golem moves only those eyes as it scans the street where we loiter.

"Don't suppose that thing has a weak spot," I say. "Looks like an unstoppable monster."

"From what Allison told me, that's exactly what it is. But the golem obeyed Sefton's commands. Who woke it up today?"

I slip my hand into his and thread our fingers, taking comfort from the simple contact while I consider his question. I'm sure it was rhetorical, but I can't help wondering. "Do you think Will did this? Could he control the golem now that Sefton is gone?"

"Maybe. He seems like a scaredy-cat, but that might be an act."

"What if he used us to find Sefton's secret journal?"

The idea only occurred to me a second ago, and I expect Grant to scoff at the suggestion.

But he doesn't. Instead, he gives me a sly smile. "You're one smart cookie, Erin. You may be right about that. I think we'll find out the answer any minute now."

The golem swerves its demonic gaze to us. The machine-beast tips his head down, then a ratcheting sound starts up as the thing slowly cranks its jaw open.

"Oh no," Grant says. "I remember what Dax said the golem does with its mouth."

"I'm guessing it doesn't sing lullabies."

"Nope." He grips my hands harder. "Time to run."

We take off in the opposite direction from the golem, still holding hands.

The ratcheting noise of the thing's jaw opening ceases.

I know I shouldn't look, but my mind has other ideas. It forces me to glance over my shoulder.

A red glow burns deep inside the golem's mouth.

"Stop gawking," Grant snarls. "You're slowing us down."

I face forward again. Between gasping breaths, I ask, "What is that thing doing now?"

"Getting ready to fire."

No chance to ask what sort of weapon the thing will fire at us. I've barely formulated the thought when the golem roars and flames shoot past us over our heads to strike the asphalt street half a block away.

Grant jerks me to a halt.

The heat of the golem's fire breath rushes over our heads, and I raise my free arm to shield myself from it. Then silence falls over the world, or at least this part of it. I gingerly lower my arm and peek out through half-closed lids.

Oh shit.

The golem has melted the asphalt ahead of us, the sidewalks too. His breath set several buildings on fire. That damn beast has blocked our way out. I glance at Grant, and he nods. We rotate to face the golem, which now stands not quite a block away.

"Should we raise our hands in surrender?" I ask. "Don't think we can overpower that thing."

Grant releases my hand and raises both of his.

I do the same. What choice do we have? For the moment, we must surrender.

The golem, which still has its maw wide open, reaches behind its head to hold its hand palm up. A small figure trots out from behind the monster's head, or maybe from inside it, and hops onto the giant metal-and-flesh hand. The golem lowers itself into a kneeling position, emitting grinding noises, and sets its hand on the ground. The small figure leaps off the monstrosity's palm to land on the roadway.

Will saunters toward us, halting several yards away. "Thank you for finding the journal for me, but I now have no use for you."

He snaps his fingers, and the sound echoes off the buildings.

That red glow fires up again inside the golem's mouth.

We are about to get flambéed.

CHAPTER NINETEEN

Grant

I MIGHT BE THE KIND OF MAN WHO MEDITATES AND DOESN'T LIKE TO argue with anybody unless it's absolutely necessary, but that doesn't mean I'm a coward. Surrendering does not appeal to me. I need to fight, but I won't risk Erin's life to do that. Sure, she can handle herself like the seasoned military vet she is. But the thought of that golem or his master injuring Erin… It makes me feel a kind of anger I haven't experienced since the day Sefton's apocalypse ripped my family away from me.

"Why are you doing this?" I shout to Will. "We helped you."

"You are tools who have outlived their usefulness."

"Did Sefton really leave those breadcrumbs for Allison? Or did you lead us to that building so we could rescue you?"

He lifts one shoulder in a slight shrug. "I was genuinely trapped in that building, and I took advantage of your presence to effect my escape. But the clues you followed were the ones my original self planted for Allison."

Will seems much more confident now, but I have an intuition that he wasn't faking when he behaved like a terrified, abused child. Maybe his success in reactivating the golem has emboldened him. I mean, the guy has a giant cyborg with asphalt-melting fire breath. That probably made him feel invincible, and the power has gone to his head.

How can we teach him a lesson in humility without getting killed in the process? I have an idea, but Erin might not like it. Well, it's nothing she hasn't done before.

I lean toward her to whisper directly into her ear. "Flirt with him."

"What?" she hisses out of the corner of her mouth. "Are you insane?"

"You did the same thing with that creature who carried us into the Echo. Why is it insane to use your special skills to distract Will right now?"

"What if my flirtation makes him angry? He's got a gigantic cyborg on his side. And I doubt the golem will fall for my charms."

"Just try it with Will. The goal is to stop him from telling his golem to squash us under his metal boots."

"They're shoes, not boots."

She just has to argue with me about everything, doesn't she?

"Whatever," I growl. "Just do it."

Erin rolls her eyes and pushes me away.

I decide to assume that means she's about to test her flirty charms on Will.

"Are we still friends, Will?" she asks. "I can't believe you were lying about everything. You like me, don't you?"

Will squints at her. "What are you doing?"

"Just chatting. We helped you, and we want to go on helping you. *I* want to help you. How can I do that?"

"You're still alive only because I need that journal. Hand it over."

Why didn't he steal that before he fled from us? He must've thought he couldn't wrest it away from me or Erin. That implies he views us as stronger and tougher than he is. Erin must realize that too. She's too smart not to figure that out. She has the journal in her backpack, but we took our packs off to meditate. They're still inside the store—a block behind us, beyond the wide expanse of melted asphalt. The road surface back there still bubbles, the heat of it warming our backs.

I hope she remembers that's where we left the journal. If she doesn't remember... No, she will.

"The journal," Will snaps, though his lips tremble the slightest bit. "I want it now."

Erin sashays a little closer to him. "I'm so proud of you, sweetie. Awakening the golem would've terrified anyone, but you did it. You're stronger and better than Sefton ever was."

"No, I—" He makes a frustrated noise. "Bloody hell, you're trying to confuse me."

His accent just switched from American to British. Had he been faking his American persona? If so, he did a bang-up job. I completely bought his performance. Or is he faking this time? Since Sefton was British, I tend to believe that's Will's natural accent too.

As if it matters.

Erin holds her hands palms out, raised slightly in front of her in a conciliatory gesture. "Relax, Will. I want to help if you'll let me. I'm your friend, remember?"

She isn't flirting, but her tactic seems more likely to convince Will than my idea would have.

"I thought we were friends," Will says carefully. "But you ran away from my golem."

"No, we ran away from his fire breath," Erin tells him. "If we'd known you were controlling the golem, we wouldn't have tried to run."

His anger softens into an almost hopeful expression. "You want to be with me?"

"Of course we do." She takes another step toward him. "Please tell me what has you so scared."

"You'll laugh at me. Sefton always did."

"No, we won't." Erin glances back at me. "Come over here, Grant. Show him we're all friends."

I approach her, and though I want to hold her hand, I stop myself from doing that. Will might not like it. And she's right, we need to placate him, not trick him. The guy was locked inside a vacant, creepy skyscraper—for months, at least. Maybe he just needs reassurance.

But I'll keep my cop senses on high alert.

Erin glances at me and tips her head toward Will.

She wants me to play nice with the guy who controls a frigging golem. Well, why not? If it stops us from getting pancaked on the asphalt, I'll give it a try. "Hey, Will, I'm glad you're okay. We were worried about you after you took off. In fact, we hung around hoping you'd turn up."

His brows knit together, and he bites one corner of his lip.

Yeah, he wants to believe us. That's a good sign.

"You must have been alone for a long time," I say. "Time moves differently in the Echo, right?"

Will gnaws on his lip for a moment. "Yes, that's right. I've been trapped here for more years than I can count."

"Trapped in that building?"

He nods.

"Can't imagine how awful that was. But you're free now. And we really do want to be your friends. What do you say?"

Will chews on his lip even harder.

I slowly approach him and nod for Erin to do the same. We halt a few feet from Will. I offer him my hand. "Friends, right?"

He stares at my hand, but then takes it. "Yes, friends."

Erin kisses his cheek and smiles.

But we still have a gigantic cyborg looming ahead of us with its maw gaping wide and its crimson eyes scanning the area. Yeah, that's not disturbing. The way every hair on my body is stiffening has nothing to do with that thing staring at us.

Being sarcastic in my own head isn't helpful.

"I do need that journal," Will says. "Please give it to me."

Erin and I exchange glances. I shrug.

She faces Will. "We left our backpacks in a store about two blocks away, on the other side of the melted asphalt. The journal is in my pack."

Will turns around to face the golem. "Get their backpacks for me, would you?"

The golem closes its mouth with a ratcheting sound, then nods and straightens. The grinding noise as it rises grates on my ears even more than the ratcheting sound had. The metal monster lifts one foot and swings it forward to stomp down on the asphalt just behind us. Its other foot whumps down a second later. The golem hesitates there, as if analyzing its options. Finally, the thing bends its knees and launches itself off the ground. The golem lands on the other side of the melted asphalt.

"How does he know which building it is?" I ask.

"My golem is imbued with tracking spells," Will says. "He knew exactly where you were the moment I awakened him and told him your names."

"But you only know our first names."

"Sefton created the tracking spells. I don't know the details, only that they work."

All this magic stuff can be amazing, but in the hands of a whackjob, it's damn annoying. Will seems a lot more reasonable than Sefton was, but I'm still balanced on that fence when it comes to our new buddy. After all, when he gets mad, he sics a golem on us.

Since he already knows why we came to the Echo, I see no reason I shouldn't ask him a question related to that. "We need to figure out what the information in Sefton's journal means. Would you help us?"

"I've already told you I know nothing about those magics or quantum physics."

"But you woke the golem up. That must've required magic."

"The spell to awaken the sleeping giant required nothing more than chanting a specific phrase. I heard Sefton recite the words when he first created the golem."

"I appreciate your honesty, Will." But if he was there when Sefton created that thing—a fact he didn't mention when we met him—then he might have more secrets.

"You appreciate it?" Will says, seeming genuinely baffled.

"That's right. I always appreciate it when someone tells me the truth. When I was a deputy sheriff, I spent every day listening to people lie to me."

He still seems confused, but I think that means he understands I meant what I said.

"We're both grateful, Will," Erin says, "that you've been upfront with us. Honesty between friends is important."

The mechanical noise of the golem on the move starts up again. Just as we turn our heads to look at the thing, it leaps over the melted asphalt, which seems to be cooling now, and lands just behind its master. The golem faces us.

And it drops our backpacks at our feet.

Saying "thank you" seems like a bad idea. Not sure that cyborg understands words, anyway, unless they're spoken by its puppet master. I kneel to unzip Erin's pack and pull out the journal. Will wants it, but if he has no knowledge of magics, I can't see what good the journal will do him. He got angry when we told him we didn't have it, and he repeatedly demanded we hand it over to him.

I rise and hold the journal in one hand. "Here it is. But since you don't know anything about magic, this thing won't do you any good. It's full of spells and alchemical junk, not to mention quantum physics. Are you an expert on that?"

Will puckers his lips while staring at the journal like it's a juicy rib-eye steak, and he hasn't eaten in days. "Please give me the journal."

"Let's find a place to sit down and go through it together. I've already spent some time studying it."

He thrusts out his hand. "Give it to me."

Okay, now I'm back to thinking he's a nutjob like the original Sefton. I am not giving up this journal without a damn good reason or at least some serious proof that I can trust this guy. I might not fully understand the info in the book, but I know it holds vital clues that might let us reverse the damage done by Sefton's apocalypse or at least stop the convulsions the Echo has experienced lately.

So no, I'm not handing over the journal.

Will's chest heaves as he blusters breaths out through his nostrils and clenches his fists tightly enough that they tremble. He clenches his teeth too, which I can tell because his lips peel back from them when he speaks, his voice raspy and harsh. "I want the fucking journal. *Now.*"

Erin raises her hands. "Take it easy, sweetie. We're friends, remember?"

"Friends do not refuse to give me what I need." Spittle sprayed from his lips when he snarled those words. "If you defy me again, I will exact punishment. Last chance."

I hold the journal to my belly and shake my head. "No dice, Will. We study this book together or not at all."

"You think you can stop me from taking it?" He makes a strange noise deep in his throat, almost like an animal growling. Then he tips his head to the side, seeming curious now. "Have you not figured out why Erin couldn't teleport you away?"

She got a massive headache but couldn't do it. That's all we know, but I won't admit that to him.

Will straightens and rolls his shoulders back, his chin lifted. "I prevented it."

Yeah, I really trust him now. He just admitted to lying to us again, didn't he? The guy keeps telling us he has no magic skills, but then he admits to awakening a golem and now, apparently, stopping Erin from whisking us away.

"I imagine she suffered intense pain when she tried to do it," Will says with a smug little smile. "Sefton might have believed I was useless and impotent, but I watched everything he did. I heard every spell he cast." Will taps his temple. "And I memorized them. I have a photographic memory, but Sefton didn't seem to realize that. He never bothered to learn much of anything about me."

A chill slithers down my spine, raising the hairs at my nape. I'm getting an inkling, but nothing I can articulate just yet.

"I must have that journal," Will says. "I'll give you ten seconds to relinquish it. Count it down for me, golem."

The cyborg emits a weird ticking noise. One, two, three…

Erin pulls a switchblade out of her pocket, flicks it open, and races up to Will. She holds the blade's glistening edge to his throat. "Stop the countdown, or I'll slit your throat."

He smirks.

She nicks his skin. Blood trickles down his throat. "Stop the countdown."

"Stop," he shouts.

The golem goes silent.

"I have a better idea, anyway," Will says. "Golem, seize them."

The great cyborg slowly bends down, stretching out a hand as if to grab us.

We snatch up our backpacks and run.

Chapter Twenty

Erin

WHERE ARE WE GOING? NO IDEA. BUT IF GRANT THINKS WE NEED TO RUN, I'll follow him anywhere. I can't teleport, which leaves us with no means of escaping except to bolt. The golem seems too slow to catch us, but since we're dealing with a magically created monstrosity, I can't rule anything out. Maybe that thing has a stick shift inside it that will push it into overdrive.

So we run, run, run.

A mechanical screeching reverberates through the city, seeming to emanate from above our heads. I risk a glance up—and my heart thuds. "Grant! It's overhead!"

He tips his head back while still sprinting down the street. "Shit!"

Yeah, lots and lots of swearing is appropriate right now because the golem is flying toward us from above. Does it have propellers? A jet engine? Given the haphazard way it flies toward us, I wonder if the thing just jumped into the air and intends to flop down on top of us. We would die, but the journal might remain intact.

"Don't watch the golem," Grant shouts at me. "Focus on the road ahead."

I do what he suggested, but my legs have started to burn and I'm having trouble catching my breath. My ears ring too. I might be hyperventilating. Who can blame me? A monstrous robot-man thing wants to turn us into red smears on the road.

Whump.

The ground shudders so violently that we both stumble and fall, rolling across the pavement because the pavement itself is rolling like waves on a turbulent sea. Cracking noises accompany the buckling of the roadway. Grant hits the curb, and I slam into him. Once the dizziness lessens, my brain manages to process what I'm seeing.

The golem lies flat on its belly on the street. Steam rises up from beneath it as if the monster slid down the roadway after crash landing on it and skidded so hard and fast that the pavement heated up. Maybe the golem got injured, and it can't get up again.

Grant crawls out from under me and struggles to his feet. He sways a little, but only for a few seconds. Then he grasps my arms and hauls me up too. "Can't run anymore. What about you?"

"My legs feel like jelly." I nod toward the golem. "Think it's damaged?"

"Kinda doubt it. We should get moving, as fast as we can. I realize that probably won't be fast at all, but still…"

"Yeah. No choice and all that jazz."

A ratcheting noise starts up, and the golem pushes up with its arms, slowly rising into a crouch.

We run. Well, it's more like a fast walk, and we weave around instead of taking a straight path. I feel a touch woozy, so I imagine he does too. My jelly legs can't carry me as fast as I need to go.

The ratcheting stops, replaced by a grinding noise that makes my ears hurt.

Dammit. We need to move faster.

Giant fingers curl around us like a barricade.

We both stumble to a halt, but we're confused for half a second too long. By the time we try to escape the literal clutches of the metal beast, its fingers have encompassed us and are closing tighter and tighter every second. I can't move my arms or legs, not with a gigantic hand wrapped around my entire body, leaving only my head and neck exposed. Grant suffers from the same problem.

The golem has caught us.

With more mechanical noises, the metal monster rises to his feet and turns around to face his master. Will stands at the intersection where we'd left him, but now he strides down the street toward us.

I can't believe I felt bad for the guy. Once a coward gets a taste of power, he gorges on it. The only way to stop a bully is to take away that power and remind him what it feels like to be the weak one. I can't stand up to him right now. Literally. I can't move my body.

The golem waits patiently for his master, standing so perfectly still that I wonder if the thing can fall asleep while standing up. Does it sleep at all? No idea.

Will halts right in front of the golem, mere feet from his mechanical slave. He tilts his head up to look at us. "You two should have obeyed me."

I want to smack him down so hard.

"Now, you have forced me to be unkind to you." Will waves a hand in a grand gesture. "Golem, take them to the palace."

Sefton had a palace? What, did he wear a crown too? I assumed nothing could surprise me anymore, not after the alchemy of worlds, but Will has done that. King Sefton died. Does his doppelgänger plan to anoint himself Lord of the Echo now? I'm beginning to suspect that what everyone, including Dax, thought they knew about Sefton was only the tip of a blood-red iceberg.

The golem starts walking. He picks up Will along the way, holding him gently in one palm with those enormous fingers half curled.

I still have my knife in my hand. If I could wriggle a bit and get a sliver of leverage, maybe I could… What? Prick the golem's finger? Yeah, I'm sure he'd collapse and writhe in agony if I did that. *Use your brain, woman. Think of something.*

Grant, who remains squished in the golem's hand with his back plastered to mine, twists his head around to see me. "Our cyborg pal doesn't seem to have a brain of his own."

"Duh." We're both speaking in hushed voices to keep Will or the golem from hearing us. "This thing is a magical construct, right? That means no brain."

"Not quite. All the Echo creatures, and Will too, are magical constructs. They have brains, even if they use them for evil purposes."

"How does this conversation help us? I hope you're not about to suggest I should flirt with the golem."

"No. But I think there might be… I don't know. Feel like an idea is hovering just out of my reach, and if I could stretch a little farther, I might catch it."

"Keep trying. We've got nothing else." I make a pained face. "My best idea so far is to get stabby with my knife."

Grant's expression goes blank. He stares at me for a moment while our golem buddy lumbers down the street and rounds a corner. Then Grant grins. "You're a genius."

"As much as I love a compliment, I think you're overdoing it. I haven't done anything genius-level yet."

"Oh yes you have." He grins. "Get stabby, baby."

Grant has never called me "baby" before. He never called me anything but my name. Well, that and "reckless." I shouldn't read too much into what he just said, though, because I doubt he means it as an endearment.

But I do what he suggested. I wriggle, though only enough to get a better grip on my switchblade, not enough to alert the golem—I hope. Once I've got my hand positioned right, I tell Grant, "Ready."

"Thrust as hard and deep as you can." He smirks. "I didn't mean for that to sound so erotic."

"Sure you didn't. I'm on to you, Larson. You're a closet sex addict, aren't you?"

"Only for you."

I need to change the subject. It's too weird for us to be making suggestive comments to each other while we're literally in the grip of a cyborg. So instead, I "get stabby." I thrust my blade as deep and hard as possible, but I don't stop with one strike. I gore the golem's hand repeatedly and even manage to slice a gash through its palm. Is that enough to distract it? Not sure, so I keep going. My blade bumps into one of the metal plates embedded in the thing's flesh. At first, I assume I can't do anything about that, but then I realize something vital. The golem's metal plates are fused to its flesh, yes, but I can slip my knife under this one. I take a deep breath and shove the blade under the plate and tug it upward to separate the metal from the flesh.

The golem roars.

And it stops moving.

Its grip on us loosens a touch, just enough that I can wriggle around and get both my hands on the knife. I manage to pry my arms free of the cyborg's grip, then slash it down toward the top of the metal plate and slice it free too. Two sides of it gape open with blood trickling down from the wound.

The golem roars again, but this time its voice has a note of pain in it.

And its fingers pop open. Not all the way, but enough.

Grant and I climb out of the beast's palm. Far below us lies the roadway. If we jump, we will probably become pancakes for real this time.

Will howls like a wounded animal. "Stop them, golem! Stop them! I command you!"

The golem pays no attention, too distracted by its own pain to worry about its master.

Grant holds our backpacks. He hands me one, and we quickly slip into them. But we can't jump, not from this height. Does he have a plan? Of course he does. Grant is amazing that way.

"Let's climb up the golem's arm and stab him on the inside of his elbow," Grant says. "That might be a weak spot." He pulls out the cutlass I'd seen him stash in his pack and slides it out of its scabbard. "With your switchblade and my cutlass, we can slay this giant. Or at least make him fall to his knees."

And then we can jump onto the ground. Damn, he's brilliant. We need to have sex again soon.

Grant and I scramble up the golem's arm while he raises his wounded hand, which means we're running downhill. I stumble and wind up sliding toward the monster's elbow, bouncing over the edges of metal plates. Grant sees what happened to me and decides to follow suit, though he slides down the beast's arm on purpose. Luckily, the golem raises his arm halfway and stops. He stares at his palm, those crimson eyes glowing less brightly than before.

Grant thrusts his cutlass into the crease of the beast's elbow, pushing it in to the hilt.

I kneel and stab my knife into the golem's flesh, hard and deep, over and over, while blood begins to pour from the wounds. Grant yanks his cutlass free, then punches it into the cyborg's flesh yet again. Even more blood pours from the wounds he inflicts. We keep piercing the elbow again and again, plunging ours blades as deep as possible and getting covered in the golem's blood in the process. It's red like ours.

The golem emits an ear-splitting sound, a cross between a howl and machinery screaming. Then the creature's knees buckle.

Whump.

The metal monster strikes the ground and starts to fall forward.

Grant and I leap off the golem's arm, landing on our feet. But we only have seconds to get out of the path of the monster's body before it crushes us. I glance back and see Will trapped in the golem's other hand, though its fingers have slackened. That gives him a shot at escaping alive, but I can't worry about the crazy son of a bitch right now. He brought this on himself.

"Hurry!" Grant hollers as he seizes my hand and half drags me away.

The golem's body seems to tip forward in slow motion, but I think that's adrenaline heightening my senses and altering my perception of time. I can smell the cyborg's blood, acrid and metallic but with a hint of motor oil. We race down the street, headed to who knows where, knowing only that we need to get far away from what's about to happen. When the golem dropped from the sky, it had nearly shattered an entire block of buildings and pavement. The creature will fall from a much lower altitude this time, but something about the way his blood smells makes me worry that we won't be safe until we get farther away.

Because I smell something I recognize, and it means big trouble.

"Run faster," I tell Grant. "That golem might have explosives inside it."

"What? Why do you think that?"

"Trust me. I worked alongside the bomb squad when I was in the Marines. I swear I smell C-4." We have to shout to hear each other over the groaning, grinding, ratcheting, roaring noises coming from the golem.

"What does it smell like?" Grant asks.

"Motor oil."

"Why would Sefton make his toy explosive?"

"No idea."

The mechanical noises end, plunging the city into a silence deeper than normal. Whatever normal is in the Echo.

Whump.

We stagger sideways as the earth shudders, but I catch Grant before he tumbles into a mailbox. They have mail in the Echo? Who knew.

The golem has fallen. But will it rise again or explode? It might just lie there on the ground, dead in whatever way a magically made construct would be. We stand still for a moment, waiting for something else to happen. I glance back the way we'd come, but I can't see anything, not even a cloud of dust. Maybe the golem disintegrated when it ceased to function.

I look down at my body and suddenly realize I'm covered in Golem blood. Grant is soaked in the stuff too.

A human roar of anguish reverberates off the buildings.

We whirl around.

Someone has rounded a corner, exiting the street where the golem had been and limping down this road toward us. The person wails again, throwing both arms in the air and tripping over who knows what. The individual manages not to fall down and keeps struggling to cross the distance to us. As the figure draws closer, I recognize that face.

Will has caught up to us. And he's royally ticked.

Chapter Twenty-One

Grant

Erin and I remain motionless while we watch our former friend shuffling toward us, favoring his left leg and cradling his left arm. When the golem fell, it must have injured Will. Though I feel like I should experience a twinge of empathy for the guy, considering how Sefton treated him, I can't pull that off. He threatened to kill us, and I believe he would have done it. Then he sicced his golem on us. So yeah, I don't feel bad for that guy anymore.

We should get out of here, but I can't move, and Erin seems to have the same problem. I think we're still in shock. About everything. Nobody has had much of a chance to deal with the losses and the horror of what Sefton unleashed on the world a few months ago. Just when we thought at least things couldn't get worse, the Echo started to freak out.

"Should we run?" Erin asks. "He sounds beyond angry."

"Yeah, but he has no leverage anymore. Without the golem, he's just a spineless nerd who can't even teleport."

"Can't believe I felt sorry for him. Or that I tried to comfort him."

"He put on a good show. His true colors only surfaced when he got out of that skyscraper."

Since I'm known as the guy who never gets upset and accepts everyone the way they are, maybe I should muster a little bit of empathy for Will. But no, I won't do that. He tried to kill me, which I find slightly annoying. He also tried to kill Erin, and I will murder anyone who endangers her.

When I glance at Erin, I feel a strong urge to kiss her. Since we're both blood-soaked, I think I'll wait. But a familiar odor wafts into my nostrils every time I inhale, a smell that reminds me of what Erin said a minute ago.

C-4 smells like motor oil.

"Do you smell that?" I ask. "On your clothes. Doesn't that odor remind you of motor oil? I assumed any explosives would be hidden inside the golem, not on us."

Erin lifts the collar of her shirt and sniffs. Her eyes widen. "Oh, shit. The golem's blood must be infused with C-4 or something similar. I kind of doubt it's actually motor oil."

"Maybe the golem needs a lot of lubrication to function."

"Grasp at all the straws you want. But if there's even a slim chance we're covered in the blood of a creature that might contain explosives, we need to act accordingly."

I ignore the limping nerd slowly coming toward us and ask, "Act according to what?"

"Decontamination protocols. We have to get this gunk off us ASAP."

"You see any bathtubs or showers around here? We can't clean ourselves off with anything but dirt."

"I know." She flattens her lips and narrows her gaze, an expression I've decided means she's thinking. Then she shrugs and shakes her head. "I've got nothing."

A shuffling sound draws our attention back to Will. He stops several yards away to pout at us. Okay, maybe his lips don't actually form a pout, but his expression and his attitude create the effect. He stands there with slumped shoulders, messy hair, torn clothes, and one shoe missing its sole. Dirt and blood spatter his body, though he's not soaked like we are.

When I glance at Erin, I know she's thinking the same thing I am. So I face Will. "Does that golem have explosive blood?"

His expression goes blank. He doesn't blink for several seconds. Then he starts laughing.

Does that mean no, the golem doesn't have C-4 blood? No idea.

When Will finally stops laughing, he wipes tears from his eyes. "Thank you for reminding me."

I don't know what that means, but I'm getting a prickly feeling on my skin that's telling me to run.

He shoves a hand into his pants pocket and pulls out a cigarette lighter. "This was the only gift Sefton ever gave me. He said it would either light my way or reduce me to ashes, and he didn't care which one happened."

"Erin," I whisper out of the corner of my mouth. "Run."

Will flicks the lighter. A small flame ignites.

And we bolt.

My leg muscles burn because I haven't recovered from our escape from the golem, but we have no other choice than to run. I can tell from the grimace on Erin's face that she feels the same agony. We both served in the military and learned how to push through the pain and fear, but nobody has ever received training in how to defeat a golem and his nutjob master, much less how to neutralize the incendiary blood of a magical construct.

An object flies past my shoulder.

I skid to a halt and throw out an arm to stop Erin.

The object is a glass bottle that shattered on impact. The makeshift wick—a piece of fabric stuffed into the bottle's neck—burns with a small yellow flame.

If I'd ever wanted to save Will, that impulse has disintegrated. Fuck him. He just tried to ice us with a Molotov cocktail. I take a step toward the bottle and lift my foot, intending to squelch the flame.

But Erin seizes my arm to stop me. "We're covered in possibly explosive blood, remember?"

I mutter a curse under my breath and retract my foot, then back up a couple of steps. "Thanks for reminding me."

"What are friends for?"

She is more than a friend, though I can't quite make myself consider the full import of that thought. Not yet. Maybe never.

I study the broken bottle while its flame fizzles out. "A Molotov cocktail has gasoline or alcohol in it, right?"

"Yeah."

"The bottle is empty except for the wick. He can't even get that right." But he could still hurt us if we really have incendiary blood on us.

Another bottle soars over our heads, smacking down on the pavement. This one lands too damn close, its flaming wick nearly grazing my shoe.

I grasp Erin's hand, and we sprint down the street.

"You won't get away forever," Will hollers. "I know this city better than you do. I'll track you down wherever you go."

He's right that we don't know the city. But we will never give in to Sefton's wimpier but no less deranged doppelgänger. We swerve around a corner just as Will lobs another bottle at us, though it strikes a building instead of us.

I see a sign up ahead and drag Erin into that building. Its wooden door is mostly intact, so I push it shut. A chair lies on its side nearby, and I grab that to brace the doorknob. In Will's condition, he won't be able to kick the door down—if he even realizes we've entered this building. He was still around the corner when he hurled the last bottle. I keep hold of Erin's hand while I take us deeper into the building, sidling around a swinging door that barely clings to its hinges.

"Did that sign say 'physical therapy'?" Erin asks.

"Yeah. This must've been a clinic at some point. Assuming anything in this world is what it seems."

"Wouldn't bank on it."

I guide us down a hallway until I see a door labeled "water therapy."

"Where are you going?" Erin asks.

"Hopefully, someplace where we can get cleaned up." I push the intact door open. "Oh yeah, this will do."

I lead Erin to the big round tub at the center of the room, which still contains water. Releasing her hand, I kneel to dip my fingers into the water. Cold, of course.

Erin crouches beside me. "Still confused, Grant. What are we doing here?"

"Do you want to rinse the potentially explosive golem blood off before it dries?"

She stares at me for a moment, then her mouth slides into a sexy smile. "You're a genius, Grant."

Genius? No, I'm not that good. "We need to get clean and get out of here before Will realizes where we are."

We strip off our clothes and jump into the pool to scrub ourselves with our hands and wash our hair out by dunking our heads under the water. Once we feel relatively clean, we dump our clothes into the water. I find a broom in the corner and use its handle to create an agitation effect like a washing machine would have. It does the trick. Now that we're cleansed of golem blood, we struggle to pull on our wet stuff. My boots make a squishing sound when I walk. We had to wash our footwear too since they got doused with golem blood too.

Instead of leaving through the front door, we leave by the rear exit and step out into an alley. To our right, it dead-ends. To our left, it's blocked by a slumped figure.

Will has found us.

Shit. Won't this guy ever give up?

"You're not getting the journal," I shout to him. "Might as well forget about it. You can barely walk, and we're in top condition."

Maybe I'm not in as top condition as I was before we jumped into the Echo, but I've got more stamina and strength than Will does. He looks even worse than he had a few minutes ago on the street. His face is pale, and he seems to be breathing harder.

"The journal belongs to me," he whines. "I am the only living version of Sefton Stainthorpe."

"He had a twin brother," I say. "That means the journal belongs to Dax now, and he wants me to read it."

Maybe I didn't actually ask Dax about that, but he won't care. Since the law doesn't exist anymore, no one can argue with my assessment of who owns the book.

"Give it to me," Will snarls while saliva sprays from his lips.

"Don't think so."

"But that—The journal is mine." He starts sobbing, and his knees buckle. He hits the ground hard. "It's mine."

I grab Erin's hand. "Try whisking us away."

"The last time I did that, it hurt like hell."

"Since when are you afraid of pain?"

"That's a low blow."

I tug her closer. "But did my evil plan work?"

She sighs and shakes her head. "Yeah, it worked."

Erin wraps her arms around me and shuts her eyes. I can tell she's trying to teleport because she always scrunches her face up when she does that.

The world shifts around us.

Will's anguished cry echoes in the alley but fades into silence as we land in another place.

Erin opens her eyes and glances around. "Where have I taken us?"

"Not sure, but it looks sweet."

We're standing inside a fancy bedroom with stone walls and a stone fireplace. Flames flicker in the hearth. A huge canopy bed with a crimson blanket sits in the center of the room, pushed against the wall. A spiffy rug fills the center of the space, extending under the bed, while two ornate dressers stand against the wall beside it.

"Where did you want to send us?" I ask. "To Cinderella's castle?"

"No." She hunches her shoulders. "I wished for us to be far away from Will and the golem, somewhere warm and comfortable and safe."

"You got all that into your one-second wish."

She slugs my arm. "Don't tick off the woman who saved your ass—again."

"I would never do that. You're a badder badass than I am."

"Very funny."

"Not joking." I cup her cheek in one hand. "You are amazing, Erin."

"As much as I love it when a man gushes over how badass I am, we should explore our new digs. Make sure we haven't crashed somebody's house."

"Good idea."

I hold her hand while we exit through the big wooden door and step out into a long hallway. Oil lanterns in sconces attached to the walls provide flickering light. A long crimson carpet covers the floor but doesn't reach the walls, leaving the stone floor visible at either side.

What is this place?

Erin and I wander down the corridor and peek inside other rooms, but we don't see anything that explains where we are. The other rooms contain various kinds of furniture but no books or other stuff that might give us a clue about…anything. We keep exploring the corridor until we reach its end.

Large wooden doors bar our way. It must be another room.

The doors swing open, forcing us to scuttle backward. In the space now revealed, I see something that doesn't jibe with the old-timey decor in this place.

Because it looks like an elevator.

CHAPTER TWENTY-TWO

Erin

A MYSTERIOUS ELEVATOR IN A MYSTERIOUS PLACE WITH NO SIGN OF life anywhere? Nah, that's not creepy. Who doesn't want to step inside a little box that goes who knows where? Down to hell, for all I know. Maybe I like taking chances and being reckless, but even I'm not stupid enough to jump right into the elevator car. So I glance at Grant. "Should we, um, go inside?"

"What the hell." He walks into the car first. "At least dying in an elevator crash would probably be quick."

"Uh-huh. I see we're back to Mr. Sunshine."

In Command Grant is the sexiest version of him, but I get why he has reverted to Mr. Doom and Gloom. This place gives me a creepy-crawly sensation all over my body.

The doors swing shut, and the car begins to move. A dial on the wall, similar to the one in Sefton's skyscraper, indicates that we're rising. We started on the second floor, apparently, and now we're heading up. The car keeps rising until we reach the fifth level, which seems like the top.

And the doors open for us.

Grant and I step out into another corridor. As the elevator doors shut behind us, we start walking down the crimson carpet, though we have no idea where we're going. Maybe I should suggest that I whisk us away to a different place, but I'm curious about where we've ended up. I know it must've piqued Grant's curiosity too. So we explore this new corridor, checking out every room we pass but not finding much of anything other than more fancy furniture.

Why did the elevator bring us here? We didn't push a button because I saw no buttons. Someone wanted us to come to the fifth floor. At the end of the hall, we find one room left to explore and push the door open.

This room is enormous. Cavernous might be a better description. It looks nothing like a cave, but it could certainly house one. As we cross the threshold, I notice a half-open doorway that looks like a bathroom. The bedroom features a four-poster bed even bigger than the ones in the other rooms we've explored. The suite also has a huge walk-in closet stocked with clothes for both men and women. Jeez, who lives here?

Grant comes up beside me. "Maybe we should steal some new duds. Doesn't seem like anybody's here, and our stuff has seen better days."

Yeah, I'd love new duds. My shorts lost their appeal after I got doused with golem blood. Though we'd washed that out of our clothes and off our skin, I swear I can still smell the motor oil odor. Still, stealing clothes from an unknown host seems like bad manners. I mean, I didn't even knock before I teleported us in here.

"Let's go into the closet," Grant says. "Just to look."

"If the door slams shut behind us and we're locked in, I'm going to beat you to death with my fists."

He chuckles. "I love it when you're vicious."

Grant used to hate that about me. Now he likes it. Maybe it was never my behavior that got to him, but something else entirely. I want to ask him about that. This isn't the time or place, though.

We set our backpacks on the floor.

As we enter the huge closet, he says, "You might still be able to teleport even if we get locked in here."

"Back to Grant the Optimist, hey? I should buy you a mood ring so I can tell at a glance whether you're going to growl at me or seduce me."

"You'll know if I want your body. No mood ring required."

As I skim through the clothes on the hangers, I realize everything here is my size. Grant is still browsing the racks when I head for the cubbyholes that house wooden boxes full of underthings. The bras and panties are also my size. I might dismiss that as a coincidence, but life post-Echo has taught me to be suspicious of everything. Magic rules the world—in the Echo and on earth.

"Everything here would fit me perfectly," Grant says. "Is the girlie stuff sized for you too?"

"Yeah. It's kind of creepy, but I've decided to be grateful I can steal some clean, fresh clothes."

"Seems like somebody expected us."

"Is Skeptical Grant gone for good? Or will he come back in a few minutes and dismiss all of this as a coincidence?"

He rests a hand on the metal bar of the clothes racks and huffs out a breath. "Do you always have to be so combative?"

"Yes. It's the only way I can get you to admit what you really think without studying the issue for a month first."

"Get changed, Erin. We need to search this place to see if anyone else is here."

Discussion over, that's what he means.

I pick a pair of butter-soft brown leather pants that mold to my thighs and have pockets where I could hide smaller weapons. I slip my switchblade into one pocket and stuff some extra rounds for my handgun in the other pocket. I've also chosen a tan T-shirt and a leather jacket that matches my pants as well as boots in the same color. One cubbyhole contains hair doohickeys, and I use a scrunchy to hold my hair back. It's harder to fight when my hair keeps falling over my eyes.

Grant and I turn to face each other.

Holy cow, he looks even hotter in the outfit he selected for himself. Black leather pants, a blue T-shirt, and a dark-blue denim jacket. His boots match his pants, which conform to every inch of his thighs and groin. The bulge in his pants draws my attention, and my breasts begin to feel swollen, the nipples taut. I want him, but not here in a freaky, vacant mystery building.

Well, okay, I want him right now despite the fact we're trapped in a freaky, vacant mystery building. Can't help it. I've never seen Grant in leather pants before.

"I see you found the wardrobe."

The female voice spurs us both to whirl toward the doorway.

A pretty blonde woman stands just outside the closet, hands clasped in front of her, and watches us with a pleasantly bland expression. "Does the clothing fit correctly? Magic isn't always the most accurate way to take measurements."

She sounds American, but I have no doubts she is not from the United States, much less the Planet Earth. Her hazel eyes shimmer with a strange golden light.

"Do you know who we are?" I ask.

"Yes." Her lips curve into a subdued smile. "You are Erin Harding, and he is Grant Larson. You entered the Echo through the gateway and brought a guest with you."

"That thing was not our guest."

She tips her head to the side, her expression turning curious. "He is not your friend?"

"No."

"I'm glad to hear that since I quartered him in the dungeon. He was…rather uncooperative."

I manage to stifle a laugh. Uncooperative? I'm surprised he didn't smash this place to rubble.

"You arrived sooner than I anticipated," the woman says. "I was never gifted with foresight, of course. But I hoped you would find your way here."

"Why?" Grant asks. "Who are you, anyway?"

"My name is Aldith. And I hoped to meet you because my ethereal senses told me you and Erin might be the ones I have waited for."

"You told us your name, but that's not what I asked. Who are you?"

She smiles just enough to dimple her cheeks. "I am the guardian of the Echo's heart."

We both stare at her blankly for a moment. I regain my senses first. "The Echo has a heart? What does that mean?"

"The closest approximation is the human heart, for this world has a pulse and arteries that throb with energy. This stronghold is the essence of the Echo, the only neutral ground within the war zone that Sefton Stainthorpe created." Aldith turns sideways and waves for us to follow her. "Come. I will show you what I mean."

Can we trust her? No way, not yet. Do we have any other choice than to follow her? Doubtful. If we attack her, she might fight back with magics. If we kill her, we might realize too late we destroyed a powerful ally. Life was hardly black and white before the apocalypse, but everything has gotten so much murkier since then.

We trail after Aldith as she leads us out of the bedroom and across the corridor to another doorway. She swings it open, marching inside. We stop just past the threshold.

Aldith gives us her neutral smile again. "This is the Heart of the Echo."

"But it's just an empty room," Grant says. "How can it be the heart of the apocalypse?"

She shakes her head. "You should know better by now. Not everything is as you assume it should be. Sefton Stainthorpe might have created this world and appropriated its power, but he never controlled the Heart. He never controlled me either, which infuriated him."

Might she really be the sole neutral element in this world? If she refused to help Sefton, then maybe she could become our ally. But I still have cynical reservations about this woman and this place. Deception is a mainstay of the Echo and the creatures it disgorged into our world.

"You remain skeptical," she says. "I understand your reticence, and I realize I cannot convince you of anything with words alone. Allow me to demonstrate."

She raises her hands, palms up.

"Hold up," Grant says. "How exactly do you plan to show us we can trust you?"

"I cannot. But I wish to show you that I'm not lying about the Echo's Heart." She glances at me, then meets Grant's gaze again. "Will you allow me to demonstrate?"

He looks at me.

I shrug.

Grant faces Aldith and clears his throat. "Okay. Show us."

He sidles up to me and clasps my hand.

My pulse revs up as Aldith closes her eyes, and I feel energies rising around us. I don't know how I can sense it, but I know these magics won't harm us. They feel warm and soft, despite the way they crackle with power. Maybe my connection to the Echo, which lets me teleport, also gives me the ability to sense that I can trust a stranger who wants to prove her sincerity to us. It's not like we have any other options.

If she fries us, I'll crawl out of hell or heaven or wherever my soul goes and punish her for hurting Grant. I don't care what happens to me, only that no harm comes to him. I won't think about why I feel that way, not now.

Glowing, golden magics emerge from Aldith's hands, the sparkling tendrils spreading upward from her palms. The energy swirls around her in a cloud that soon envelops her so we can't even see her face. I feel the magics licking at my skin, but it isn't a bad sensation. In fact, it infuses me with a sense of peace and contentment I've never experienced before. I don't want it to end, but I know it must.

The magics dissipate, revealing Aldith. Her lips spread into a joyous smile as she lowers her hands. "The Heart is here in this room with us."

"You are the Heart," I say. "You control this place."

She shakes her head as her smile softens into something gentler and almost beatific. "No, dear, I am but the servant."

"You said the Heart is here."

"And it is." She walks up to us, glancing back and forth between me and Grant. Then she lays her palm on Grant's chest. "You are the Heart of the Echo."

Grant stiffens, and even his fingers go rigid, though they still clasp mine. "No, you're wrong. I can't be—I don't have the Echo power."

"Of course you do." Aldith lays one hand on his cheek and the other on mine. "You, Grant Larson, are the Heart. But Erin Harding is the Lifeblood."

My mouth falls open. "Excuse me? That's insane. I'm not the Lifeblood of anything or anyone. I'm just the crazy chick who takes risks no one else would. I kill Echo creatures. Unless spilling blood is what you mean, I am not this…whatever it is."

"Your bravery and your willingness to fight for the world you love are what proves you are the Lifeblood." She moves her hands to our shoulders, and her cheeks dimple again. "You don't believe me yet, but you will. Why do you think I sent signs to guide you?"

"Will sent those signs. For Allison."

"No, dear. He wanted you to believe that, but even Will knows that's not the case." Aldith takes two steps back. "The signs were for you and Grant. The Heart has been without its Lifeblood for too long, and the time has come to reunite the elements."

"What purpose do these elements serve?" Grant asks.

"You have noticed the tremors in the Echo."

"Sure, but—"

"And you came here to stop them. To do that, you must first unite with the Lifeblood."

"How?"

Aldith laughs softly—because we both look stunned and confused, I'm sure. "Make love to her, Grant."

Chapter Twenty-Three

Grant

A STRANGER JUST ORDERED ME TO HAVE SEX WITH ERIN. WHAT THE hell? I don't even know for sure that this woman knows anything or if she's giving us the biggest snow job in history. The Heart? The Lifeblood? This is all starting to sound like bullshit. I can't be the heart of anything since my own heart has felt cold and empty ever since the Echo invaded our world. I lost the love of my life and my precious son. I can't "unite" with Erin.

Maybe I fucked her once. But that's irrelevant.

Yeah, right, it's irrelevant. What a stupid jackass I've become.

"I can tell you are resistant to the idea," Aldith says. "You need time to realize the truth."

"Why are we in this room?" I ask. "There's nothing in here."

"As I said, the Heart of the Echo resides in this room. Right now, it is nothing but a collection of energy. It needs you and Erin to become complete and alive."

"If it has a heart, arteries, and blood, then it is alive. What are we supposed to do for it?"

Can't believe this is what my life has become. A quest for alchemical secrets and magics I don't understand. I was a logical, hardworking deputy sheriff, and now I've become enmeshed in forces I can't comprehend.

No way could I be the Heart. It's crazy.

"Your first task," Aldith says, "is to stop the convulsions in the Echo that have bled into the mortal world. Only then might the end of the apocalypse be within sight."

"The end?" I freeze with my gaze glued to Aldith. A strange shiver races over my skin, though it's not fear. "Are you saying Erin and I could destroy the Echo and end the apocalypse?"

Aldith aims her bland smile at me. "You shall not be the ones to end what Sefton began. But you are important organs within the body. Only your connection might stop the convulsions and begin the healing process."

"This all sounds too convenient. We get naked, and the Echo stops convulsing? Come on."

Aldith shrugs. "You found your way to this place. That means you are the necessary elements. Time passes differently in the Echo, so your friends on Earth might be enduring more spasms while you linger here."

Now she's issuing vague threats. I think. Or maybe I'm just way too cynical these days.

"You mean time moves faster here," I say. "But we already knew that."

"No, not faster. Not necessarily. It might slow down, speed up, hover, or even rewind. The Echo itself decides which way it will allow time to move." Aldith bows her head. "I regret that I have been unable to affect the conditions here or on Earth. Sefton retained that power by removing the Heart and the Lifeblood. And Will appropriated the power when Sefton died. But he could not take control of the Heart or the Lifeblood. Only you and Erin possess that power."

"If nobody's in control here, how can the Echo keep going? A heart and blood seem like critical things for any living…entity." I try not to cringe when I say that, but all this talk of mystical hearts and blood makes my skin crawl.

"Yes, it is critical. The black hearts of the worst Echo creatures have sustained this realm thus far." Aldith raises her head. "They cannot be allowed to continue their reign of terror. Feed the Heart, and the balance of power will shift."

"But Erin and I can't stop the apocalypse."

"Not alone. But that is a tale for another day." Aldith spreads her arms wide. "This room has contained the Heart until its proper owner could claim it. The Echo has been waiting for you, Grant."

"But—No, I can't—"

Finish a sentence? No, I can't do that anymore. This is sheer insanity. I'm not a good enough person to deserve this honor, if it is an honor. Maybe it's a trick to turn us into evil puppets for Will. We have only this woman's word to go on.

Aldith clasps her hands. "You may, of course, teleport out of here at any time. Nothing will stop you from leaving."

Erin shuts her eyes for a moment, then looks at me. "I can teleport. Didn't try it all the way, but I can feel it will work if we want to get the hell out of Dodge."

"Do you want to leave?" I ask.

"No. I'm starting to believe Aldith."

As much as I hate to admit it, I won't lie to Erin. Despite my reservations, or maybe my fears, I need to speak the truth. "Yeah, I'm starting to believe her too."

Erin shifts her gaze to the floor. "So do you want to, um…"

"Get it on? Might as well give it a shot."

She scowls at me. "Well, if it's that much of a trial for you to screw me, we can just hop on back home."

"I didn't mean it like that."

Aldith clears her throat. "This is my cue to leave. If you require anything, simply call my name."

The woman disappears. Literally. Poof, she's gone.

How can I still be surprised by the freaky things magic can do? Of course a woman can vanish into thin air, and of course Erin can teleport us straight into a safe zone. Naturally, we need to have sex to save the world. Makes perfect sense.

Erin and I awkwardly cross the hall and go into the bedroom, then awkwardly stop to glance at each other sideways. I kick the door shut while she starts to sit down on the bed, but jumps up again. Why should this feel weird? We fucked earlier today. Now we both act like virgins who don't know how sex works.

I grasp Erin's shoulders and turn her toward me. "Are you sure you want to do this?"

"Yeah. I'm sure. Sort of." She winces. "Well, being ordered to screw each other is…weird. I want to be with you, but I can't help feeling like Aldith will be watching us."

"I get that. This feels weird to me too." I slide my hands down to her upper arms. "But we're attracted to each other, and we had amazing sex just this morning. That means we have chemistry. We just need to relax and forget about the circumstances."

"Are we going to meditate again? That was surprisingly hot."

"Yeah, it was." I raise a hand to brush my fingers over her cheek. "I wanted you right there in that dilapidated building. I wanted you in the physical therapy clinic too, when we stripped and washed our clothes. You are beautiful, Erin, and the sexiest woman I've ever seen. I love your body."

"I love your body too." She lays a palm on my chest and glides it down to my waistband. "Maybe we don't need to meditate this time. Maybe all we need is to focus on each other and forget about the rest of the universe."

"That's called mindfulness, Erin. It's meditation too."

"No half Lotus position this time. We should meditate on each other's bodies."

I have no idea what that means, but my dick loves the idea. It jerks and starts to stiffen. The sultry tone of her voice has always done this to me, even before we had sex or kissed. I've wanted her since the day she walked into Sanctuary. Making love to her won't be an onerous duty as long as I avoid thinking about everything except for Erin's body.

"Let's undress each other," I say. "Slowly. Sensually. Like we have all the time in the world. Maybe we do. Let's see if we can freeze the clock while we make love."

"Oh God, I want that. With you."

Erin backs away just far enough that I can see her entire body, then takes hold of the hem of her shirt and slowly lifts it. She exposes her flat belly inch by inch while I track her every movement and she shimmies her hips just enough to make my dick jerk again. My breathing grows heavier, and I clench my hands into fists to avoid grabbing her so I can tear her clothes off and sink my cock into her body. I want her like crazy, but I can't focus on why, not right now. It would ruin this moment.

She pulls her shirt up over her head and tosses it onto the floor. Her lips tighten into a sexy smirk while she lays her palms on her upper chest and glides them down her body so slowly that I'm breathing even harder, my chest rising and falling while I struggle not to hyperventilate. She palms her breasts through her powder-blue bra, then slides her hands down her belly to grasp the button on her brown leather pants. Damn, she looks incredible in leather. But I'm so excited to see her naked that I need to remind myself to keep taking slow, even breaths.

Erin unhooks that button and eases her zipper down, revealing her powder-blue panties.

"Fuck," I growl. "You're driving me insane."

"Good. Insane is better than snippy." She kicks her boots off and shimmies out of her pants, leaving only her skimpy blue panties and bra. I see glimpses of the hairs on her mound through the semi-transparent fabric.

And now I'm rock-hard.

She pushes her panties down over her hips and wiggles until they fall to her ankles. While she steps out of her underwear, she unhooks her bra and tosses it away.

I barely have time to salivate over her tits before she turns around, leaving me to admire her taut ass. But when she bends over to remove her socks, I hiss, "Hurry the fuck up, would you?"

She spreads her legs just enough that she can gaze at me through the gap between her thighs. Her head hangs upside down, though that elastic thing in her hair keeps it from falling around her face. "Getting a little overexcited, huh?"

I wish she weren't speaking in that sultry tone again. It's eroding my willpower even faster. Like I had much willpower left, anyway.

Erin removes one sock, then the other, doing it slowly on purpose while she flashes me upside down smiles between her legs.

I rip my clothes off so fast that I probably tore a few seams, but I don't give a shit. Stripping at lightning speed due to extreme sexual frustration isn't the brightest idea. I forget that I still have my boots on and try to yank my leather pants off while the boots are still on my feet. That results in me crashing into the bed, kind of bouncing off it, and tumbling to my knees on the floor.

Erin laughs. Loudly.

And I growl. Seriously, I do.

But I take a few slow, deep breaths and channel my Zen side, closing my eyes while I listen to my heartbeats decelerating.

Something tugs on the button of my pants.

I open my lids halfway.

Erin is kneeling beside me, undoing my pants while seeming intently focused on the task. I can't resist staring at her tits and the way their stiff peaks point slightly upward.

She casts me a sideways glance. "Like what you see?"

"Hell yes."

"You've been seriously pent-up, haven't you?"

I suck in a sharp breath when she drags my zipper down, which makes her fingers graze my cock.

"Think you can get yourself undressed now?" she asks. "I mean without the Three Stooges solo routine."

"Yeah, I can do it. Please get on the bed, Erin. It's taking all my meditative skills not to flip you onto your back and fuck you right here on the floor."

She kisses me sweetly, then climbs onto the bed and pulls the covers back. With a quick jerk of her hand, she ditches the scrunchy thing that had held her hair up. Now the lush, dark waves cascade over her shoulders and kiss her breasts.

This time, I manage to remove my clothes without acting like a buffoon. Finally naked, I crawl up the bed on all fours until my body hovers over her. Christ, she's beautiful. I feather my lips over hers, flicking my tongue out to taste them. Her breaths tease my mouth, and I swear I can almost taste her lips. But it's another part of her I need to devour now.

I lay my body on top of hers and shimmy backward with deliberate slowness, licking and nibbling on her flesh while I move. When I pull one nipple into my mouth and gently lave it, she arches her neck. But when I flick my thumb over the other peak while I suckle this one, she moans, and her back bows up. How many times can a woman come before she's too exhausted to take it anymore? I plan to find out.

Right now.

Chapter Twenty-Four

Erin

GRANT KEEPS TORMENTING MY NIPPLE WITH HIS MOUTH AND HIS hand, and all I can do is moan repeatedly and thrust my fingers into his thick, silky hair. Every time he gently nips that peak, I gasp and moan again, sounding so desperate that it's pathetic. I don't care. I love what he's doing to me, and I never want it to stop.

He removes his mouth from my nipple, but then touches his lips to the rigid tip and groans. The vibrations from that sound penetrate my skin and send a bolt of sheer pleasure straight down my nerves and into my core. He licks the peak and blows a gentle current of air across it while pinching my other nipple. I'm struggling to catch my breath, and the way my sex has started to tingle and throb doesn't help.

Grant swallows my nipple and the areola, then flicks his thumb across my other peak in swift, light motions that drive me insane in the best way. The most incredible sensation sweeps down my nerves from my breast straight into my clit, and my entire body goes rigid. I cry out as the orgasm rushes through me, softer than a regular climax but no less satisfying. I've never come this way before, but I love it.

The man with my tit in his mouth releases my flesh and grins. "Ready for round two?"

I'm still breathing hard from what he just did, but yeah, I need more. So I nod.

He slides down my body, licking a trail in his wake until he reaches my hips. His breaths tease the hairs on my mound, and my gaze has become riveted to his every movement. When I glance at his face, our eyes meet, and he winks. "Don't look at my face. I want you to watch me fucking you with my mouth."

I want that too, but I can't speak to tell him so.

Grant spreads my folds with two fingers and holds them like that. First, he blows a breath over my slick flesh, making me moan, then he flicks his tongue out to tease my clit. I jerk and gasp. He slides his fingers up and down, licking at my nub, and my gaze tracks the movements of his tongue while he coils it around my clit again and again. Holy shit, watching him do that ramps up my arousal until I feel like I might turn into a raving lunatic if I don't come soon.

"You taste so damn good," he murmurs. "I could feast on you all day and all night."

He drags his tongue up and down my cleft while his nose rubs against my nub. I fist my hands in the sheets and spread my legs for him, silently begging him to take me right now, then I bend my knees too and thrust my hips up. He buries his face between my thighs to seal his mouth over my opening, then plunges his tongue inside over and over while I thrash and cry out and clutch the sheets so hard that I hear a ripping sound. Screw the sheets. I need him inside me so badly that I hear myself begging him to do it.

Grant shifts his mouth to my clit. His face glistens with my slickness. He licks his lips and smiles at me with so much heat and hunger that it makes my nub throb, then he pushes two fingers inside me and starts pumping while he latches on to my clit and suckles it fiercely.

The orgasm slams through me like a wrecking ball, shattering my self-control. I scream his name and thrash beneath him, my eyes squeezed shut as I ride out the spasms. The intensity of the climax wrenches my whole body, and my screams turn into hoarse cries.

When the orgasm finally fades, I lie here limp and gasping.

Grant kisses my belly. "Catch your breath. When you're ready, I'll make love to you."

He lies down beside me and combs his fingers through my hair while I come down from the most amazing climax I've ever experienced. How does Grant Larson know what to do, what to say, to make me wild with desire for him? I've never gotten this excited with any other man. But every time he touches me, I melt for him.

Once my breathing normalizes and my ears stop ringing, I turn my face into his palm to kiss it. "Thank you for that."

"We're not done yet."

"Good. I'd be disappointed if that's all we do. I need to feel you buried inside me again, for longer this time so I can watch your face while you take me."

"I want that too." He rolls onto his back and pats my hip. "Get up."

"What?"

"Get up, Erin." He grasps his rigid erection and strokes himself slowly. "I want you to ride my cock."

Just the thought of that makes me grow wetter.

He slaps my thigh. "Get up and fuck me already."

I rise to my knees and crawl over to straddle his hips. Then I need to take a moment to appreciate the masculine beauty of Grant's body. He has defined pecs and abs that make me want to bend down and lick every line of those muscles, and his thighs look powerful too. I already knew he had strong biceps, but what really catches my attention now is that dick. Wow. It's thick and smooth, and the rosy head just begs to be licked and sucked. But I'll do that later. For now, I need to take him into my body and feel that gorgeous cock nestled inside me.

I let myself revel in the look on his face while I grasp his length and slowly pump it. His eyes have gone hooded, his lips are parted, and his chest heaves.

"Hurry, baby," he almost growls. "Don't wanna go off before you've even mounted me."

But I wait a few more seconds, just to watch him squirm and grimace. Then I waddle forward and hold the base of his dick to get it positioned just right. A breath gusts out of him. I bend my knees until the head of his erection nudges my opening. My clit throbs, but I hold my position for several seconds until Grant fists his hands in the sheets and makes a sound I can only describe as a desperate snarl.

Okay, enough torturing him.

I lower myself onto his cock until I've got him seated fully inside me. Oh God, this feels even better than I'd hoped it would. I rock my hips gently, letting us both enjoy the sensation of our bodies merging and my wetness dribbling down his dick. He gasps and grunts, his gaze riveted to the intersection of our bodies.

"Faster, Erin, please."

I speed up the pace, but only a little, and rise up until his crown just nudges my entrance, then I slam back down. The way his cock glides in and out has me teetering on the verge of another orgasm already.

"Erin," he hisses. "Can't wait—ah—much longer."

"Me either." I throw my head back and ride him harder, fondling my tits. "Oh God, Grant, yes."

He surges up, seizes me around the waist, and flips us both over with me beneath him. Staring into my eyes, he plants his hands on the mattress at either side of my head and begins thrusting into me so hard and fast that I come within seconds. While my body convulses around him, he punches into me twice more and freezes, shouting as he goes off. I swear I can feel his release erupting inside me, and it makes me come harder.

Though we've both found our release, he settles his body onto mine, and we just lie here without moving. His dick has softened, but I still feel him inside me. I love that sensation. But I love the way he's gazing at me even more, because his expression resembles affection. Just yesterday, I would've laughed at myself for thinking such a thing, considering the way Grant has behaved toward me. Coming to the Echo changed everything between us in ways I still don't understand—especially since we found the Heart of the Echo. This place feels magical. It's more than the supernatural energies that suffuse the building. I sense a different kind of magic between me and Grant, a sizzling and sweet kind that makes my throat go thick and my chest ache in the best way.

He brushes hair away from my face with two fingers. "Hey, are you all right? I know that was intense, but…"

"I'm fine." Grant seems less than convinced, so I touch my lips to his. "Really, I'm good. Feel fantastic, actually."

"Me too. Which seems wrong somehow, since we're trapped in the Heart of the Echo."

"Whatever that means." I fold my arms around him, and he rests his head on my shoulder. His breaths tickle my throat. "Not sure sex gave us more power."

"Maybe we should try it again."

"You don't need to do that. If sex with me didn't rock the worlds the first time, I doubt it will do the trick the second time either. I must not be the Lifeblood after all."

"Bullshit. You are that and more."

I run my hands up and down his back, not minding at all that his full weight still bears down on me. It feels right, lying here with him. "Thanks for the vote of confidence, but for all we know, Aldith didn't mean me specifically. She might've meant that any woman who found a way into the Heart of the Echo could become the Lifeblood."

"Shut up and listen." He lifts his head to aim his beautiful blue eyes at me and sweeps his thumb over my lips. "I didn't make love to you because a weird girl told me I should. I wanted to be with you, Erin."

"Yeah, but—"

"No buts. You are as critical to the salvation of both worlds as I am, or as Dax and Allison are. Maybe I never believed in magic before the apocalypse, but I've witnessed what it can do—the good and the bad." He shifts his weight so he can clasp my face in his hands with his elbows braced on the mattress. "You are good, Erin. Amazing, actually. Sorry it took me so long to realize that and admit to it. If anyone is the key to reversing or at least stopping the apocalypse, of course it's you."

"What do you mean of course it's me? That makes no sense."

"No, it makes perfect sense." He dips his head closer until our noses touch. His eyes bore straight into mine, imbued with an intensity that takes my breath away. "You're a warrior, a hero, a role model to Willow, and the smartest, bravest person I've ever met."

"But you hated me until earlier today."

"No. I never hated you." He presses his lips to mine and licks at the seam of my mouth until I moan softly. "Later, I'll explain to you why I treated you the way I did. But right now, we need to make love again, this time for real. That means I'll do it slowly so I can show you how I really feel before I try to explain it in words."

"Grant, I—"

He kisses me again, pushing his tongue between my lips, though he doesn't go any deeper. Not yet. He glides one hand down my side, all the way to my hip, then he kneads the hollow there while he explores my mouth with sensual movements of his tongue. I feel myself growing wetter, my body softening as I realize what he wants to do now. This won't be hot sex. Well, okay, it will be hot for sure. But he told me what he wants in the most literal terms.

Grant Larson is about to make love to me.

Chapter Twenty-Five

Grant

SOMETHING HAS CHANGED BETWEEN ME AND ERIN. SCRATCH THAT. EV-erything has changed. I don't fully understand why or how, and I have no clue in what ways making love inside the Heart of the Echo will affect us both. But I don't care. Right now, I need to show her what I've been afraid to admit—to her and to myself—because this feels like the right time to let go of the past, at least for a while.

I've never gotten hard again while still inside a woman. Never thought it was possible. But the more I kiss Erin, the stiffer I get. The blood doesn't rush to my dick all at once, though. I feel myself gradually hardening while I let myself revel in our kiss and the way she strokes my back while our tongues tease each other. The first time we kissed, I hadn't wanted to stop. Here and now, in this weird and mysterious place, I know we won't stop until we've both shared our true feelings by kissing and touching and getting lost in each other's bodies.

Erin knows how to kiss. That's one thing I've learned about her. I move my hand up to caress her breast while I dive deeper into her mouth and groan at how good this feels. Damn, I could lie here for days just enjoying the taste of her mouth and the sensation of our tongues melding and separating, over and over, while our bodies start to writhe of their own volition. My dick shifts inside her, and she crooks her nails into my back. I think she tried to gasp, but my mouth prevented her from making a sound. With our mouths still fused, I begin a measured pace of thrusting into her while her body molds to my cock and the scent of her cream teases my senses. I never thought I'd want anyone after Adele, but I won't think about that right now. In this moment, I'm giving myself permission to relish the feel of a woman's body wrapped around me.

I pull my mouth away so I can gaze into Erin's eyes. She looks at me too, and something sizzles between us, something I won't even try to describe. Magic? Maybe. But we don't need spells or Echo power to create a connection between us. It was always there, even when I refused to see it.

"Grant," she murmurs while she grips my biceps. "Oh, Grant, this is—"

"Hush." I graze my lips over hers while I thrust with more power. "Just let it happen, baby."

I can feel her body tensing up, the way it does right before she comes. Her breaths become soft gasps as she struggles to lift her hips into my movements, and her nails dig into my skin. Every time I plunge inside her, I blow out a breath, and when I pull out, I groan. She arches her neck and squeezes her eyes shut, but then seems to force herself to look at me as if she can't stand not to do that. The pressure inside me grows with every thrust, and I raise onto my straight arms to push even deeper inside her.

When she comes, it unfolds in slow motion. Her mouth falls open, and her body freezes. While we gaze at each other, the first spasm of her climax grips my cock. The pressure to come barrels down my spine faster and faster, but I need to make sure she jumps off that cliff first. So I reach down to separate her folds with my fingers, then settle onto her again while rubbing against her clit with every thrust. She cries out, her muscles clenching me in a pulsating rhythm, and I can't hold back one second longer. I shout while machine-gun spasms fire through my cock, punching into her body until I've spilled everything I have inside her.

Then I go limp on top of her.

Erin's chest rises and falls while we both try to recover our ability to breathe without gasping. Even when I make love to her sweetly, we wind up breathless and spent. Guess we just can't help it. Sex with Adele was never quite this…intense.

"Wow," Erin says after a moment. "That was less athletic than the first or second time, but no less mind-blowing."

Yeah, it was that and more. Now it's time I told her why. I slide off her body onto my side and hook an arm around her waist. "I've wanted you since the day we met, but I was afraid of what it would mean if we had sex."

She rolls onto her side to face me. "What did it mean? Aside from Aldith's claim that we can become one with the Heart of the Echo."

"I'm not talking about that." I cup my hand over her hip and move my thumb in lazy circles. "The alchemy of worlds robbed me of my family, and I convinced myself I'd be a cheater and a traitor if I let anyone else into my heart besides my wife. Adele was the love of my life, and our son meant everything to us."

Erin tips her head down so I'm looking at her scalp. "Yeah, I get that. Don't worry. I won't demand you announce to the world that I'm your girlfriend."

Does she think I'm ashamed of what we've done together? I must've given her that impression since I fucked her in the car, then just walked away like nothing had happened. Erin is a strong, capable woman. But even the strongest of us can feel vulnerable when our emotions get tangled up. I can't believe I treated her that way, or that I kept snapping at her and calling her reckless. Her bravery saved us here in the Echo. When she leaned out the car window to fire machine gun volleys at our horny monster friend, it was the sexiest thing I'd ever seen.

So I tell her the truth. "You are amazing, Erin. I've never met anyone as brave, intelligent, resourceful, and unstoppable as you are. We survived traveling into the Echo because of you, not because of anything I did. We wouldn't even be here now if you hadn't taken a crazy risk that turned out to be the smartest thing you've ever done."

The top of her head gradually rises until I'm gazing into her eyes again. They shimmer with the slightest hint of tears. Erin crying? Just last week, I would've said that could never happen. But now, she looks at me with her eyes full of an emotion I wouldn't have tried to describe before tonight. I understand at last because I finally realize what I need to do.

"Never thought I'd say this," I tell her. "But I'm ready to move on. With you."

Her eyes widen. "What? You don't even like me."

"Were you not listening a minute ago? I waxed poetic about how wonderful you are."

"Sure, but it sounds like you mean—Well, it can't be that. What exactly do you mean? Move on? From the Heart of the Echo. That's what you must mean."

"I meant what I said the way I said it, no reinterpretation required." I cradle her cheek in my hand. "Adele might've been the love of my life, but I can't spend the rest of whatever life we have left pining for her. She wouldn't want that. Adele will always be in my heart, but I have room for more than one woman in here." I clasp her hand to my heart. "Got a spot waiting for you, if you want it."

Tears trickle from her eyes, but she doesn't even try to wipe them away. "I want that. If you're sure."

"I'm sure, Erin." I kiss her softly. "It's time we both moved on. The apocalypse taught me that life is too damn precious to waste it on obsessing over the past. Let's live for today, tomorrow, and whatever comes after that."

"Sounds like a plan."

What I need to say next seems moronic in my head, but maybe she won't think it's as stupid as I do. "Aldith mentioned that you and I can stop the convulsions of the Echo. We can control the Heart, that's what she said. Do you think that, uh, we did that when we had sex?"

Erin bites her upper lip while her body quivers.

"You're trying not to laugh at me, aren't you?" I say. "I know it sounds dumb—"

She seals my lips with two fingers. "Not laughing at you. The idea that getting it on will save the world sounds insane. That's why I was trying not to laugh."

"Oh. Good." I scratch the back of my head while avoiding her gaze. "I'm, uh, glad to hear you weren't laughing at the idea of having sex with me."

She smiles and taps my lips with her fingertips. "You are adorable when you're flustered."

"Don't think I've ever been flustered before. Isn't that something only girls do?"

Erin pokes me in the belly. "Don't insult the 'girl' who saved your ass more times than anyone can count."

"I didn't mean it that way." My lips curve into a smile that I'm sure conveys my real meaning. But I palm her tit just to make sure she gets it. "Should we try again just to make sure we've connected with the Heart or whatever the hell we're supposed to be doing?"

"Are you implying sex with me was just a tool for saving the world?"

"No, I—" I'm about to apologize when her expression changes. Her smirk spurs me to slap her ass. "Will you ever stop harassing me?"

"Afraid not."

"Good. I've gotten used to it, and I'd probably die of shock if you stopped."

She slaps my ass. "Are you always this cheeky?"

"You've been hanging out with Dax too much. 'Cheeky' is a British thing."

Erin's expression turns serious, and she exhales a weary sigh. "Do you honestly think we can stop the Echo's convulsions? We had sex, but I don't feel any different. I mean, I don't feel like I've developed the supernatural power to control the Heart of the Echo." She scrunches up her face. "What would that feel like, anyway?"

"Not a clue." I sit up and stretch, feeling better than I have since before the apocalypse. "Let's go across the hall and see if we can get into that other room. The Heart room or the Lifeblood room or... I have no idea what to call it."

"The creepy-ass room?"

I raise my brows. "Doesn't that term apply to this whole building? This whole world?"

"Yeah, I guess it does." She sits up too and stretches, the action lifting her tits. "Guess we should get dressed."

My brain thinks now is a good time to stare at her breasts, or maybe that's my dick's decision. Either way, I can't form any words. I love her body. I love fucking her. I'm starting to think another round of hot workout sex might be just the thing right now.

Yeah, that's definitely my dick talking.

Erin smacks my cheek, though not hard. "Wake up, Grant."

I clear my throat and rub my jaw, though I can't stop staring at her chest. "Sorry, I got distracted. Your body hypnotizes me."

She busts out laughing. "There's a line I've never heard before."

My attention shifts down to her hips and the hairs on her mound. Did I just groan like a man who found a juicy morsel after starving for six months? Erin turns me into a ravenous beast. I won't say that out loud, though. I swear I've never behaved this way before.

Erin pats my chest, her cheeks dimpling. "You really are adorable."

"Uh, thanks. That was a compliment, right?"

She laughs again, though not as raucously as before. Then she clambers off the bed to stand at the foot. "Are you coming?"

No, but we could both be doing that if I just... I squeeze my eyes shut. "Shit."

"What's wrong now?"

"I can't stop thinking about sex." I open my eyes and wince. "Maybe it'll help if you get dressed."

She salutes me. "Sir, yes, sir."

Erin marches into the huge closet where I can't see her anymore. She could've put on the clothes she'd been wearing before we jumped into bed together, but I guess she's a typical woman in one respect. She needs to try on lots of outfits.

I get up and get dressed too, but I stay away from the closet and wear the same thing I'd had on before we got naked.

The woman I can't stop fucking ambles out of the closet. Okay, I have stopped fucking her, but I want to do it again. And again. And again. It doesn't help that she's wearing skintight jeans that hug her hips and a top that stretches barely past her belly button. It has extra-short sleeves too. She holds a denim jacket draped over one arm and taps the toe of one hiking boot on the floor while she angles her head to the side to study me.

"Didn't want clean clothes?" she asks.

"I only wore this outfit for a little while before we, uh..." My gaze darts to the bed and the rumpled sheets that must still smell of sex and Erin. "Well, you know."

Suddenly, I can't speak the words "had sex." Can't say "fucked" either. Even "made love" sounds like a weird thing to say. I know this is just anxiety because I haven't been with anyone since my wife, not until today. The feeling will pass.

I grasp Erin's hand, leading her across the hall to the creepy-ass room.

Chapter Twenty-Six

Erin

I'VE ONLY EVER THOUGHT OF NERDY GUYS AS BEING ADORABLE, BUT I've called Grant that twice. He is not a nerd. I mean, geeks can be hot too, but the words geek and nerd don't describe the man I just got down and dirty with a few minutes ago. Grant can be surprisingly sweet and almost shy at times, which I'd previously seen only when he was with people other than me. But here in this bizarre place, I finally experienced the sides of him everyone else knows well.

But nobody else gets to experience how incredible he is in bed.

What we shared was more than mind-blowing sex. It meant something, though I don't have the time or the brainpower to figure out exactly what it meant. He told me he's ready to move on and that he has room for another woman in his heart. I've never been in love, not really. I had boyfriends I cared about, but those relationships never turned into a commitment. I lived in my apartment, and they lived in theirs. With Grant, I feel…ready for more. Before the apocalypse, I would've thought I should take a lot more time to decide how I feel about Grant. I still don't know exactly what this is between us, but I do know I want to be with him, even if we wind up not working out as a couple. I need to give us a shot.

Like Allison says, the pace of life post-apocalypse has accelerated. I won't second guess what I feel. But I'll still ride Grant's ass if he does something I disagree with—or if we're naked. Yeah, different kind of riding in that case.

We walk into the creepy-ass room and find Aldith already there, standing in the center of the space with her hands clasped and her head bowed. She raises her head when we enter. Her lips curl up the tiniest bit, which seems like the closest she gets to smiling. Well, if I'd been stuck inside a weird place like this, I might have trouble summoning a real smile too. That thought leads to a question, and I decide to ask it.

"Just curious," I say. "Can you leave this building?"

"No. I am bound to the Heart of the Echo until someone else takes control of it." She turns toward us as we stop near her. "Did the ritual engender a feeling of oneness?"

"Um, what?"

Grant squeezes my hand. "She wants to know if sex made us feel any different, like we have Echo power."

"Oh." My cheeks start to feel warm. I never get embarrassed, but I've done that today thanks to the most intimate and powerful sexual experience of my life. Grant gave me that. But did it amp up my Echo power? Not sure. "How can we know if we have the ability to control the Heart of the Echo now?"

Aldith's almost smile curls up a bit more. "There is but one way to know. You must attempt to take dominion over the Heart."

"Good plan," Grant says," but we have no idea how to do that."

"Employ your intuition. It brought you to the Echo, did it not? And it guided you toward your destination."

"You mean this place," I say.

Aldith approaches us, placing one hand on my arm and the other on Grant's. "It is time to channel the strength of your newfound connection and seize control of the Heart. Time is running out."

"What do you mean?" Grant asks. "How is time running out? And for who?"

"For everyone in both worlds. Creating another world and merging it with the earth required magics of such scope and power that it could not be sustained for long. The cracks are beginning to show."

"You mean the convulsions. We saw those in our world."

"Similar incidents have occurred here as well. The fabric of the Echo is falling apart."

I think back on our journey through this world, and I have to point out something. "Where is it falling apart in the Echo? The Capital City seems fine. Empty, but intact except for what seems like damage incurred during the first waves of the apocalypse."

"Let me show you." Aldith turns sideways to us and waves a hand toward the wall. A window appears. "Take a look. The Heart has a panoramic view of the entire Echo."

Hand in hand, Grant and I approach the window to peer out at the totality of the world that invaded our home and wreaked uncountable costs in lives and destruction. The structure in which we stand seems to hover in the sky, far above everything else in this world. Our bird's-eye view reveals exactly what Aldith meant when she said the fabric of the Echo is falling apart. I see the Capital City in the distance, untouched and vacant. Smoke streams up from many locations elsewhere in this magically constructed world, but that's not the most disturbing aspect.

The sky pulsates with shades of purple and black that seem to split and slither around like blood cells in a body. Lightning slams down intermittently, scorching the ground and making buildings explode.

"Without the Brain," Aldith says, "the Echo is without guidance. Sefton Stainthorpe was the Brain, the cognitive entity keeping this world in some semblance of order. Well, perhaps 'order' is an inaccurate description. He kept it from completely disintegrating."

I can't tear my gaze away from the shocking view below us, not even when I speak to Aldith. "So killing Sefton killed the Echo too, or at least injured it badly. Must've taken a lot of energy to hold a magically made world together."

"Yes. That's why Sefton grew weak enough that Dax and Allison could stop the alchemy of worlds."

"Or maybe they were more powerful to start with."

"It is difficult to differentiate the two causal factors."

She talks like a scientist, but we are not discussing physics or mathematics. Those disciplines might have inspired Sefton Stainthorpe, but they didn't lay waste to the earth. Magic did that.

I turn toward Grant. "We need to try. See if we can take control of the Heart."

He rotates toward me. "Yeah, we do need to take control. Right now."

I glance at Aldith. "Do you help us? Or should we try this with just me and Grant?"

"The power is yours alone. I am a caretaker, not an integral element of the Echo."

"Okay." I clasp Grant's hands. "Let's do this."

He threads his fingers through mine and draws me a little closer. "You've used the Echo power before. That means you should get this party started."

"Party? We'll throw one of those once we stop the worlds from convulsing."

"I'll track down some warm champagne for us to celebrate with."

He said "warm champagne" because we don't have ice post-apocalypse. I really miss having a nice cold drink on a hot day. But I need to focus. My task is to somehow start the process of taking control of the Heart so we can stop the Echo's convulsions. I have no clue how to do that. Magic is all about mental power, right? That's the way I've understood it when Allison explained it to me and when Grant explained the alchemy of worlds. Magic isn't something you accomplish with a wrench or a computer. Not that computers work anymore.

Snap out of it, woman, and do your job.

Yeah, babbling in my head won't save anybody. I need to ease my anxiety. So I close my eyes and focus on the feel of Grant's hands in mine, the warmth of his skin, the roughness of his palms. I can hear the whispering of his breaths, and he gently strokes my palm with his thumb. The tension inside me unwinds little by little to relax my shoulders first, followed by the rest of my muscles, until I feel as soft as butter in the sun. My awareness of the world around me recedes, though I still sense Grant with me, and the anchor of his presence keeps me from drifting away into a trance.

Relaxation, check.

I don't realize I've moved closer to Grant until I feel his cheek grazing mine. If Aldith is telling the truth, Grant and I need to channel the energy of our lovemaking to tap into the Heart. Instead of logically trying to figure out how to do that, I let my body sag into him and relive the moment when he'd given me the sweetest, most beautiful climax I'd ever experienced. Right before I came, he'd whispered, "Hush, just let it happen, baby." Those tender yet sensual words had pushed me over the edge and suffused me with a feeling of completeness, like I'd always been meant to share a supernatural connection with this man.

Maybe this was our destiny.

Grant slips his arms around my waist to tug me closer, but he doesn't try to kiss me. He just holds me while I rest my head on his chest and listen to the steady thump-thump of his heartbeats. My heart thumps in time with his, as if we've synchronized our souls. Don't care if that sounds crazy. I know something binds us to each other, something more than our bodies touching, more than the words we might speak. I wrap my arms around him and revel in the deep intimacy of this moment, this connection.

Power sizzles through me.

I feel it, though I can't describe the sensation. Every fine hair on my body shivers and stiffens as a luscious tingle spreads through me from head to toe and dives deep inside my sex. I could almost climax just from that sensation. Grant's dick thickens against me, and I know that means he's experiencing the same effect. Without opening my eyes, I slide my hands up his chest and loop my arms around his neck, rising onto my toes to press my mouth to his.

The second our lips meet, that power zings through me again.

Grant plunges his tongue between my lips and devours me like I'm the last morsel of food in the universe. While our tongues tangle, he grasps my ass to lift me onto my toes and thrusts his hips into me, rubbing the iron length of his cock into my mound.

A crack of thunder explodes overhead, rattling the building.

I stumble backward, out of Grant's arms. "What was that?"

"Though I am far from an expert," Aldith says, "I believe you two just took dominion over the Heart of the Echo."

"How can we tell for sure if that's what happened?"

"Try to halt the convulsions, I suppose."

Grant and I look at each other. He shrugs. I shrug. Some amazing superheroes we are.

I grasp his hand and turn toward the windows, where we can see the convulsions racking the sky. Then we glance at each other again, and I know he understands what I want to do. I know what should be done, but I also realize I can't accomplish the task intellectually. I need to feel it. We both aim our focus out the windows and just do it. Energy crackles on my skin, diving beneath the surface, racing through my body and straight into Grant's at the exact moment when a similar energy rushes out of him and into me.

Another, louder crack of thunder resonates through the Echo. It vibrates in my bones and makes the building shudder so powerfully that we both stumble backward.

Then silence falls over the world.

And the sky no longer roils. It has turned a deep shade of azure that I've only seen once before—when the alchemy of worlds began on earth. This must be the natural sky of the Echo. The sun burns less brightly than in the mundane world, but it still illuminates the entire land. I don't know if the Echo is a globe or just a flat surface, and I suppose it doesn't really matter right now.

"Did we do it?" I ask, not caring who answers my question. "Seems like we did."

"Yes, you have done it," Aldith says. "The Echo is once more stable, though the apocalypse has not subsided."

"At least the worlds won't be destroyed. Right?"

"Correct. You have stabilized the earth as well."

We actually did it. But I still have a few questions for our eerie friend. "We've taken dominion of the Echo's Heart. But what does that mean? Is it a one-time thing or a permanent change?"

"I believe you will remain in control unless and until you die."

"Can we use our shared power to make things better in both worlds?"

"That I cannot answer." She tips her head to the side, and her gaze goes distant. "There is another, more pressing matter you should attend to. I sense Will is out there, desperately seeking a way to find you and secure Sefton's journal for himself."

Great. I'd really hoped I would never need to see that dweeb again. He set his pet golem loose on us, after all.

Aldith's eyes flare wide. "Oh my. He is rather angry with you two, and I fear he can feel that you have dominion over the Heart of the Echo. He is not well pleased."

Sometimes she talks like a medieval person. Or at least the way medieval people talk in the movies.

"Okay, so Will is ticked off at us," I say. "Does he still have magic?"

"Yes, though not as much power as you and Grant have."

"Can he cause major trouble with his magics?"

Aldith puckers her lips as if she's considering the question. "I can't say for certain."

"Well, that leaves us with one option." I turn to Grant. "I know you agree."

"Yeah, I do." He smiles. "Time for some reckless Erin tactics."

Chapter Twenty-Seven

Grant

SOMETHING ABOUT TAKING CO-DOMINION OVER THE ECHO HAS changed my perception of Erin and myself. Why else would I suggest we employ her gonzo tactics to find and stop Will? Either that, or sex with her has melted all my brain cells. The weirdest part is that I don't mind at all. Lunacy sounds pretty damn good today. The apocalypse has made everyone a little nutty, but no one more than Sefton Stainthorpe's doppelgänger.

Before we head out into the unfamiliar world of the Echo, I need a few more answers from Aldith. "Is Will as dangerously nuts as Sefton was?"

"Perhaps. I've had no direct contact with him, so I can't give you a definitive response."

"Okay. Then can you tell us whether the golem is up and running again?"

She shrugs.

"What *do* you know?" I ask. "You tell us all kinds of vague stuff and… What? We're supposed to decipher it on our own?"

"I regret that I cannot be more helpful. I once did have more knowledge to impart, but Sefton managed to delete most of it from my memory."

The way she phrased that statement makes me wonder. "Are you a computer?"

She laughs softly. "No, I am a living being. Though I am different from you."

"In what ways?" I'm getting sick of her vague statements, and I want answers before Erin and I go out there to track down Will. "Come on, Aldith, tell us the truth. Stop making us drag it out of you."

She bows her head and wrings her hands. "The vision you see of me is not what I really am. I didn't wish to upset you, so I used what little magics I do have to create a more palatable image."

"Palatable? You're being vague again."

Aldith raises her head to look straight at me, though she bites her lower lip. "I will show you. Please don't panic. I mean you no harm and only wish to help."

Why would we panic? I have a sinking feeling I know the answer.

She takes a deep breath and exhales it.

The image of a cute, petite woman evaporates, replaced by what I assume is the real her—an Echo creature with scaly, flesh-covered skin and small spikes on her head. She has eerie green eyes that almost glow and inner eyelids that flick out every so often. I've seen much weirder and more disturbing Echo creatures than Aldith. The others I've come across were created by Sefton to resemble their human counterparts, which means I need to ask more questions.

"If you're an Echo creature," I say, "why aren't you trying to murder us? Those monsters are evil."

She shakes her head slowly. "Do not paint all of us with the same brush, Grant. Those of us who are not bent on wreaking bloody havoc will do you no harm. In fact, we will help you whenever possible, for even we wish to escape this world."

Not sure inviting Echo creatures to come home with us is a good idea. But I'll worry about that after we stop Will from doing whatever evil things he's plotting. Being a cop didn't prepare me for this. Neither did the army. All the combat experience on earth couldn't prepare anybody for living in a post-apocalyptic world full of magic and monsters.

But now I have magic powers. *Holy shit.*

"Do you have a counterpart on earth?" I ask Aldith. "A twin who's not a scaly being."

She considers me for a moment. "I would assume so, though I've never ventured into that world."

"Let's grab our backpacks," I tell Erin. "Then try to get out of here."

We retrieve our packs from the bedroom and return to the creepy-ass room where Aldith waits for us.

I clasp Erin's hand. "You should teleport us out of here, and see if you can take us directly to Will. I might have powers now, but I don't know how to whisk us away."

"Like I do? Well, maybe I've gotten better at doing that. But I'm no expert."

"You're more of an expert than I am. I know you can do this. Go for it, Erin."

A smile flickers across her lips. Then she shuts her eyes, and I do the same. Don't think I want to see whatever ether or wormhole we go through to reach our destination. I've had enough surprises over the past few months. A man needs some downtime once in a while, but I doubt I'll get any of that. I wince as I feel the change happening, though it's more of a mental sensation than a physical one.

"We're here," Erin says. "You can open your eyes now, Grant."

I peel my lids apart, which seems to take more effort than it should because I swear my eyelids have become glued together. But when I open them, I get to see the best sight in any world—Erin's face. "Hey, beautiful, you did it."

Her lips twitch, but she doesn't quite smile. "You were worried I'd screw it up, weren't you?"

"No. I have total faith in you, just not in magic."

She stares at me. "Total faith? In me?"

"Yeah, of course." I pull her close. "Sorry I acted like such a dick around you. That's over now. For good."

"I'm glad you feel that way. Because I need my partner to trust me all the way. That's how I feel about you."

"Ditto. Now let's find Will."

We're standing in the middle of a street that seems deserted, but I don't think this is the Capital City anymore. That means we will see Echo creatures and probably have to fend them off. At least I have a solid partner by my side for whatever comes next. I do trust Erin, all the way, because she has proved to me I can. Not by trying to do that. Just by being herself. Yeah, I finally appreciate her way of doing things, even if in the future I might sometimes disagree with her actions. She's been right too many times lately for me to doubt her ever again.

A noise, faint but distinct, catches my attention. I tip my head to the side and listen. Is that growling? Yeah, definitely. Whatever creature is making that sound, it doesn't seem like the friendly type. Erin and I have no weapons. We left them on the street where Will and his golem found us. Escaping from a cyborg didn't give us time to snatch up our weapons, though at least we still have our packs.

"Do you hear that?" Erin whispers.

"Yep, I hear it." I'm speaking softly too, though for all I know, these creatures have super-hearing. "We have no way to defend ourselves."

"We can punch and kick them."

I rotate my eyes toward her. "Hand to hand won't work with Echo creatures. They're too damn strong, and at least one of them has an armored torso. We need real weapons."

"Do you think I can magically create guns for us? Come on."

No, I don't expect her to conjure weapons out of thin air. I have a different idea. "Try teleporting our backpacks to us. You remember where we left them."

"Don't know if I can teleport objects."

"Give it a try. You can do it, Erin, I know you can."

She nods and shuts her eyes. Her shoulders bunch up, and her face does that too. But then a breath gusts out of her as her shoulders flag. She glances at me. "Didn't work. Sorry, I tried."

"That's okay. I have an idea."

I cradle her face in my hands and kiss her.

She relaxes against me and exhales a breathy moan.

Though I'd love to keep kissing her, we have important things to do. So I pull away and glance down at our feet, where our two backpacks slump on the pavement, and I grin. "You did it, baby."

She grins too. "Yeah, I did."

The growling noise I'd heard a few minutes ago has grown louder, clearly closer than before. I yank my cutlass out of its scabbard and shrug into my backpack straps. Erin grabs her machine gun, then gets her pack in position. Whatever is coming for us, it doesn't sound like a friendly Echo creature. Aldith never behaved like a monster, which wrecks my belief that all creatures are vicious killers. How many nice Echo beasts are out there? Don't know, and I can't risk finding out right now.

I lead Erin down the street. "Since you brought us here, I'm assuming Will must be someplace nearby."

"Hopefully. I'm new to this teleporting thing, so I can't swear I got my targeting right. We could be miles away from him."

"No, we're close. I can feel it. Besides, I trust your magics even if you don't."

"You have magics too, Grant. After all, you are the Heart of the Echo."

I don't like hearing her call me that. I'm not crazy about the title, but every time I think about what it means, I get a creepy-crawly sensation all over my body. I never wanted to become a vital link in a chain I can't see or understand. Sefton Stainthorpe served as a part of that chain too, and he was a whackjob.

As we reach an intersection, I notice shapes moving around in the semi-darkness on a side street. Though we stopped the convulsions of the Echo, the apocalypse has not been reversed. The sky above seems darker than it did when we were high above it inside the stronghold where we found Aldith. Just like on earth, here in the Echo, all the buildings have suffered devastating damage. I can't help wondering why, since this world only came into existence maybe a week before the alchemy of worlds began. Then again, Dax and Allison have talked about how he spent five years in the Echo before Sefton ignited the process of merging the worlds. Time moves differently here, just like Aldith said. For Dax, it moved more quickly. What effect will the time distortions have on me and Erin?

I can't worry about that right now.

The sun seems to be setting, which explains why the figures of creatures seem like writhing shadows rather than silhouettes. The buildings on the side street cast darkness on the ground too, adding to the ghost-like ambiance. We both stay aware of our surroundings as we keep walking, hyperalert to every sound and shadow. The sinuous outlines of creatures become more defined as they inch ever closer to this street. In a matter of seconds, we will have left the intersection behind us—but not the creatures that stalk us. I wish they'd just come out and attack. Waiting and wondering is the worst part.

We've traveled halfway to the next block when it happens.

A horde of creatures rushes out into the next intersection, blocking our way.

Erin and I stop to survey the area. The creatures behind us, who had been mere shadows, now reveal themselves and line up in the intersection behind us. I see every kind of Echo creature—horned, spiked, scaly, fishlike, and other things I can't describe.

"Maybe we can command them," Erin says. "We are the Heart and Life-blood of the Echo."

"Great idea. How do we do that?"

She grasps my hand. "Magic, of course."

To control the Echo, we had to get naked. I'm not doing that out here in front of ravenous beasts. I doubt I could get an erection, anyway. The potential for imminent and horrific death is not conducive to getting turned on.

We don't get the chance to argue about her suggestion. The creatures rush at us as one, like a wall of spiky, scaly, gnarly monsters ready to pummel us. I lash out with my cutlass at the first beast that reaches me, aiming my blade straight for its heart, but the creature hops backward. Then I see it. A figure standing in the doorway of a wrecked building. The person standing there steps out onto the sidewalk, giving me a clear view of him.

It's Will.

I slash my blade toward the creature again, but then I stop. "Need some space, Erin, just for a minute. Can you handle that?"

Erin smirks and fires off a volley of rounds from her machine gun, scattering the creatures.

That won't hold them back for long. I have seconds to do this. So I shout, "Will! Get your ass over here. I've got what you want." I shrug out of my backpack and pull out the journal, but I also grab the cigarette lighter I'd found in the store where Erin and I spent our first night in the Echo. I flick the lighter, igniting a flame, and hold it near the journal high enough in the air that Will can see. "Call off your dogs, or I'll torch this thing."

He steps off the curb onto the street but halts there. "No, you won't. You need it if you're going to reverse the apocalypse."

Clearly, he doesn't realize Erin and I have dominion over the Heart of the Echo. He thinks we're still just two earthlings he can order his minions to trounce.

I move the lighter closer to the journal and flip it open to show the pages. "Call them off, Will."

"No."

The creatures make a move in unison, but Erin blasts them with another volley.

I don't want to reveal too much to Will, but I need to make him under-stand I will burn the damn journal. Erin's life means more to me than any book, no matter how magical and vital it might seem. I'd also realized after browsing the journal that it contains nothing more illuminating than the ramblings of a nutjob. So yeah, I'll give it up—but only to get what I want.

To make my point clear, I light the first page on fire.

"No!" Will screams as he races across the street to reach us. He glances at the creatures. "Back off now! I command you!"

The monsters retreat to either end of the block. Will halts several yards away from us.

I douse the burning page by laying it facedown on the ground and stomping my foot on it. Then I raise the damaged journal again. "I'll light it up good next time if you don't cooperate."

Will grinds words out between his clenched teeth. "What do you want?"

"Give us your golem."

Chapter Twenty-Eight

Erin

MY RECKLESS, INSANE BEHAVIOR MUST BE RUBBING OFF ON GRANT. WHY else would he suggest that Will should give us his golem? What would we do with that thing, anyway? Maybe we could order it to crush the creatures that surround us with its big metal feet. Not sure what else a golem is good for if you aren't a megalomaniac bent on destroying two worlds.

"Are you off your rocker?" Will asks. "Why would I give you my golem?"

"To get the journal," Grant says. "Before I torch it—for real this time."

Grant had been saying that the journal must hold the key to undoing the apocalypse. But now that we control the Heart of the Echo, maybe he thinks the journal isn't necessary anymore because we have all the power we need. Unfortunately, I can't read his mind to find out the answer.

"What's your decision?" Grant asks. "The journal or the golem?"

"I could have my creatures or my golem destroy you," Will says. "You'd be dead before you realized what happened."

"Go on, do it. But I can torch this book faster than you can shout orders to your troops."

Yeah, Grant has definitely absorbed some of my crazy behavior. I should prepare to whisk us both away, just in case.

Will studies Grant for a moment, his expression unreadable. Then he glances at me and lifts one brow.

I have no idea what that means.

"All right," Will says. "You may have the golem. If you can summon him."

Will seems quite smug now, as if he's positive we have no chance of summoning the metal beast. Yeah, he must not know we took control of the Heart, otherwise he would never give us the golem. Sefton's doppelgänger doesn't seem to have the vast magics that the original madman wielded.

Grant moves closer to me and whispers, "Got any ideas about how to summon the golem?"

"No. This was your idea. Don't you know how to do it?"

"Guess we'll have to wing it. Should we make out to improve our chances?"

Since he's smirking, I know he doesn't really think we should do that. Making a joke during a dire situation might've seemed inappropriate to me before the Echo, but life after the apocalypse has rewritten all the rules of etiquette.

And I love it when Grant teases me.

We face each other and hold hands, our gazes connected by an invisible tether that I can feel as a pulsing thread of magic. Just yesterday, I would've denied magic existed. Today, I'm relying on it to save our lives. How bizarre. But I push all other thoughts out of my mind and focus on the task at hand—how to summon the golem. Grant's blue eyes transfix me, almost as if he's hypnotizing me, and I gaze into those irises as I take a deep breath, letting it out slowly. Everything else fades from my perception. I see only him, feel only his hands grasping mine, while we concentrate on a single thought.

Come to us, golem.

I swear I hear Grant's voice in my head while we concentrate on our task. *Come to us, come to us.* A metallic grinding noise emanates from somewhere farther away, faint at first but growing louder with every passing second. Monstrous footfalls draw ever closer. *Whump. Whump. Whump.*

Grant releases my hands.

When I open my eyes, he's smirking again. Cocky Grant turns me on even more than Zen Grant. So yeah, I feel like having sex right now, which is beyond inappropriate.

Whump. Whump. The golem strides ever closer.

Now I glimpse the crown of its head as the cyborg trudges up the side street, heading for us.

Will sputters. "No, you can't—It's impossible. Only I can summon the golem."

Grant chuckles. "We just did, asswipe. Not as all-powerful as you hoped you were, huh?"

I shake my head. "Even Sefton wasn't omnipotent. And you, Will, are nothing next to the mad genius."

"Remember when he whimpered and whined because he heard our horny friend coming for us?" Grant asks me. "This guy is a loser."

Why are we both insulting Will? I think Grant is trying to knock the dweeb off balance, and I'm all in for that. The more upset he gets, the more mistakes he'll make. Will believes he has more power than we do.

Think again, doppelgänger.

Our golem lumbers into view, turning the corner to head for us. It steps over the line of creatures that bars the intersection and halts maybe twenty feet from where we stand, then faces us and just waits. For instructions, I assume. Guess whoever summons the golem gets to command the cyborg.

Will throws an arm out to indicate us. "Kill them, golem. Kill them now. I am your master."

Not anymore. The golem ignores Will as if he doesn't exist.

I sidle closer to Grant. "Um, what now? We summoned that thing, but I'm fuzzy on the rest of your plan."

"No plan," he murmurs out of the corner of his mouth. "Winging it, remember?"

"I'm open to suggestions."

Will stomps toward us, but the golem takes one small step to block his path. He lets out a loud, frustrated cry. "Give me the fucking journal!"

"Sure thing." Grant tosses the book to Will, but the guy fumbles his catch and nearly falls over in his zeal to snag the journal. He gives us a smug look. "You are incredibly stupid, aren't you? This book allows me to control the Echo—all of it."

I stifle a laugh. He really has no clue.

Will flips through the book, his expression turning almost manic.

Since Grant doesn't have a plan, I decide to enact my own idea. I wave my arms in the air to get everyone's attention—well, everyone except Will—and wait until I've achieved my goal. All the creatures watching me snarl and gnash their teeth.

I take a deep breath and go for it. "Listen up, everybody. If you want to live, better run for it right now. The golem will crush anyone who sticks around. Last chance. Go now."

The creatures scoff at me.

Oh, they'll regret that. I crane my neck to look up at the golem. "Would you mind sweeping away these annoying cretins for me? Please?"

The golem swings his foot out and sweeps it leftward.

All the creatures scatter, fleeing in various directions to avoid getting bowled over by the cyborg's foot.

"Golem, stop!" Will almost shrieks. "I command you!"

The golem ignores him and shuffles around to swing his foot at the line of creatures behind us, but they've already started to flee. The only living things on this street are me, Grant, Will, and the golem.

Wow. My idea worked.

Grant grins. "Nice work, Erin."

"Thanks. But we lost the journal."

"Don't worry about that. It's useless, anyway. The ramblings of a madman."

"Useless?" I lodge my hands on my hips. "Why didn't you tell me that before now?"

"Didn't know how you'd react. I mean, that was our only lead for how to stop the Echo convulsions." He rubs the back of his neck and winces. "I'm sorry. Should've told you as soon as I realized the journal wouldn't help us. I was, uh…"

"Embarrassed?"

"Yeah."

"It's not your fault the journal doesn't help us. But maybe we don't need it now, anyway."

No, I won't say out loud that maybe our newfound shared power is better than Sefton's ramblings. Not in front of Will.

"Better run," Grant tells Will. "Or we'll ask the golem to please crush you under his foot. You've got the journal, so go."

Will scowls briefly, but then takes off down the street.

"Should we have just let him go?" I ask. "That guy might be whiny and annoying, but he has Echo power."

"Not as much as we do. I'd rather not kill anybody unless it's absolutely necessary." He lifts his brows. "You asked the golem to chase the creatures away. What happened to killing every last one of them?"

"I guess your Zen attitude has rubbed off on me."

"And your gonzo tactics have influenced me. That's why we make such a good team."

The golem turns around to face us, his head tipped down as if he's watching and waiting for us to command him again.

Maybe this creature captured us earlier, but I don't think he meant to hurt us. I can see the scars where we slashed him in our attempt to escape. The golem has been a slave, first to Sefton, and then to Will. We asked him to come to us, which skirts the line of enslavement. Not all Echo creatures are evil, as Aldith proved to us, and that makes me wonder.

I suddenly have an idea that's so bizarre I'm sure Grant will balk at it.

"What are you thinking?" Grant asks. "I can practically see the gears turning in your mind."

"I have a radical idea that might get us killed."

"Your favorite kind of plan. Tell me about it."

"Let's release the golem from his magical enslavement."

Grant stares at me, his face blank.

Yeah, I figured this plan might be too radical for him.

But then he smiles and kisses me. "You're a genius."

I can't help laughing. "Genius? No, I'm just the kind of girl who loves insanely bad ideas."

"You're an optimist in disguise, huh? Your wacky ideas usually work, after all."

"Are you saying we should do it? Free the golem?"

He glances up at the metal beast. "Yeah, I think we should. Maybe if we give him autonomy, he'll realize we only hurt him earlier because we needed to escape from Will. We should apologize for that, to get the ball rolling."

"Okay. Let's do that. Can the golem speak?"

"Not sure." Grant sucks in a big breath and hollers, "Golem, can you speak to us?"

The creature shakes its head slowly, emitting a metallic noise.

Grant looks at me and shrugs. "Guess we play twenty questions with the big guy. Yes or no responses only."

"Okay. Let's start with that apology." I clasp Grant's hand as we both tip our heads back to meet the golem's glowing red gaze. "We're sorry we hurt you. If we'd had any other option, we would've taken it. Do you accept our apology?"

The golem nods.

"We really appreciate that." I pause to think of what to ask him first. "Are you enslaved by magic to do your master's bidding?"

He nods.

"And we are your masters now, right?"

Another nod.

"We would like to free you, but we aren't sure it will work. Do you want us to try?"

The metal beast nods yet again.

"Okay." I turn to Grant. "What else should we ask him? He served Sefton and Will, so maybe one or both of those guys blabbed useful info to the golem. What do you think?"

"Worth a shot." Grant clears his throat. "Golem, do you know how Sefton Stainthorpe created the Echo?"

Our new friend shakes his head.

"Did Will mention anything about how to stop the apocalypse?"

The golem shakes his head again.

"Let's try to free him," I say, "then maybe ask him a few more questions. It would be a show of good faith from us to give him the option of answering rather than forcing him to do it. I assume we are forcing him, though we don't mean to do that."

"Good point. Let's free him."

We face each other, our foreheads touching, and hold hands again, lacing our fingers. I gaze directly into Grant's eyes while he gazes right back at me. Power crackles between us, an almost palpable force, as I feel the magics gathering inside me. Grant must experience the same thing. An erotic warmth ripples through me, suffusing my body, but I no longer care about whether it's bizarre or wrong to get turned on every time Grant and I use our shared power. It feels right.

Our hunger for each other empowers us.

I can't describe how I sense it, but I know we just freed the golem. He is autonomous now. The risk we've taken might get us killed or earn us a solid ally. Time to find out which way the big metal guy will swing.

We return our attention to the golem, and I say, "You're free now. No one can enslave you again."

I know that's true, though I can't explain why. Magic doesn't come with a user's manual.

"Do you have a name?" I ask.

The big guy shakes his head.

"Would you like to have one?"

He hesitates, then nods.

"You can make one up yourself, or we could help you. Would you like us to do that?"

The golem nods.

Grant gives me a brows-raised look, probably because he thinks it's weird that I'm going to give our new friend a name. I could let Grant do that, but I've already got an idea. "Would you like to be called Jarek? It means strong, which definitely applies to you. But it can also mean spring, as in renewal and rebirth. That suits you too since you're now an independent being. What do you think?"

The golem nods.

"You like the name Jarek?"

He gives me a thumbs-up sign, his metal joints creaking as he forms the gesture.

Well, that's weird. "Okay, I hereby christen you Jarek."

The golem opens his mouth a little, and I swear his lips curl up the tiniest bit as if he's trying to smile. I hadn't realized he had lips until just now. They're thin and gray, not at all like a human mouth. I briefly wonder where Sefton got the flesh to create the living machine, but then I realize I don't want to know.

Jarek kneels amid a cacophony of metallic noises, then touches a fingertip to the ground. He draws a pattern on the asphalt by gouging it out.

The golem has written, "Thank you."

I approach him and settle a hand on his gigantic arm. "You're welcome."

When I glance back at Grant, he's gaping at me.

"Something wrong?" I ask.

"You…made friends with a golem."

"Uh-huh. I took a page from your book and went for a peaceful resolution."

"I don't make nice with Echo creatures, in general. Not wanting to murder every last one of them isn't the same as a peace treaty." His gaping mouth shifts into an appreciative smile. "You are an amazing woman, Erin. I never would've realized that if we hadn't come to the Echo."

He's impressed, I think. What I've done with the golem didn't emerge from a plan or even serious consideration. I had a hunch and followed it. Now we have another ally besides Aldith.

I move to stand beside Jarek's hand, laying both of mine atop his index finger. "Maybe we can work together, hey? Grant and I want to make both worlds better."

He uses the index finger of his other hand to gouge out his response in the asphalt. "Me too."

"Did you like Sefton?"

Jarek shakes his head.

"Didn't think so. He sounded like a total bastard."

My new friend does that sort-of smiling thing again and nods.

I pat his hand with both of mine. "Now you've got friends. If we stick together, maybe we can change the worlds."

Jarek's lips curl up a teeny bit more.

Yeah, my plan worked. But we still have a serious problem. Will is out there somewhere, angry and humiliated, and I have an intuition that he wants revenge.

Chapter Twenty-Nine

Grant

WHAT'S LEFT FOR US TO DO NOW? ENDING THE ECHO'S CONVULSIONS in this world should have stopped them on earth too, though we can't know that for sure unless we go home. But I have no doubts Will is running around searching for a way to get his revenge on us. We shouldn't just go home and forget about this world, especially since we learned the Echo houses decent creatures alongside the murderous ones.

I can't help thinking of Aldith and Jarek. Okay, the golem is right beside us, so of course I think of him. But we left Aldith in the stronghold, alone. What if Will finds a way to get inside the Heart of the Echo and hurt her? Jarek has the size and strength to squash a skyscraper, so I doubt we need to worry about his well-being—unless Will invokes even stronger magics to stop the cyborg.

When I look at Erin, she smiles. "I know what you're thinking."

"Do you? I'm not entirely sure of what I'm thinking. I'm positive I have no idea what your thoughts are."

"Baloney."

"What do you mean 'baloney'?"

She laughs softly. "Haven't you noticed? We share a telepathic bond that started before we took dominion over the Heart of the Echo. I felt it when we meditated together. Didn't you?"

My thoughts rewind to our time in that auto parts store when we got in a meditative groove. I did feel like I could hear her thoughts and sense her desire like a palpable force inside me. Before we breached the Echo, I would've dismissed the idea as ridiculous. Now, I can no longer brush it off. "You're right. We do share a telepathic bond."

"Does that bother you?"

"No. I like it."

"Me too." She glances up at Jarek, then looks at me again. "Now that we've taken control of the Heart of the Echo, I think we should go home. Don't you? We need to check on our world and make sure the convulsions have stopped there too. Even if we can't reverse the apocalypse, maybe we can use our new powers to make things a little better for everybody."

"I agree."

"But I worry—"

"About Jarek and Aldith, and any other nice Echo beings."

Erin raises her brows. "Yeah, that's exactly what I was thinking. Guess we have telepathy even when we aren't having sex or meditating."

"Let's ask our big buddy what he thinks." I turn to face the golem, and Erin does the same. "Hey, Jarek, we need to go home to check on our friends. Would you be okay if we go?"

He nods, then scrawls a big message on the asphalt—*Help your friends.*

"You are a friend too," I say. "And we'll be back to find Will. Can you keep an eye out for him while we're away?"

Jarek nods.

"Maybe you could come home with us." I just thought of that option.

The golem nods, then shakes his head.

"Are you saying you want to come with us, but you can't?"

Jarek nods again.

I clasp Erin's hand. "It's time to go home, but I feel bad for leaving Jarek and Aldith here."

"We'll come back for them." Erin faces the golem. "Can you help us get out of the Echo?"

Instead of responding, he bends down to offer his hand to us, palm up, like he wants to give us a ride.

Erin and I climb into his palm.

Jarek jogs down the street, but we get a surprisingly gentle ride despite his swift gait. As we leave the city, heading out into barren countryside blackened by the apocalypse, I can't help feeling like we've scored a major victory. Our trip into the Echo netted us awesome new powers, new friends in Jarek and Aldith, and more information that might one day help us undo the damage Sefton inflicted on the earth. Maybe we can save the good Echo creatures too.

A dark smudge in the sky enlarges with every massive stride the golem takes. That's the doorway to the Echo. Or from this side, the entrance to earth.

When Jarek halts, we find ourselves face to face with the roiling black disk of the doorway. Our golem buddy raises his hand to his chin level to look at us.

Erin scrambles to her feet and leans over to kiss his cheek. "Thank you, Jarek. We won't forget about you."

The golem stretches his arm out until the doorway lies only feet away, then he pushes his arm through the opening to set us down on the ground. His giant limb retracts, and we can't see him anymore.

Erin and I stand on the Paddock Viaduct, the bridge that crosses the Trinity River and marks the area where the alchemy of worlds had begun. Before we can whisk ourselves away, an external force yanks us out of Fort Worth and teleports us to Sanctuary. It must be noon on the Lost Coast. As we adjust to the bright sunlight, having come from the epicenter of the apocalypse where the sunshine is always muted, I realize Dax and Allison stand a few yards away.

"Welcome home," Ally says as she races over to hug me and then Erin. "Dax was getting pessimistic, but I knew you'd come back eventually."

"How long were we gone?" I ask.

"Ten days."

"Wasn't that long for us. But we met a nice Echo lady who told us time in that world can slow down, hover, or speed up."

Dax stalks up to us. "Slow down? I only experienced the acceleration, though it didn't seem fast to me. Be grateful you weren't trapped in the Echo for five years."

"We are grateful."

He slaps my arm. "Glad you didn't get eaten by Echo creatures."

"Yeah, me too."

Erin gives me an odd look, and thanks to our new bond, I know what she wants to ask me. But not out here in front of everyone. We've touched down in the central commons of our camp, and other people loiter nearby.

"Have the convulsions ended here?" I ask. "They did in the Echo."

"Yes, the conniptions are over," Allison says. "We haven't experienced any of those in several days."

"Good. We have a lot more to tell you guys, but Erin and I need to have a private talk first. If that's okay."

"Of course." Ally eyes me and Erin as a knowing smile curves her mouth. "You two aren't arguing anymore. In fact, I'd say you've gotten to know each other really well."

I claim Erin's hand. "Yeah, we're a couple now."

Ally grins. "That's wonderful. I knew you were meant for each other."

Willow rushes up to us and hauls me into a bear hug, then does the same to Erin. "I missed you guys soooo much."

Erin tousles the girl's hair. "Yeah, we missed you too, sweetie. Have you grown since the last time I saw you?"

"No," Willow says with a laugh. "I'm fifteen. That means I'm too old to grow anymore."

Though Willow wants to know "absolutely everything" about our time in the Echo "including the gross parts," we excuse ourselves to go into my tent. After offloading our backpacks, we sit down on the cot.

"Why didn't you mention that Aldith also said time can rewind?" Erin asks.

"Not sure if we should tell anyone about that."

"But why?"

"Don't you get it?" I fold my hand around Erin's and gaze into her luminous eyes. "Rewinding time to stop the Echo from ever happening would mean you and I never met. We never came to Sanctuary and made all these friends, and Allison and Dax wouldn't be having a baby. Do we have the right to erase the good things we've found since the apocalypse hit?"

"Maybe our new powers will give us the skills to erase only the bad parts."

"We aren't good enough with our powers yet to know what we can or can't do. Until we figure that out, I suggest we keep some stuff to ourselves."

"I guess you're right. We don't know the rules of being the Heart and the Lifeblood of the Echo."

Now that we've agreed to keep a few secrets, we head back out to the commons, where Dax is grilling fish for lunch. I can't even remember what time of day it was when we left the Echo, but I'm famished. Those fish smell like heaven. Willow gives us a detailed description of how Dax took her net fishing this morning and they caught enough to feed the entire camp for lunch today.

But after our meal, we inform Dax and Ally that we need to go back to Fort Worth and make sure the convulsions have really ended there. Dax whisked us away before we had a chance to look around, not that we're complaining. Coming home feels damn good. Dax wants to go with us, but we assure him he should stay here with Allison. Only Erin and I will risk returning to the epicenter.

We emerge near the viaduct.

"Don't see anything weirder than usual," Erin says. "How long should we hang out here?"

"Let's tap into our shared powers to determine if things are stable here."

We hold hands, close our eyes, and focus on our task. I can feel the convulsions have stopped, though I can't explain how I know that. But I trust my intuition, more than I ever had before the apocalypse.

Erin and I look at each other, and she says, "It's all good."

"Yeah, it is."

The doorway to the Echo hovers high above our heads, seeming to be in stasis.

"Should we hang around for a while anyway?" Erin asks. "Just to be sure."

I shrug. "Might as well."

Erin turns to head away from the viaduct toward other parts of the city. I lag a little behind her, mostly so I can watch her sexy ass. Maybe we should waste a little time by having sex while we loiter in this city. Yeah, that's a solid plan based on sound reasoning. It has nothing to do with how much I want to fuck her again.

Erin glances back at me. "Hurry it up, Larson. Are you turning into an arthritic old man?"

"As soon as we find a comfortable spot, I'm going to prove to you how not arthritic I am."

She grins at me over her shoulder. "Can't wait."

I grin too.

But then pressure bears down on me as if someone dropped a big iron blanket over my body. I freeze, suddenly unable to take another step. I manage to open my mouth just enough to squeeze words out between my clamped teeth. "Erin, help."

She whirls around, gapes at me for a second, then rushes over to grasp my shoulders. But she can't do that. Her palms meet an impenetrable and invisible barrier. As hard as I try to break free, I can't do it. Sweat streams down my face from the effort. Erin pounds her fists on the unseen wall, shouting wordless cries of frustration.

The world disappears.

I spin through a dizzying void and pop out into muted sunlight. My brain needs a moment to sort through what I see around me. Devastated buildings. An eerily azure sky. Creatures gathered on the street before me, snarling and gnashing their teeth, ready to chow down on their meal.

Me. I'm their meal.

The creature Erin had tricked into transporting us into the Echo hunkers at the front of the congregation—and Will stands beside him.

At least the force field around me has evaporated. I could run, but I have no clue where I'd go. Without Erin, can I teleport? Or use any magics? I wish somebody had given us an instruction manual.

Will limps up to me, smiling smugly despite the gray pallor of his face and sweat dribbling down his temples. He's breathing hard too, almost wheezing. That's exactly how Sefton had looked after using a shitload of Echo power. Maybe I can exploit his weakness. No clue how, but I need to think of something. Since I don't have my backpack or any weapons, I have little chance of beating these Echo creatures in a fight.

"You ran away," Will says, and even his voice sounds weaker, though no less nasty. He hobbles closer to me, and spittle sprays my face when he snarls, "Give me the real journal."

"I did. You've got the genuine ramblings of the original Sefton Stainthorpe. Not my fault he was a raving lunatic."

"That's rot."

"Sorry the truth doesn't make you happy."

He flaps a hand toward the horny monster. "Seize this arsehole and transport him back to the palace. Now. I need to torture the truth out of him."

The horny beast pulls me into a bear hug, though not the cuddly kind, and his massive arms restrict my ability to inhale. I can pull in only shallow breaths. He lopes down the street. When I glance back, I see Will climbing into a vehicle. Soon, he's driving after us. I try to teleport, but nothing happens.

My only hope is the newfound bond between me and Erin. But will she hear my telepathic cry for help? I have no choice but to try.

Erin, help, I'm trapped in the Echo.

Chapter Thirty

Erin

GRANT IS GONE. HE VANISHED IN A HEARTBEAT AS IF HE'D TELEPORTED, though I've never known that type of travel to involve an incapacitating bubble that envelops the traveler. Something or someone ripped him away. To where? And why did they do it? We stopped the convulsions and gained new powers and new insights into the Echo. We should be celebrating. Why Grant? I don't understand anything that just happened, and I've become frozen in this spot, inches from where he had stood seconds ago. Is he dead?

No, he can't be. I will never believe that.

Tears burn in my eyes, but I swipe them away and take slow, deep breaths. Grant showed me how to meditate, and I need to do that right now. But my hands are shaking, and I feel like I might throw up. No, no, no, I need to keep it together. So I shut my eyes and imagine Grant's voice leading me through mindfulness meditation, the way he had back in that building in the Echo. His soothing tone. The sensation of our minds touching. The intimacy of the connection. I can almost feel him, almost, not quite, so close…

I throw my head back and shout curses at the heavens.

This isn't helpful. What should I do? Go home to Sanctuary and tell everyone I lost Grant? He must be in the Echo. I need to get in there, but my teleportation won't work.

Suddenly, I have an idea. A crazy one. Grant would call it a "gonzo" plan, and he'd be right. I sprint onto the bridge, halting at the center, and bend my head back to glare at the entrance to the Echo. Since I've had no luck contacting Grant, I'll try getting in touch with someone else.

I take a big breath and scream, "Jarek!"

Nothing.

"Jarek!" I scream even louder. "I need you, Jarek. Come and get me."

Growling and snarling noises originate from behind me. I've roused the Echo creatures, and I have no weapons I can use to defend myself.

Don't care. "Jarek! Help me. Please."

The doorway to the Echo telescopes open, and a large metal-and-flesh hand reaches down to pluck me off the ground. Jarek cradles me in his palm as he pulls me into the other world. The doorway shuts, and he sets me down on the asphalt surface of a street.

No time for pleasantries. "Have you seen Grant?"

Jarek shakes his head.

"What about Will?"

He nods.

"Do you know where I can find him?"

Jarek shakes his head.

Damn, I wish he could talk. Yes or no responses are so limited.

Erin, help me, I'm trapped in the palace.

Grant's words slam through me, making me stumble sideways as if they exert a physical force. But I heard those words in my head, in his voice. Maybe our telepathic link only works in this world, since I couldn't contact him until Jarek brought me here.

I tip my head back to gaze into the golem's red eyes. "Do you know where the palace is?"

He nods.

"Thank you for bringing me here," I say. "But I need another favor. I'll understand if you don't want to do it."

Jarek bends his knees and touches my nose with the barest pressure from his enormous index finger, which I think means he wants to assist me.

"You will help?" I ask.

The cyborg nods his assent.

Relief makes my entire body sag, and my knees almost buckle, but I catch myself. "Please take me to the palace. Grant is there."

Jarek offers me his hand, and I climb on for the ride. As he jogs down the street, I have nothing to do but think. Maybe my telepathic bond with Grant only works when we're in the same world. Does my teleportation have a similar limit? Or could I bring something from earth into the Echo using my powers? Might as well try.

I close my eyes and focus on my connection with Grant. The warmth of it rushes through me, and I know we are connected now. So I summon all our shared power and picture the object I need, picture it appearing on my lap. At first, nothing happens. Then a weight settles on my thighs. I open my eyes and grin.

My backpack sits on my lap, with my sword still in its scabbard.

Unzipping the pack, I dig around until I find the rest of the grenades Grant and I had scrounged up in that big store. I have three left. That's not my entire arsenal, though. I also have two more magazines for my machine gun and my switchblade, as well as a handgun.

Oh yeah, this will do.

Up ahead, I see a structure squatting atop a mountain that has steep sides. The closer we get to the building, the more detail I can see. It looks like a castle straight out of a fairy tale. Sefton must have thought Allison would live there with him and they would rule the Echo together. Now Will has holed up in that castle. What is he doing to Grant?

At the base of the mountain, Jarek halts. He raises his hand high above his head, reaching up to the peak. I step off his hand onto a rocky but mostly flat area not far from the castle and pull on my backpack. I wave down at Jarek. "Thank you."

He nods, then assumes an upright posture I take for the golem standing guard.

I race toward the castle, leaping over boulders and holes. By the time I reach the gates, I'm almost out of breath. I allow myself ten seconds to recover, then I knock on the massive wooden door.

Nothing.

Screw this. I fist my hands and clench my jaw, willing myself to zip straight to Grant. The gates vanish, and I find myself inside what looks like a prison cell.

Grant sits on the floor, knees bent, hands on the floor, gaze downcast.

"You needed a hand?" I say.

His head jerks up, and he grins. "Erin. I knew you'd find me."

My pulse accelerates, and every hair on my body lifts. I did it. I found Grant. "Are you okay?"

"Yeah. I've only been here for a few minutes. Will locked me up and left."

"It's only been a little while for me too."

Grant heaves his body off the floor and pulls me into his arms to kiss me. "I love you, Erin."

A thrill chases over my skin, and I can't help grinning. "I love you too, Grant."

The door bursts inward.

We turn toward the figure limping across the threshold. Will props himself up with a gnarled wooden stick, and he seems even paler than the last time I saw him.

"You don't look so good, Will," I say. "Maybe you should dial back the magics and give yourself time to recover."

"No, I will not," he snarls. "Give me the real journal."

"We did. Not our fault you refuse to believe the truth."

Our horny friend the Echo monster hovers just behind Will.

"I want the journal!" Will shouts, but his voice has become hoarse. "Tell me the truth!"

Grant pulls my sword out of its sheath and clamps my hand around the grip while he keeps his palm around mine. "Time to end this."

Somehow, I know exactly what he wants us to do. While both gripping the sword, we lunge forward as one to pierce the exact center of Will's heart.

"Want to know the truth?" I ask. "Grant is the heart. I am the Life-blood. You are nothing."

I know he understands what I mean. I see it in his eyes.

Grant and I combine our strength again, pushing harder than ever to punch the sword straight through until the hilt meets Will's chest with most of the metal protruding from his back. We marshal that physical power again to thrust the blade into the Echo creature's heart too. Will is shorter than the creature, but somehow, we knew the exact angle that would let us kill him with the same blade.

The linked bodies of Will and the beast crumple to the floor.

Grant extricates the sword and wipes the blood off using Will's clothes.

It's over. We prevailed.

But I don't feel like celebrating. I experience a powerful sense of relief, as if the weight of two worlds had settled onto my shoulders but now has been removed.

Grant gazes down at the dead man. "Guess we own this castle now."

"Don't think I want to live here."

"No, but maybe we'll find more answers hidden somewhere in this building."

"Maybe." I grab his shirt and pull him closer. "But not today. We've earned a vacation from death and mayhem."

"Let's get out of here."

"Jarek is waiting to take us home."

Chapter Thirty-One

Grant

EIGHT DAYS HAVE GONE BY SINCE ERIN AND I ENDED WILL'S MANIC reign in the Echo. Everything seems to have calmed down, though I doubt we've been given a permanent reprieve. However much time we have to relax, I plan on making the most of it. That means Erin and I go down to the beach for a saltwater bath in the nude. Naturally, that was her idea. We also told Dax to discourage anybody else from visiting the beach until we come back. Nobody says no to Dax—except for Allison. So we climb up to the crest of the mountain and make our way to the shore.

Oh yeah, I plan on making love to Erin on the warm, golden sand.

We amble down the gentle slope that leads to the beach hand in hand, reveling in the sunshine and the sound of waves lapping on the shore. Life might not be what it was before the Echo, but we've carved out a nice little haven here on the California Coast. All I want to think about now is what I want to do to Erin once I get her naked. We've just passed the spot where I had erected a makeshift camp when I first landed here, not long after the apocalypse hit. It seems like such a long time ago.

Erin stops and points toward the shore. "What's that?"

I halt too and follow the track of her finger. A lump lies on the sand. No, not just a lump. A human being. I drag Erin along with me as I sprint toward the figure lying sprawled at the edge of the beach, where waves splash over the person who lies facedown there. We crouch at either side of the person and gently turn the body onto its back.

We gaze down at a woman's face.

She's breathing, though she seems rather pale and scratches mark her arms. I pat her cheek, but she doesn't respond. Checking her pulse, I feel a strong rhythm. So I slide my arms under her body and lift her into a sitting position, then scoop up a handful of water to splash it on her face.

The woman's lids flutter several times, then finally open. She gazes at us blearily. "Who are you?"

"My name is Grant, and that's Erin." I nod toward her. "What's your name?"

Her faces goes blank. "I don't know."

An amnesiac? We've never had one of those show up on our doorstep before.

I pat her hand. "Don't worry, we'll take care of you. If you feel like you can't walk, I can go get a stretcher from our camp. We made one out of tree branches, in case we ever needed it."

The woman bites her lip. "I'd rather walk."

"All right. If you get weak along the way, just let us know."

Erin offers the stranger a bottle of water, and the woman takes a few sips. Then we help her get up. Her dress is dirty and frayed at the hem, but otherwise undamaged. We take it slow as we make our way back to the camp. Everyone is happy to see a newcomer, though they all wonder what caused her memory loss and how she wound up on our beach. Those questions will wait for another day, though. Right now, we need to take care of her.

Naturally, Dax wonders if the woman's amnesia is a trick. I don't blame him for being skeptical, but Erin and I both feel we can trust the stranger. No concrete reason why. We just know it's true. Erin and I share control over the Heart of the Echo, but the parallel world remains a dangerous place. Now that we have allies in the Echo, we all experience something we haven't known since before the alchemy of worlds.

We have hope. And these days, that's the most precious gift of all.

**The apocalypse isn't over yet. Get ready for
the epic conclusion to the trilogy in *Echo Unbound*.**

ANNA DURAND IS A BESTSELLING, MULTI-AWARD-WINNING AUTHOR OF contemporary and paranormal romance. Her books have earned best-seller status on every major retailer and wonderful reviews from readers around the world. But that's the boring spiel. Here are some really cool things you want to know about Anna!

Born on Lackland Air Force Base in Texas, Anna grew up moving here, there, and everywhere thanks to her dad's job as an instructor pilot. She's lived in Texas (twice), Mississippi, California (twice), Michigan (twice), and Alaska—and now Ohio.

As for her writing, Anna has always made up stories in her head, but she didn't write them down until her teen years. Those first awful books went into the trash can a few years later, though she learned a lot from those stories. Eventually, she would pen her first romance novel, the paranormal romance *Willpower*, and she's never looked back since.

Want even more details about Anna? Get access to her extended bio when you subscribe to her newsletter and download the free bonus ebook, *Hot Scots Confidential*. You'll also get hot deleted scenes, character interviews, fun facts, and more!

VISIT ANNADURAND.COM TO SIGN UP.

www.ingramcontent.com/pod-product-compliance
Lightning Source LLC
Chambersburg PA
CBHW070957180726
48291CB00004B/1332